PRIDE AND
JOI

GAY G. GUNN

Genesis Press, Inc.

Indigo Love Stories

An imprint of Genesis Press, Inc.
Publishing Company

Genesis Press, Inc.
P.O. Box 101
Columbus, MS 39703

ISBN-13: 978-1-58571-265-6
ISBN-10: 1-58571-265-5
Manufactured in the United States of America

First Edition 1998
Second Edition 2007

Visit us at www.genesis-press.com or call at 1-888-Indigo-1

DEDICATION

To my pride and joy…

my sons, Tré and Marc…

Dites moi qui vous aimez, et je vous dirai qui vous etes.

(Tell me whom you love, and I'll tell you who you are.)

—Creole Proverb

CHAPTER 1

Joi picked up the dollar bills and slid the change into her cupped hand as the ladies left. They'd taken an hour and a half to eat, and lollygagged another forty-five minutes before gathering their overflowing shopping bags and leaving her a fifteen percent tip, exactly. She hated them. Joi wanted to be one of them. She was supposed to have been one of them by now, but life surprised her by dealing her a trilogy of terror: the untimely deaths of her brother, her father and her fiancé. She hated when things beyond her control took control. If Joaquin had lived she would have him, a college degree, a career, two children and leisure time to lunch with her friends. She would be the served, not the servee. Now she was forced to wait upon the woman she should have been. This area of Detroit was in transition and now attracted these new patrons with their imported leather pants, silk blouses, manicured nails and designer bags—women who used to lunch on linen tablecloths in posh restaurants where ferns flapped in their faces, and a prissy waiter recited the specials of the day after introducing himself as "Sean." Now these luncheon-ladies forsook ambience for good food; Joi had heard one of them remark, "The place is seedy, but the food, reminds me of my grandma's…before cholesterol worries."

In one motion Joi stuffed the tip into her pocket, picked up her pad and moved in front of some of the lunch usuals who had watched the beautifully coifed, sweet-smelling black women leave. Shorty, Goldie and Edgar—these were the guys this place was built for, Joi thought—and Louie had been serving them for generations.

"They got nothing on you," Brown-eyes, their new friend, said.

"Just a million bucks," Joi remarked, then asked, "What'll you have today?" She patted the pockets of her pink, white-aproned uniform for a pencil, and found it perched over her ear. She stood in front of their booth and rubbed her left ankle with the scuffed-up white shoe of her right.

"Joi, you looking mighty dandy today," Shorty said.

"Cut the crap," Joi sassed. "The usual?"

"What's the special?" Brown-eyes asked. She had been ignoring his name stitched on the pocket over the Ford emblem for over a week now.

"Can't you read?" She motioned over her right shoulder to the blackboard. "Liver and onions, mashed potatoes and peas," she recited, knowing it would be easier to tell him than to have him decipher Louie's scribble.

"I'll have that, then," Brown-eyes beamed. Joi moved on to Shorty and the other two without paying attention to his smile.

"Oh, man, I wouldn't eat that mess at home let alone out and pay for it," Shorty teased. "Gimme the usual," he said. The other two men agreed.

"And four beers," Goldie added.

"Make mine a milk," Brown-eyes said.

"Figures," Joi mumbled, pivoting away from them and slapping the next booth with menus. "Burn three cheeseburgers, fries and slaw…and one 'special' for Mr. Special," she told Louie as she joined Ella at the waitress station toward the back.

"My man Pride with those bedroom brown eyes is still checking you out," Ella informed. Joi sipped water without looking at him. "Been three weeks now," Ella continued. "Where did that fine brother come from? Umph, umph, umph."

"The factory, like everybody else in this joint," Joi said. "I'm going out back for a smoke."

"Seems to me if I had some fine brother like him scoping me out, I'd give him some play," Ella said, following Joi out to the alley where Chantel, the third waitress at Louie's, was already puffing away. "He's nowhere, going nowhere, and I've been there and I ain't going back." Joi lit up a Winston and took a long, satisfying drag. "Where has he been all this time?" Ella asked. "He knows the guys, so he's not new."

"Used to go to Pops around on Jackson, the only place the brothers could go, back in the '40s and '50s," Chantel chimed in. "His father went there and so did baby boy before they closed it down last month."

"Loyalty," Ella sighed. "I like that in a man." She let a saucy smile graze her lips.

"Breathin'. You like that in a man," Chantel teased.

Joi rolled her eyes at them both, took another long drag and said, "Tradition. His father worked in the factory, he works in the factory and his children will work in the factory. Like I said, a nowhere guy going nowhere. Son of a man who was born to lose. Born losers. I want more and I'm gonna get more for me and mine." No child of mine will have to drop out of college because a parent dies, she thought.

"They make good money," Ella said.

"He managed to tell me that just last week. He came in for a cup of Joe and left me a five dollar tip," Joi said. "I told him that was too much. He said he made 'plenty money' and had no one to share it with. You know niggas always got to let you know how much money they make…trying to impress. I assure you that his definition of 'plenty' is not mine. I let him know coffee was all he was gettin'." She dragged on her cigarette, remembering how a slow smile had lifted his mustache.

"He was just trying to be nice," Chantel said.

"Yeah, right," Joi said on a stream of smoke. "He doesn't have enough money for me and mine. He's a dead-end man. A factory worker—"

"He may be just a factory worker," Chantel interrupted, "but did you notice how his work boots are always spit-polished? I can see my reflection in them. And his work pants have a crease in them sharp enough to cut Helen's sweet-tater pie. He's always clean-shaven and his mustache is as neatly trimmed as his natural." Joi and Ella eyed one another with mild amusement at their colleague's study of the brother. "And do you see how his body fills the doorway? Six-foot four inches of solid—"

"Got dirty fingernails," Joi declared, then sucked on the thin white cane.

"What?" Ella managed before Louie banged the screen door open.

"What you girls think this is?" he barked. "Beverly Hills? You got orders backed up!" Joi flicked off her cigarette and blew out the last of her smoke as she followed the other two in. "She sure does know a lot about the man," Joi said to Ella as she yanked up the coffeepot from the hot plate. "She talks to her customers. You oughta try it sometime. Especially a brother that fine, that buff," Ella said, devouring Pride with her eyes.

"You should date him then," Joi said.

"Umph, don't think I wouldn't in a heartbeat. The age difference wouldn't bother me none. I could show a young pup like that plenty." Ella let a sly grin glide across her aging brown face as she shoved a piece of gum between her ruby-reds. "I betcha he's a good lover with a slow hand, and look at those lips. Umph! But," Ella said and swung her gaze to Joi, "it's not me he's interested in." Ella winked at Joi. "Ha! Oooh, to be thirtyish again. The thought makes me wet with anticipation."

"Ella!" Joi reprimanded her friend, then turned to serve the foursome their food.

Joi checked on her other customers trying not to think about the events which led her to Louie's—trying to deal with the unexpected death of her soul-mate, trying to maintain the grades to keep her scholarship, then losing it anyway; trying to deal with rejection from the university, from financial aid and from loan officers. Trying to scrape money together to finance the tuition herself, but each time she saved up enough, something would come along to siphon it away: the car that died six years ago and she didn't have the money to repair or replace it; the incidentals not covered by her mother's medical or homeowner's insurance or her three days per week, part-time job; her mother's dental work; her mother's foot surgery; the furnace; the hot water heater; the roof. There was always something that kicked Joi's dreams into the backseat. Her younger sister Noel and her husband provided half of everything, but Joi's half was harder to come by. Joi tried not to think about any of this but certain times of the month and some times of the year made her more sensitive than others. She knew she had to get her act together before she could attract a brother with an act of his own. But when would she get a chance at her old goals? The handle to life's offerings was as elusive as a butterfly and as slippery as a greased pig. No matter how hard she tried, she could never get a firm grip.

When she returned to the waitress station in back, her gaze fell upon Brown-eyes. For a change she eyed him. His combat boots were Army regulation clean. His pants ironed, creased and crisp, and on his workman's shirt by the Ford emblem—embroidered in black—was his name—"Pride." She'd heard the others call him Joe. Ordinary Joe—plain, everyday, common Joe. Even his parents had no imagination.

She warmed her standing cup of coffee and Pride's vision filled her view once again. There wasn't a thing ordinary about him—not that muscle-hard, tall lean frame, or that deep voice; not those high cheekbones which plunged into hollows and ran along his strong, square jaw. Those soft brown eyes were hooded by a tangle of thick, lush eyelashes which reminded Joi of her daddy; he had had a forest of light brown lashes like that. And he would give her butterfly kisses as he dropped her off at school every day and again at bedtime after she said her prayers. I bet Pride could give good butterfly kisses, she thought absently.

Twice Joe Pride had come to Louie's for dinner, alone. Tonight would be his third. Joi showed him no partiality; in fact, she tried distancing herself from him. His gaze was always unsettling, drawing her in closer than she wanted to be, drowning her in their satin softness. It wasn't the sweeping, lustful look of most men; she could handle them with a mouthy retort that left their pumped-up egos totally deflated. In Joe Pride's eyes she didn't see lust—she saw longevity, and that terrified her. She didn't want a relationship with any man. Three years ago, her thirtieth birthday had sent her into the arms of Dr. Geoffrey Rollins. But he was married and when Joi found out she gave him an ultimatum. He wanted to keep his wife and keep Joi, literally. No dice. She was not raised to be the "other woman." She was raised to be the only woman in a man's life. For the past three years, she'd been nobody's woman. There was a certain safe, uneasy comfort to that. After the catastrophe with Dr. Geoff, Joi swore she'd be more practical next time. Her mind was clear and focused; she didn't need her body messing things up. No question Joe Pride was fine. But she didn't want the complication of his attention now, or the toll it would take to extricate herself from him later.

Luckily, Pride sat at the counter, which was Chantel's station. Joi served the last piece of peach pie to her customer, parted the curtain which separated the diner from the employees lounge and went in to the back room for a break. She sat at the table with a glass of orange juice.

"What you reading?" Pride said, startling her.

"*National Geographic*—on Paris," she said, looking around nervously and fiddling with the magazine's edges.

"I've been there."

"Lemme guess. In the service, right?" she asked sarcastically, looking up into his eyes only a moment before her own quickly danced away.

"Yeah."

"Figures," she mumbled and returned to her reading.

"You got something against the Army?" he asked.

"Listen, you're not suppose to be back here. It says 'Employees Only.' " She looked straight at the table, not wanting to see those soft brown eyes again. His deep velvet voice was arresting enough.

"Sorry."

"Whatever," she said, flipping him off with her hands. She didn't know what it was about him, but he made her uncomfortable. After the curtain closed behind his frame, she looked up at where he had just been standing, then returned to strolling down the Champs Elyseés. Louie barked her back to reality.

❧❧

The next day Joi served the foursome their usual lunches.

"What's that?" Joi asked Pride before she realized it.

"This? A bracelet." He held up his wrist so she could see the metal configurations around the jasper stones and composed marble. "You like it?"

"Yeah, it's cool."

"He made it," Shorty offered. "He got all that stuff at his crib. Got a whole workshop."

"Really?" Joi tried to play off her fascination with its design. "It looks like that intricate silver and turquoise jewelry that the Zuni Indians in the southwest make."

The foursome looked at her numb and stupefied, wondering what Zuni was. "Pride got some Indian in him, don't you Pride?" Goldie joked. Everyone laughed but Joi, who simply left them to their ignorance. A few minutes later, Chantel left Joi and Ella at the back station and went to the booth to see his bracelet.

"Damn," Joi said to Ella. "Now he thinks we're over here discussing him." She watched him look over Chantel's shoulder to the pair of them.

"Well, we are," Ella said, cracking her gum.

Embarrassed, Joi went into the back.

⤎⥋⤏

"Night, Louie," Joi said.

"See you tomorrow," Louie said over his shoulder as Joi pushed the glass door open on the frigid night air.

She gathered her coat collar against her neck and

fished in her pocket for a cigarette to keep her company for the half-block walk to the bus stop.

"Want a ride?" Joe Pride asked, sliding his long, maroon-brown LTD to a halt at the bus stop.

"No thanks," Joi said, stopping her dance-to-keep-warm long enough to answer. She hated when she worked this shift; when she left in the middle of everyone else's, she couldn't catch a ride and had to take two buses home.

"It's pretty late," he said, leaning over from the driver's side to talk to her. "Mighty chilly for just September."

"I know what time it is, the month and the bus to take. I've been taking it for five years before you came along, and I intend to continue taking it. Good night."

She threw up her head and looked north for the bus, as the raw wind stung her nose. She rummaged for a tissue, turned her back to him and the wind, and blew. When she turned back, he was still there.

"Would you move your car? My bus is coming."

"Maybe some other time," he said, and when she didn't respond, he pulled off.

Climbing onto the bus, Joi slipped her fare into the slot and listened to the familiar clink to the bottom, then she took a seat. She smiled; one of the small pleasures in her life was to have a bus seat all to herself.

She unfurled her *National Geographic* and continued to bask in the sun at a cliff-side villa, which clung to the coast of Amalfi in sunny Italy, high over the Mediterranean Sea. She had been all over the world on the Detroit bus routes. Her heels had clicked across the soap-stone steps of the Taj Mahal. Her index finger had dipped into a canal as a handsome gondolier sang "O Solo Mio" through the waterways of Venice, depositing her at her five-star hotel. She had taken the same barge trip down the Nile as Cleopatra. On the Arabian Peninsula in Oman, she had participated in *Lailat al henna*, the woman-only celebration to honor the bride on the eve of her wedding. She had gambled in Monaco, shopped in Morocco, been on safari in Kenya, dug for the Chinchorro mummy in Chile, and been inside the life of a geisha. She had spent a week in the Fiji islands, the jewel of the South Pacific, where the flora and fauna belonged in aquariums and the natives had Afros bigger than Huey Newton's. Many nights she'd been so engrossed in her travels that she had missed her transfer point or her final bus stop altogether. But not when it was cold like this. She hated winter, and with the weather getting this cold, this fast, it meant this city was in for a doozy.

She rang the bus bell, stashed her travel log into her pocketbook and lit up another cigarette—her escort for the two blocks home. She walked past neat, well-kept houses to her apartment building, which surrounded a courtyard like a huge U. The elevator groaned to the sixth floor and she opened the door to her efficiency.

"Home," she said.

⤛⤜

Through the diner window, Joi stared absently into the frigid noon sunshine. Most folks welcomed the change of seasons, but the advent of winter meant the dying of warmth and the promise of severe cold, and left Joi silently cursing its imminent resurrection. Every year here she vowed would be her last. Every year she greeted the reappearance of winter with hopeless animosity and resignation. The years were going by so fast. Too fast. Like a kid trapped on a carousel, she couldn't get off the never-ending circle which had become her life. She took orders, served food, counted tips, wiped tables, took breaks and went home to a microwave dinner. Her life was not anywhere near what she had planned it to be. Year after year, instead of motivating her to change, the knowledge, despite her futile attempts to grab hold of her life, just weighed her down, and during wintertime she was most vulnerable. She fought being lethargic and resigned. She wished she still had access to Dr. Morton, the college psychologist who was helping her cope with Joaquin's death and getting her life back on track. She had told Joi that she would forever be haunted by her brother Chip's unfinished life, and that her father's and then Joaquin's deaths had left her feeling abandoned; that each death resurrected the others and Joi had to be constantly vigilant and not let depression become a loyal companion. She and Dr. Morton were going to work on Joi's hyper-anxiety of letting anyone get too close for fear that they too would eventually die or leave her in some way. But she lost her scholarship and her psychologist. Joi wished she could hibernate like the bears—sleep though all the crappy weather and sunless days, and awake refreshed and ener-gized with the advent of spring. Sometimes it was all she could do to pull herself out of bed and face another day and her perpetual battle to retain her status as one of the working-class poor.

Shorty followed Pride's gaze to Joi standing by the window. "Man, give it up," he suggested. "The girl ain't gonna give you no play." The men quieted when Joi served their three beers and milk and sauntered away. "You are not her type," Shorty concluded.

"She's something special," Pride said.

"You can say that again, but you ain't got what she's in the market for, brother. She wants a man with long money and a edumacation, who can take her to all those places she's always reading about. To Broadway shows and the opera and do."

"And a house in Sherwood Forest or Indian Village," Edgar added.

"And that ain't none of us sittin' at this table," Goldie said.

"Or working in the factory, even with your big time promotion," Edgar said.

"She even speaks French," Shorty said, then yelled, "Hey Joi, speak some French."

"No," she quipped back with an accent and a roll of her eyes.

"I know you'd drink muddy water and sleep in a hollow log if she'd give you some, man, but you ain't got it, Pride. Give it up," Shorty advised the son of his old friend.

Joe Pride couldn't hear them as he watched Joi move gracefully from table to table—balancing plates, taking orders, returning change, counting tips. Her mocha-chocolate body was poured into that pink and white uniform, which fit too loosely; he was sure she wore it that way on purpose so as not to attract the wrong kind of attention. Her dark, chestnut-brunette hair was swept back into a short ponytail, but by lunch, soft tendrils had broken loose from the rubber-band constraint.

They sprang into big, shiny-brown ringlets that were highlighted gold as she passed the window's sun. Her features were beautiful enough to support such a short curly coif. Her almond-shaped eyes, set in that toasted caramel skin, were crowned with long, lazy lashes as naturally arched as the eyebrows that set off the exotic symmetry of her face. He was spellbound with the divot between her nose and upper lip. He'd never seen one so pronounced, so deep that sweat would rest there when she was overworked or agitated. She'd wipe that delicate dip with the back of her index finger, then send it to brush her hair back from her faces—a gesture she came to own. But that sexy divot hiked up her sensuous top lip into a perpetual, heart-shaped pout. And as if God wanted to know how much more a man could take, He had heaved more character onto her face by accenting her heavenly mouth with a deliciously cavernous dimple on her left cheek. She was simply gorgeous, a natural beauty. Well, maybe she wore some lipstick to keep the saucy pair from chapping, he thought.

When her back was turned to him, Pride let his eyes sweep down from the nape of her head, where her hair rested in smooth swirls against her neck, down her body to those shapely brown legs hideously camouflaged by nurse-white support hose stuffed into equally ugly, run-over shoes. Still, she was someone special. He had never known anyone who read books for pleasure, or did cross-word puzzles for relaxation. She was fascinating, beautiful, smart, and the mere mention of her name sent shivers up his spine. The nearness of her sent him into adolescent orbit. He never thought he'd ever feel this way again about a woman. But he did, and her name was Joi Martin.

He'd come into the diner three weeks ago to eat lunch with the fellas, never expecting to find this Nubian treasure. At thirty-four, he was too old for love at first sight, but there she was. She glided across the linoleum floor like it was a Paris runway. She could fan a fire with that backfield in motion.

"Hello, boys," she had said with a low, sultry voice, like a weary jazz diva getting ready to sing her signature song, totally unaware of the effect she had on her audience. Mellow—that described her as she slid them their menus and went on to the next booth. She had smiled at him, and it was all over for Joe Pride. She rocked his world. Just by being, she showed him how empty his life was—a life he thought was filled to the brim with ten hour workdays, football, basketball, baseball, bowling and trophies to prove how good he was. Joi Martin screamed E-M-P-T-Y, and he drew a red circle with a scarlet slash through it, indicating no life without her. He had merely been existing—breathing, marking time until this black bombshell blew his world apart. With her he saw all the possibilities. Over the next few weeks, he had imagined all they could be together. Only problem was, she wasn't buying it.

"Joi, your mama," Louie said, holding up the receiver as the overhead light bounced off his bald head.

"Yeah, Ma," Joi spoke into the telephone, sighed and listened. She ran her fingers through her hair and said, "The eagle flies on Friday, Ma, so tell Dr. Abrams he'll get his money then." Joi looked at Ella disgustedly, and then turned to the wall so her friend couldn't see the frustration in her face. "Blood from a turnip, Ma. Okay. Okay!" Here come those circumstances beyond her control taking control again, she thought. "Weird," Joi said aloud as she hung up the receiver and blew hair away from her face.

"You mean your mama or Joe Pride?" Ella teased, as she eyed her friend, then Pride, before returning to paint her lips red.

"Both."

"Well, I agree about your mama," Ella said and they laughed, "but you just got Pride's nose is all. Give him some and he'll leave you alone."

"Heffa," Joi said to her playfully.

"It's been three years since you had any, so your stuff has got to be rusty. Nothing will chase a black man off quicker then a bad lay."

"For a black man, there's no such thing as a 'bad lay,'" Joi quipped as she let her eyes swing over to look at him. For once, he wasn't eyeballing her. She turned to her wise old war-weary friend. "Why me, Ella?"

"Who knows? You just got it like that. He likes what he sees and he wants to get to know you."

"Weirdo," Joi said, letting her curious glance turn to ice as she yanked up the coffeepot from the hot plate. "Born loser."

"Just keep telling yourself that, and maybe you'll believe it," Ella said, peeling away to pick up an order. "That's one of them defense mechanisms ain't it?" Ella winked and popped her gum. "I dated a psychologist once. He was so stingy in bed. So calling Pride names makes it easier don't it?" she said, passing by her friend again. "Keeps him at a distance, huh?"

CHAPTER 2

"What is that mess in your hair?" Joi accosted Pride one afternoon as she slid Shorty his fries. It was only the second time she'd ever asked him a direct question.

"I put a little texturizer in to—" he began.

"It looks Gawd-awful," she spat, putting a spin on the catsup so it landed right by Goldie's burger.

"It looks like yours," Shorty teased.

"Mine is natural and so should yours be," she said to Pride. "God gave you what he thought you should have."

"He's just trying to get it like mine so he can attract the ladies," Goldie said, fingering his limp, greasy wet curls. "You like mine?"

"It's about as classy as that gold tooth stuck in your mouth," Joi sassed before returning her gaze to Pride. "Don't let these yahoos get you in trouble," she concluded, then moved on to the next booth.

❧

Pride had missed lunch with the guys but came by that evening. Like subtle radar, Joi knew he was there before she saw his frame leave no space in the doorway.

"Aw, great," she sighed when she saw him working his way toward one of her tables. But when he passed it and came straight for her, her heart pounded and her legs turned to jelly. She was pissed. She didn't know why. She rolled her eyes in exasperation and opened her mouth to protest. "I got something for you," Joe Pride said, stealing her thunder. He handed her a little box with a stick-on bow.

"For me?" Joi looked at him skeptically. She couldn't remember the last time someone had given her anything.

"Go on, open it. It won't bite."

She reluctantly took the box, self-conscious about the other patrons who could not see around Pride's large frame. Slowly she lifted off the lid. On a bed of cotton lay a bracelet. "Oh, it is beautiful."

"I noticed you didn't wear silver, so I made this in gold with mosaic stones. Pink, to match your uniform."

"It's really beautiful." She was at a loss for words as she slid it on her wrist and held it up against the flashing neon sign that blinked "Louie's."

"That was really nice...thoughtful of you." She twirled it around her slender wrist. "You know, you could sell these to those new little shops up on the hill."

"Yeah?"

"Sure. There are all kinds of little, unique doodads in there. Bracelets, pins, earrings. You could do matching kinda things, make extra money. Not that you need to." She was talking too much now, a sign that she was nervous. His soft brown eyes with the canopy of lazy lashes flustered her even more. She looked away again. She didn't want to feel anything for him but grateful.

"Joi, pick up!" Louie barked.

"Thanks, this is really nice. I gotta go," she said as she wiped her divot and brushed hair back from her face.

"Need a ride home?" he asked, as she backed away from him.

"No. Chantel's taking me home. Thanks."

"See you tomorrow then," he said, and left.

⟡

The door to her efficiency squeaked open. She held her shoe to it and yanked the key from the lock. Her new bracelet stared back at her. She took off her coat and threw it towards a hook, walked out of her scuffed-up shoes, turned on the television, removed a Lean Cuisine from the freezer, threw the carton in the trash and popped the frozen block into the microwave. She shed her uniform, washed her face and looked in the mirror.

"Katmandu," she answered Alex Trebeck, who gave her $1,000 *Jeopardy* dollars.

She raised her wrist to rest beside her face. She smiled at her friendship bracelet and then sighed. She wasn't ready for a relationship, especially with somebody like him. She had vowed that when she started this dating thing again, she had to be serious. Joe Pride would have been a good way to pass the time in her younger days, but she needed to concentrate on heavyweights now, contenders for the championship wedding ring, men who had to be able to provide well for her in a manner she planned to grow accustomed to. While Pride had many positives, he didn't have the background or the foreground she was looking for. Still, they could be friends. Maybe.

⟡

Over the next two days, Joi's assessment of Joe Pride escalated. She admired him for giving her the bracelet without the boys from the peanut gallery being around, and for not making a fuss over it at lunch the next day. It was three days before Shorty noticed it.

"Yo, hold up! What have we here?" Shorty said, taking her hand. "I never knew you to be into jewelry."

"You could fill the Detroit River with what you don't know about me," Joi said. "It's a gift from a friend." She snatched her hand back.

"C'mon, Joi, you know you too ornery to have any friends," Goldie said.

"Looks like a Pride original to me," Shorty said, to which neither Joi nor Pride commented.

After more teasing, Pride finally said, "Cut it out. You're embarrassing her."

"We at lunch and you ain't my boss now," Edgar replied playfully.

"What's that song them white boys sing about driving him crazy?" Shorty continued his teasing as he flipped through the jukebox selections. They were laughing when some classy luncheon-ladies entered and temporarily took the threesome's minds off the jesting at hand.

Then Shorty found what he was looking for and punched P8, the Fine Young Cannibals' "She Drives Me Crazy." Joi eyed him suspiciously, knowing he was up to something, as she continued to serve her customers at the counter. As the record began, Joe Pride sipped water and perused the menu while Edgar began a rhythmic hand clapping, Goldie beat on the table like drums and Shorty picked up his air guitar. It was amusing for all the customers to watch the antics of these grown men as they mouthed words to a song they obviously did not know. They reminded Joi of folks trying to fake "Lift Every Voice" at a Black History Month luncheon. But when the record and the trio got to the refrain of the song, they began to shout the words and point at her and Pride—something about her driving Pride crazy like nobody else.

"Ooop ooop, and he can't help himself!"

Joi was embarrassed, then mortified, then livid and finally angry. She looked over to the nonplussed Pride before she went over and yanked the central power from the second chorus and stormed to the back.

Ella followed her. "I think that's kinda cute. A live show at Louie's—maybe tips will be better."

Joi held her head, shaking it in disbelief.

"They don't mean no harm," Ella said in her all-knowing tone. "Men are children, that's what makes them so much fun in bed." She snapped her fingers with a thought. "Lemme call and see if Tony is free tonight." She went to finalize a nocturnal tryst with one of her longtime beaus, leaving Joi sitting at the break table.

Pride eased his way to the back where Joi sat.

"I'd prefer Stevie Wonder's 'Knocks Me Off My Feet,' " he said to announce his presence, his voice as soothing as a caress.

She flashed her furious jet-blacks at him before returning them to the magazine she wasn't reading. Her anger denied her tongue expression. "Hey, Joi," he said.

When she looked up at him again he concluded, "Don't let these yahoos get you in trouble." He winked and left.

Joi took a deep breath and blushed a smile.

❦

Pride's new promotion kept him busy so that sometimes he missed lunch with the fellas, and Joi missed him at dinner when she had the breakfast-lunch shift. She tried convincing herself that she didn't mind not seeing him, but she did. Trying not to think of him made her think of little else, missing the attention once it was gone.

Winter came with a vengeance and took up permanent residence in Detroit. She trudged into the diner one day when the snow was light and falling in fluffy flakes, but by three o'clock businesses were shutting down, and by five the darkness of the sky was made bright by the unexpected blizzard. Louie lived ten miles the other way so Joi stood at the bus stop, hoping she wouldn't have to use her key to reenter the diner and spend the night in the back room as she had done during the blizzard of '91. She just knew she'd miss all of *Jeopardy* tonight. Not a bus in sight, not even any cars. The suffocating white flakes whipped her nose and clung to her brown knit cap. She noticed, in the distance, a long dark vehicle crawl haltingly against the crystalline snow. The snow-covered car slowed to a stop in the middle of the street. The window slid down.

"I know you need a ride tonight," Joe Pride said. He smiled and his soft brown eyes shone in the snow-filled night.

"Sure." It was the best offer she'd have tonight.

Joi negotiated the drifts that were shoved against the curb, her legs as frozen as her feet. She slammed the door shut and slapped encrusted snow from her coat and feet. "Thanks," she said begrudgingly. It was more like a reflex from good home training than genuine gratitude.

"My pleasure," he said, turning the heat up for her and adjusting the radio volume. "As bad as the blizzard of '91."

"Yeah."

Joi tried not to shiver, but the wet of her clothes meeting the warmth of the car set her teeth to dancing. The car inched a few blocks and Joi stared out at the blanket whiteness.

"Ah, Marvin Gaye!" Pride identified the song on the car radio and turned up the volume. ' "Pride and Joy'—that's us. Pride and Joi." He smiled and sang off-key.

"Oh, brother. Your are so corny."

"Corny." He mimicked her voice with a nasal whine. "What kind of word is 'corny?' "

Joi had to smile.

"That's not a Mo-town word," he said. "Where are you from anyways?" When she didn't respond, he continued. "Me, I'm born and raised right here in Detroit. From Duffield Elementary to Miller Junior High to Cass Tech High School. You must be one of them St. Martin de Porres Catholic High School girls."

"Who told you?" Joi hated people in her private business.

"Who knew?" He smiled at his ruse.

Joi thought about it, then realized that no one knew about her de Porres days. "Lucky guess."

"No, I'm psychic. I know these things…just like 'Pride and Joy' is us. Joe Pride and Joi Martin."

"Cheeze," she said, but didn't call him corny again. "Mind if I smoke?"

"Actually, I do. This is a smoke-free car. But have a piece of candy." He slid open his ashtray where assorted hard candy stared back at them.

"Good grief, are you for real?" she said. "I want a smoke, not a sugar-hit!"

"It's bad for you. You should take better care of yourself."

"If I'd known a lecture went along with the ride, I'da refused." She returned her gaze to the white nothingness. "No, you wouldn't have," he said softly as he steered through the blinding flakes.

"I'm sorry. It's a bad ending to a bad day. Oh, I love this song!" She turned it up without asking. " 'Some Kinda Wonderful' by the Drifters," he identified. "Yeah."

She stopped singing long enough to answer. "My brother loved the Drifters. He taught me how to cha-cha on them." She smiled, remembering, and listened until it was over. "He was ten years older than me, but he was a good guy. You remind me—" She stopped cold. "Yeah, a real good guy," she finished vaguely. She didn't want to share.

"Where is he now?"

"Dead. Trying to stop a fight. Good Samaritan—got himself killed," she said sotto voce, then shook off the unpleasant memory. "Boy, he could dance—and handsome? Whew! All the girls in New Orleans loved Chip."

"I thought you were from here?"

"We moved up here when I was ten. Been here ever since," she said with a heavy sigh.

"So 'corny' is a New Orleans word?" he asked. Joi chuckled. They ploughed on for another treacherous block; the visibility was nil in front of them. "Where do you live exactly?"

"East Irving," Joi answered as the car skidded to a halt.

"I don't think we're gonna make it."

"You're telling me." The ocean of white was smothering them.

"I don't live far from here. If you don't mind, we could make it there."

"Whatever," Joi said, more terrified of the weather than of him.

The car struggled the next eight blocks until the LTD turned onto Phoebus Road; it got stuck halfway up the driveway to his house. Heading toward the porch, Joi stepped into the footprints Pride created in the powdery wet snow, tracking some into the living room. She stood in a puddle of her own making as he turned on the light and disappeared into the kitchen to start a pot of coffee.

"Make yourself at home!" he called back to her. Joi removed the knit cap and pulled the scarf from around her neck as she surveyed the room.

A neat, clean, masculine house, devoid of knickknacks

and full of comfortable furniture: a worn recliner was aptly poised in front of the TV. Trophies stood on the mantle where pictures usually live. It wasn't a fancy house, but it was solid, straightforward, well-built with gleaming hardwood floors. Beyond a menagerie of plants, unlined drapes piggy-backed tasseled shades at the pristine windows, which now mirrored spotlight-white back into her face. Wood was stacked in the fireplace, ready for igniting, while two perfect piles sat on either side of the opening, waiting to be used. The smell was neither of antiseptic nor sweat socks, but was an inviting, lived-in scent of homey aromas—baked cookies, beer and dish detergent.

"Come in!" Pride urged her as he reentered the living room with a book of matches and knelt on the hearth. "A fire is in order on a wintry night like this, and candles in case of a power outage."

"This is nice," she said quietly as she clutched her coat instead of removing it. She watched him kneeling to build her a fire and fought the feeling of easy welcome.

"Thanks. It's not much, but it is mine. You hungry?" He looked up at her, catching her by surprise. "Relax, Joi." He stood and walked toward her, unclutching her hands from around her neck. "I'm not going to hurt you."

"I know that," she said boldly, challenging his eyes with hers.

"You must be cold," he continued as if he hadn't heard her. "Why don't you go upstairs and get out of those wet clothes? I have some old flannel shirts in the closet of my room, socks in the top drawer and a bathrobe hanging on the back of the bathroom door. Go on." He urged her to the flight of stairs. "Bathroom is straight ahead."

Joi tipped up the steps and, through the railing, glanced at two other bedrooms. They were also chock-full of trophies and as neat as the master bedroom, which faced the front of the house. His big bed was made.

"Find everything okay?" he yelled up the stairs.

"Yeah, sure."

"I'm making turkey sandwiches, okay?"

"Yeah," she said as she opened the closet door. His work shirts hung on hangers as did his pants—all evenly spaced, facing the same way. His shoes were lined in a row facing out. "Neat freak."

The socks were folded in vertical columns in the first drawer of his dresser, where Canoe, English Leather and Eternity were arranged in an arc around his comb, brush and a change valet. Just as he had said, the robe hung on the door of the spotless bathroom—no ring around the tub. She checked out her image in the mirror before draping her wet clothes on the shower rod.

"Cheeze," she said, feeling domestically inept as she put on the robe without compunction. If his house was this clean, his robe must be hospital ready.

She returned to the first floor and stood in the living room in the too-big robe with the sleeves rolled up twice and the hem kissing the floor.

"Better?" he asked. "You want to eat in the kitchen or by the fire?"

"Fire" was no sooner out of her mouth when he produced two TV trays and set them up. "You get the coffee."

"Sure." She looked around the kitchen. This cleanliness was getting monotonous; this room was just as sparkling as the rest of the house. She smiled when she saw the chipped porcelain sink-like chinks in his perfect armor.

They passed each other and she settled in on the couch as he returned with a bowl.

"I whipped up this salad," he said.

"Can you turn on *Jeopardy*?" she asked.

"What's that?"

"The TV show."

He turned on the television and handed her the remote. She grinned when she saw the familiar blue blocks and bit into the sandwich. "This isn't turkey, is it?"

"It's not lunch meat."

"You made this turkey from scratch?"

"Only God can make a turkey from scratch. But I did buy a whole, raw turkey and cook it. Doesn't always have to be Thanksgiving," he teased.

He watched her eat and become absorbed with Alex Trebeck's questions. "Next in line," Alex read the answer to the Presidents category, "Lincoln, Jefferson, Franklin D. Roosevelt."

"George Washington," Joi replied before the first contestant buzzed in and got it wrong.

"Correct," Alex told her. "Denominations of American currency. Pick again."

"More than just a pretty face," Pride said with sincere admiration. He was amazed by her intelligence.

"*Mea culpa,*" Joi answered Alex.

"French?" Pride asked.

"Latin," she said, poised for the next question in languages. "*Raison d'etre,*" she answered Alex. "French," she said to Pride. "Means 'reason for being.' Ibsen," Joi answered.

"I'll just be quiet so as not to show my ignorance," Pride said, but she didn't hear him.

She answered "Absolute zero" to a math question and "Pericles" to another category. She missed Final *Jeopardy.* "God...I knew that;' she said, and slapped her forehead with the palm of her hand. And, as if reentering the domain called earth, realized how she had been ignoring her host and became immediately self-conscious again. "The sandwich was really good. Thanks."

"My pleasure."

"Can I call my mother? She'll be worried."

"Sure. Right over there."

Joi punched in her mother's number, reassured her she was safe and concluded "...I'm fine, Ma. I called you so you wouldn't worry. No, there is no number here. I'll call you tomorrow, Ma. Bye." She hung up the receiver as Pride put the last of the dishes in the kitchen. "Damned if you do and damned if you don't," she said. It was impossible to ever please her mother, Jacquleen St. Marie, unless Joi hit the lottery or married a multimillionaire. Joi followed him into the kitchen and sat at the counter.

"Your mother alright?"

"Nothing a lobotomy couldn't cure," Joi said, half-jokingly.

"You're lucky to have somebody," he said, sinking his hands into hot sudsy water.

"I don't know about that." She automatically picked up the teatowel and began drying. "But she is 'all I have left,' as she constantly reminds me." She accepted the plate and his nonverbal invitation to continue. "My father was shot when his cab was robbed. What about you?" she asked before he could respond to her tragedy. "Any family?"

"None. Both parents dead. Two brothers dead—one chose to ride the white horse to hell, and the other a car accident. I'm the last Pride. That's a lot of pressure."

"From whom? You got no family." She was sorry the moment it left her mouth. It had always been one of her problems—open mouth, insert foot. She was not oblivious to the pain her caustic remark must have caused. "I'm sorry."

"No need to apologize."

⊷⊶

Lulled by the monotonous news reports of the surprise blizzard that had paralyzed Detroit, Joi fell asleep on her host's shoulder. The scent of burning wood, the crackle of the fire all wrapped in nature's cocoon that a heavy snowfall always brought had soothed her. She was awakened by the television station sign-off. Her head jerked from Pride's shoulder which roused him moments later.

"Go on upstairs and pick any bed you like. Whichever—I promise I won't lay a hand on you," Pride said.

She brushed her hair back from her face. "I'd like to stay on the couch. I like the fireplace." She looked into his eyes and fought the feeling blooming there. It was easy to be lost in his seductive gaze but she wanted to keep her way and keep her distance from him. With the nearness of him, she was getting mixed signals; her brain was telling her one thing, and her body something else.

"Okay. Couch and fireplace it is," he agreed.

When she returned from the bathroom, Pride had gathered two pillows and blankets from the closet and made her a bed on his sofa. "Sure you'll be comfortable here?"

"Positive. Thanks." She gave him a quick, nervous smile. "Okay. Holler if you need anything." He backed away from her towards the stairs. "Good night."

"Night."

When he went up to bed, she snuggled beneath the matching blankets, watching the fire dance before her. She relished being here—the privacy and security of being in a house. No nocturnal sounds of a whining elevator with loud passengers. No neighbors walking overhead or partying beneath her. No smells that she did not create and was left to wonder what they were. No odd toilet flushes, arguments or dogs barking. Joi was seduced by the peace, quiet and tranquility of this house and the man who slept upstairs.

❧❧❧

He almost never woke in the middle of the night, but he did this night. Pride tiptoed down to the fifth step and looked at his couch. Huddled underneath the lump of cover, bathed by the fire's glow, was Joi Martin. He couldn't see her, but knowing she was there, in his house, made him happy. He envied his robe that lazily melted over the contours of her body. She stirred, and her bare foot found its way outside the comforter. He smiled and fought the urge to tuck it back in. To touch her skin, to let his hands slowly inch from that foot up her shapely calves over her supple thighs and cradle her behind in his hands. As his desire hardened in his cotton briefs, he smiled again, not daring to venture on with this deliciously wicked fantasy. He couldn't wait to feel the length of her against him; to taste that succulent, sassy mouth, to stroke and explore every love-hungry crevice of her lithe, nude body. He longed to make her shimmer, shake and vibrate with satisfaction.

With his own body now responding more virilely to his imagined tryst, he stopped his mental fantasy. For he wanted more from Joi than just satisfying his sexual curiosities—wondering how she liked it done and what kind of noises she made. He pledged that he would give Joi Martin all the time she needed to join him where he already was; he was in love. He admitted it to himself for the first time. And he would take whatever time he needed to crack the tortoise-hard shell she'd built around herself, and get to the luscious marshmallow goo inside— the ultimate reward for a brother patient enough to go after the prize. Pride didn't know why or who had caused

Joi to construct this protective veneer around herself, but he would get her to trust and then love again. He smiled at himself…and then at her on the couch before he retraced his steps up to his cold, crisp sheets. He was making progress. First the couch, then his bed, then forever. Those were his plans for them. Pride and Joi.

Another foot of lake-effect snow had fallen during the night and assorted power outages dotted the immobilized city, which hadn't begun to dig out. Schools, businesses, the factory, all stood as silent centurions against the pounding blizzard which made snow-bunnies of the few trucks that tried to plow the white before the city called a halt to their unproductive efforts. Early that afternoon, Joi devoured a huge breakfast before volunteering to chop vegetables for Pride's turkey soup. As it simmered on the stove, perfuming the house, they ventured outside to attempt to shovel snow, but when that proved futile they built a snowman on the porch which launched into a snowball fight. When they tried to make snow angels, Joi was almost suffocated by the whiteness. They returned inside. While she showered herself warm again, Pride made cornbread, and they ate in the kitchen without *Jeopardy*, and without cigarettes. Joi hadn't missed either. They were caught up in the natural conversation of two friends exploring their pasts and getting to know one another.

"You from Louisiana and can't cook?" he teased.

"I was going to have maids when I grew up. My mama did it all," she said.

"My mama taught us all to cook, iron and sew. She

didn't want us depending on nobody for nothing. Said when we marry, we're to marry for love, not for a house-keeper."

"Is that why you never married?"

"Who said?" Pride mock-challenged with a smile. "I was married once. We were both too young."

"Was this her house?"

"Nope. Bought this two years after we split."

"You have children?"

"Not a one," he said and sipped his coffee. "What about you? Never married?"

"Nope." She countered him sip for sip, not wanting to give him any false hope. "Right man hasn't come along yet." She rose from the table. "I'll wash this time," she volunteered.

"Will you know him when he comes along?" he asked, joining her at the sink and reaching for the teatowel.

"I'll know." Her eyes rose to challenge his, but unable to sustain the intensity of his mesmerizing stare, she looked away. "When he comes along."

After the kitchen was restored to its usual tidiness, Joi asked to see his workshop.

"Really? No woman has ever asked me about my hobby. Now, it's not as clean as the rest of the house," he apologized, opening the basement door, cutting on the light and leading her down the steps.

"There's hope for you yet, huh?" She looked at his work bench and the bust of a woman. Her image was spun from clay and it sat on a separate pedestal, finished, and Joi wondered why it wasn't upstairs on display.

"Who's that?"

"My mother, best as I can remember. She died when I was fifteen."

"You look like her." Joi inspected the sculpture, not knowing why she was glad it wasn't a bust of his ex-wife.

She settled in on a stool by his side and watched him fashion a pin from mother-of-pearl, glass beads and wood. As he spoke easily, admitting to not having much time to spend on this pastime recently, Joi's eyes scanned the rest of the basement: a pool table, a bench with a set of weights, a punching bag suspended from a ceiling rafter, and an open door through which a washer, dryer and ironing board could be seen.

According to the news, the snow broke a twenty-six-year record as it continued to fall, so Pride built her a fire and left her on the couch for another night The next day snow fell anew. As spaghetti sauce simmered on the stove and Pride went through his paces on the bench with his weights, Joi played around with the pool cue. She tried to ignore his bulging biceps which rippled in response to the tension and release rhythm of his lifting. A "v" of sweat darkened the center of his thin, cut-off t-shirt.

"That's it," he said, and sprang up from the prone position. Joi tried not to stare and went back to her awkward pool stance. "Hey, lemme show you how that goes," he said. He walked over and placed himself squarely behind her. She flinched from the nearness of him, and he said, "I guess I smell a little ripe. I'll take care of that in a minute. But this goes come-sa."

He laced her fingers over the long, slender pool stick.

At his touch, she inhaled deeply and couldn't breathe out. It had been so long ago that she had had a man that close to her—a man of his stature, his presence, his intimacy. This man she had pigeonholed as a nowhere nuisance was now filling her senses. His fresh, manly musk was intoxicating; she thought she'd explode. She was glad she wasn't facing him. As his hands slid up her arms, the house plunged into sudden darkness. Rescued by the night, she allowed a puff of breath to escape her lips.

"Power outage," he pronounced, seemingly unaware of the havoc he was creating through her body. "C'mon." He took her hand and guided her toward the basement steps and up into the snow-lit kitchen. He unhanded her and expertly lit candles while she tried to emotionally regroup. She thanked the Lord for the darkness and Pride's excusing himself to take a shower.

She concentrated on the fire shimmering in its place and fought the urge to imagine his polished mahogany body being soaped up, then rinsed clean. She absently leafed through a sports magazine, forcing the unnatural inclination of thinking of him as only a friend, like Dante. Pride had been a perfect gentleman over the past two days. He hadn't made any advances, although Joi almost wished he would, so she could label him a predictable predator and reaffirm her unsavory opinion of all men— that they were interested in only one thing. Instead, Joe Pride was seducing her without touching her; a lethal, slow dance of heart and soul. As Joi looked at his trophies, she realized that Joe Pride wanted it all. And he was used to getting whatever he wanted.

That night they ate spaghetti, broccoli and garlic bread by candlelight—compliments of Mother Nature and Detroit power. The red wine had made her woozy, but Joi remembered Pride laying her on the couch and tucking her in. As firelight licked the side of her face, he said, "Good night, Joi."

She lay back on the soft cushions and watched his lean, muscled body stand over hers, then leave. She bit her bottom lip, closed her eyes and went to sleep.

On the third day, Detroit dugout and her idyllic world evaporated with the sunlight that began to melt the snow. She hated to go home. She wanted to stay here forever; she wanted to leave, fearful that her resolve was beginning to fray.

"Thanks, Joe Pride," she said as he eased his car in front of her apartment building. "Wanna come up?" she asked, knowing there was no place to park on the snow-packed street.

"Sure. Lemme find a spot for my car."

"No!" Joi exclaimed, not expecting him to say yes." I mean, let me out, I got no boots." She stepped into the snow pile that ate her legs up to her thighs. She turned to him and said, "6C—straight up."

"Okay."

Joi bolted up the six flights, leaving the sluggish elevator to its own devices. She slammed open her apartment door and the smell of garbage smacked her in the face.

"Aw, damn!"

She stuffed the plastic bag closed and threw open her

windows, then reached for a can of air freshener. She kicked her National Geographies under the sofa bed and tried forcing her blankets into the fold, transforming her unmade bed back into a couch. She realized it looked lumpy, but ignored it and started jamming one week's worth of underwear into the hamper. She spotted the dirty dishes across the room and charged back to the kitchen and desperately began hiding them in the cupboard.

"Aw, crap!" She sighed in resignation when she looked over at the wreck of the room where most people bathe. She slid across the parquet floor to the bathroom door.

"Aw, man," she lamented, eyeing the caked deodorant drying out from exposure. The razor for her legs sat on the tub where deflated suds were encrusted around the perimeter. Bobby pins on the floor, an open tube of toothpaste, and white stockings hung from the shower rod like nylon icicles. Hell, she'd just close the door and hope he wouldn't have to go. The doorbell rang just as she sent crossword puzzles flying under the TV.

"Welcome to my humble abode," she said breathlessly trying to cover the chaos.

"Airy," he said, sauntering in. Expecting warmth, he bristled at the blast of cold air.

"Oh, the window." She went to close it. "I feed the birds sometimes," she lied. She looked around at her disheveled efficiency and thought of his perfect place. "Okay. I cannot tell a lie. I'm a slob," she admitted. The best defense was an offense.

"Opposites attract," he said." I couldn't get a space, so

I'll have to take a raincheck. You cook." He walked to the door and she followed.

"Lean Cuisine," she countered and smiled genuinely for the first time since he'd come.

"I don't think so. We'll work something out. See ya, Joi."

"Bye, Joe Pride, and thanks."

She closed the door behind him and walked to her picture window, which dominated the efficiency. She knelt on its generous windowsill and saw his car's hazard lights blinking gold into the surrounding snow. When he got to his car he waved, and she shrank back, not realizing he could see her, before she waved back. She cut on the TV, got a pail, poured some detergent into it and fished for her cigarettes as the water foamed suds. She stopped. She hadn't missed smoking in three days. She threw the half-empty pack in the trash and commenced cleaning her apartment.

≈≈

Pride didn't call that night and Joi was beginning to think it was all a fluke that lean, mean, clean Joe Pride would really be interested in her. She just wanted him for a friend. After he made his play—men always did—she'd tell him that she didn't like him in that way but she enjoyed his company. They could become platonic friends. Joi had it all figured out. But now, after he saw how she lived, why would he call? He was a man of substance, property and pride. She lived in an untidy efficiency. She was a waitress. Still, she checked the telephone a few times to make sure there was a dial tone. She endured a call from her mother about everything in general and nothing in particular. Once her mother had decided that Joi had stayed with Ella, the character assassination of "that old, fast waitress" began. Joi rather admired the woman who was closer to her mother's age than hers, but still had that joie de vivre to keep a tight body and a healthy interest in the opposite sex. If her mother were to do the same, she'd have less time to concentrate on her daughter. Joi listened as her mother continued to tie up the line and sap her energy, while she silently wished for call-waiting, then told herself she didn't care if Pride called or not. She had enough friends.

She slept fitfully that night, only to be jerked awake early the next morning by the doorbell. Halfway hoping Pride would come back, since the apartment was now ready for him, she opened the door. It was a telegram which read:

There are twelve J Martins in the telephone book. You are not one of them. Please call me at 555-1389. JP.

Joi smiled.

CHAPTER 3

When Detroit finally dug out, Louie's reopened. within the week, things had returned to normal. Pride and Joi were circumspect as they traded secret glances and knowing smiles. Joi's respect for him deepened; she liked the way Pride never let on that they had spent three days and two nights together. But over the next few days, Joi became dimly aware that the guys had started noticing little things; her giving Pride the steak sauce without his asking for it. And at dinner, his coffee, black with two sugars, came that way so he didn't have to add a thing. They observed that she saved him a big piece of peach pie after she had told them she was out. Their smiles and the subtle, peripheral looks were clocked as the guys noted their movements.

Joi bit her bottom lip and shifted her weight from one scuffed-up white shoe to the other as the sun caressed the side of her face and disappeared into her dimple. She had enjoyed being distantly friendly with Joe Pride over the past week, but now…the pressure.

"Joi?" Pride brought her back from her quiet musings.

"Yeah, I heard you." She wiped her forehead of imagined sweat and slid her thumbnail between her front teeth.

A date. It had been years since she'd been asked out. She hadn't missed it. She'd been to the Hot Spot a couple of times with Ella and Chantel, which always reconfirmed for her that she'd rather be home with a bag of microwave popcorn between her legs, an old black and white movie on television and a roll of toilet tissue. But now that he was asking her out, she had to worry about what to wear, the hair and the makeup—then he picks her up, and the expectations at the date's end…

"Joi," Pride interrupted her thoughts again, "it's just a surprise birthday party Shorty's throwing for his wife, Ruby—"

"I know." She looked up into his waiting brown eyes and relented. "Okay," she said, shrugging her shoulders and wiping sweat from the divot under her nose before brushing hair from her face. "Why not? We're just friends."

"Just friends," he reassured her with a wide grin. "Now, lemme see you smile."

"Don't press your luck. Okay?"

"Okay."

After they exchanged quick smiles, Joi went back to work. Pride was content with her backward glance. He refused to let her go to that place of hers where she closed the door behind herself. Pride knew women and he sensed in Joi not deprivation, not complacency, but a quiet, controlled fear bred from a lack of trust and practice.

≪≫

Joi eased her key, then her shoulder, into her front door.

"Hello, Lovey," Dante sang out, sliding on his gold slippers across the hallway and stopping right at Joi. "Here, I'm returning your earrings." He opened his hands and the rhinestones sparkled in his tanned palm. "Maybe one day you'll get a chance to use them."

"Maybe I will," Joi quipped. She went in and hung her coat on its hook, ignoring Dante's perfectly arched and raised eyebrow. Her friend and neighbor was at least ten years her senior, and despite his proclivities, was still a handsome man, though on the canvas of his smooth nutmeg-colored skin, faint character lines were beginning to etch themselves around his eyes and mouth; but they in no way diminished his stunning and flamboyant style. His nails were always manicured and his hair fastidiously coiffed, but that was expected from the owner and head stylist of Dante's Inferno, the hottest beauty salon in Detroit.

"Do tell, Lovey." He followed her into the kitchen as she placed a bag of groceries on the dinette table. He swiped, then popped a can of birch beer. Joi shot him an intolerant glance. "Who held your hand after you found out the louse was married?"

"Am I gonna pay for that all my life?" she asked, shedding her shoes and sweater.

"Small price—Oh, you've cleaned up!" Dante noticed. The room crowned by the picture window was almost immaculate. He couldn't see into the closed bathroom door, but the kitchen and its dinette were spotless. "Are you ill?"

Joi stepped out of her uniform without answering and put on an oversized St. Martin T-shirt, a gift from Dante's latest Caribbean jaunt. She took out one microwave dinner and motioned toward the other, silently asking

Dante if he was staying for dinner.

"How can you eat that mess?" he huffed. "You need a good man like I have, to take care of you."

"Maybe I do."

"Alex Trebeck?" Dante aimed sarcastically. He crossed his shapely, clean-shaven legs at the ankle.

"No." She smiled slyly at him.

"Did the lee Princess meet a welder?"

"He's just a friend."

"I'll take him. Besides, Lovey, that's how it starts. Details?"

"We're just going to a birthday party for one of his friend's wives."

"Oh, how-plebeian. But nice."

"Look, I remember when you were still Regi from Tupelo."

"Ouch. No need to get bitchy. Maybe he'll be your sugar daddy, like mine. We're all about reinventing ourselves, Lovey."

"Don't get happy. I'm just going to a house party, okay?" she said, pointing a bunch of carrots at him.

"Oh my," he replied. "I don't believe I've ever seen you with fresh veggies before. This is more serious than even you realize," he teased. "Is he the reason for the redecoration?" He fanned his graceful hands expansively around the apartment like a wand. "I like him already."

"He's mine, okay?"

"Would I do that?" Dante took a mock-wounded stance, his hand to his chest. "Well, we'll have to get something appropriate to wear." He dashed off to her closet.

"I just want to eat, watch Alex and crash, okay?"

"Oh, how dismal," he said, ignoring her and assessing the state of her wardrobe. "We'll have to go shopping. True, the '70s are back, but let's not wear the originals. Okay?"

Already this one date was negatively impacting her life. She found herself spending her precious weekend off-hours in the company of Dante and Ella on their single-minded mission to find her the perfect dress. They dragged her from store to store until they settled on an ecru sweater dress designed to showcase Joi's fine curves. They rounded out the purchases with hose that matched, new shoes—heels—and a camel hair coat.

The pair followed her home and continued playing their Professor Higgins to her Liza Doolittle, but Joi flatly refused to let Dante put a "little relaxer" in her hair to "tame the curls and add some weight." Dante volunteered to do her nails if she would stop biting them long enough to grow some by next Saturday night.

She finally put them out and closed the door on the well-meaning duo who were going to Balzac's for coffee. Ella and Dante were exhausting enough alone, but together, overwhelmingly suffocating. Once they were gone, Joi was left with her new frock and her old worries. She kept telling herself Joe Pride was just a friend. It had been so long since she had cared about anyone, and she didn't have the time or energy to sustain a man in her life again. Her last foray into romance had been a disaster. While she was well over it and him, she just couldn't go through all that drama again in this lifetime—the ultimate disappointment and the void he left. It was all so tiring and hardly worth the effort.

"But Pride is just a friend," she reassured herself aloud. He could ease me back into the dating scene so when I'm ready I won't have to take a remedial course, she thought. "I'll be okay. I have to start sometime. Somewhere. Why not him?" she reasoned with her mirror-image.

∽∾∽

"Shorty, teach me to cha-cha?" Pride asked as they walked to their cars at the shift's end.

"Say what? That old dance, why not just form a Madison line?"

"I wanna learn by Ruby's birthday party." Pride turned up his collar against the hawk blowing from the river.

"You not cha-cha-ing with my wife," Shorty teased, and they chuckled as they dodged cars.

"Well?"

"Damn, man. The cha-cha?" Shorty's scowl receded and he shook his head. "That was a smooth dance, though. A nice groove-two bodies swaying together. Folks don't dance together no more. Okay, man. Who you bringing?"

"Let's just say Ruby won't be the only one surprised."

A couple of nights that week, Pride drew the shades of his office and put on the "Drifters Greatest Hits" CD while Shorty showed him, "One, two, cha-cha-cha."

"You pretty light on your feet for a big guy, Pride," Shorty teased.

"Hush, man, or people will start to talk," Pride

quipped back.

"You got it and I'm outta here, man." Shorty let Pride's door squeak open and echo in the quiet, cavernous hallway. Seeing the coast was clear, he inched his squat body into the corridor. "Just keep practicing. Later."

"One, two, cha-cha-cha," Pride counted as his body moved in syncopated cadence, his tall frame silhouetted against the dingy yellow shade. He walked to his car cha-cha-ing. With a market cart in front of him as he shopped, he practiced. From his driveway to his front door, he practiced. But he broke loose in the sanctuary of his living room. As the Drifters blared from his stereo, he mastered the turns, the hesitations, imagining the fine brown frame of Joi Martin securely in his hands and responding to his every command. He was ready.

⤙❧⤚

"Surprise!" everyone yelled and engulfed the birthday girl as her husband fell back, leaving his wife to the well-wishers.

"Well cut my legs and call me Shorty. You were right, Joe Pride," Shorty said in greeting, looking at his friend who was standing proudly next to Joi. "The surprise is on me. Miss Martin, how nice of you to come."

After they all retreated to the basement where the food and drink were as plentiful as the music, Pride said, "I think they're playing our song." He led Joi to where they had pushed back the rug to expose the linoleum dance floor.

"Well," Joi said as Pride turned her while they cha-chaed to "Some Kind Of Wonderful."

"Surprises are all around tonight. Where'd you learn to cha-cha like this?" She was impressed.

"I'm an athlete and dancing is a sport." He spun her again in synchronicity; they ended up in the same rhythm and the crowd cheered. "Just a little something I picked up." They danced together like seasoned veterans until the last note. ' "Sand in My Shoes' by the Drifters," he identified the next song. "Know why I had them play that? 'Cause I got a contract with that boutique for my jewelry."

"Really? That's great, Pride." She was happy for him. He would make big bucks with his gorgeous jewelry.

"Thanks to you, Joi." He double-turned her.

"You're the one with the talent."

"Yeah, but you saw something in it I didn't. Thanks."

The music stopped and the revelers sang Happy Birthday before Ruby cut the cake. Everyone laughed when she threatened to kill her husband if he told the guests how old she was. She opened her gifts and thoughtfully acknowledged all the givers. Ruby thanked Joi for the bath salts, but "Oooohed" loudly, along with everyone else, over Pride's ethnic necklace.

"It's inspired by the Masai Tribe," Pride said as Ruby fingered the metallic leather, the brass strips and the cowrie shell charms. "They signify wealth."

"Lord, are you listenin'?" Ruby asked with a hearty laugh.

"Let's get this party jumpin' again," Shorty, with the help of Jack Daniel's, yelled. "I know!" He snapped his fingers, put on a record and sang a few bars of "She Drives Him Crazy" before Ruby told him to "cut that mess off."

"Hey, hey, you ain't running this show," Shorty told her and she kissed him playfully. "Now," he said in his most dignified voice, "we have a little something special for our second guests of honor," Shorty said eyeing his wife. "Marvin Gaye's 'Pride and Joy' for our own Pride and Joi. You'll start it off. This is like the Soul Train spotlight dance."

"Soul Train didn't have no spotlight dance, fool," Ruby teased.

"But we do! Go 'head. Cut a rug, you two."

Like the phoenix, the party rose again. Appetites surfaced and were satisfied again, accompanied with stories from the factory. The dance music was replaced by the blues, and some of the tall tales turned to James Pride—what a good man he was, hard worker and trusted friend—and ended with how proud he would be of his baby boy, Joe. At about 3:30, while BB King plucked "Lucille," Pride and Joi said their good-byes.

"Shorty loves his blues," Ruby said with a smile.

"Thanks for coming, Joi. Sure hope to see you again." Shorty winked. "We pitched a wang dang doodle tonight didn't we?" Shorty asked as Ruby punched him playfully.

"I like them," Joi said as she sat close to Pride on the ride back home.

"Yeah, they're good people."

"And when Edgar went into that crazy dance—"

"The slop—"

"Yes…" They laughed for the last three blocks to her

front door. "You want to come up?" She looked into his soft brown eyes with their lush-lashed awning.

"Yes," he said quietly. The glow from the streetlight caressed her face the way he wanted to. He found a space big enough for his LTD, parked with aplomb, then walked around and opened the door for Joi.

They held hands from the car to her front door. She gave him the key and watched him open her door. She hung up his coat on a hook as he walked to the middle of the room. The light from the street lamp commingled with the moon, funneling the lunar rays into a giant muted spotlight. She walked past him and clicked on the stereo, deciding they didn't need more light.

"Coffee?" she asked.

"No," said he, "but how about a dance?" He held out his hand.

"Sorry, no cha-cha," she said of music. She took his hand and moved in instinctively to fit into the contours of his body, only to be embarrassed when she realized the song wasn't a slow drag.

She chuckled nervously as he rearranged her body, putting one of his hands around her waist and lacing his with hers in front of them. They did a shuffle step to begin the mid-tempo dancing as Pride proclaimed, "I couldn't have picked a better groove. You like this? All 4 Ones', 'I Could Love You Like That.' " He began singing with the group.

Joi followed Pride with ease as she picked up on some of the lyrics about Romeo and Juliet, Cinderella and a Prince Charming rescue, liking romantic movies, making promises, tenderness, understanding, moving heaven and earth if you were my girl and dreaming of a love that's everlastin'. Pride then sang the title with the group again— "Can Love You Like That."

More than his voice and the words, Joi noticed the sincerity of it all and fought the feelings he was conjuring up in her. But when this one song blended into the old Boyz II Men's "I'll Make Love to You," she found herself surrendering, intuitively moving into him for the long awaited slow drag. Her body sought refuge in his. He felt good to her; he smelled good and made her feel relaxed, safe and comfortable. He silently reciprocated in kind as the length of his desire said hello to her thigh. She was glad she had put fresh sheets on her sofa bed. It would be easy for him to push the coffee table out of the way and slide open their trampoline for the night. She smiled. At the song's end, his full, luscious lips sought hers, and they kissed. His lips were as firm and soft as she had imagined; his moustache tickled as his hands ran heatedly across her back. She whimpered. Her nipples tensed and her womanhood expanded as juices began to flow in anticipation of an unrehearsed night of passion.

"I better go," he said.

What? her inner self yelled; her outer self was too stunned to speak.

"Maybe we better take it slow," he said. He waited for his manhood to cool down and catch up with his mental decision, and the gap between his physical and mental state made his voice thick and hoarse. He kissed her again, and she looked directly at him. Her eyes twinkled like wet onyx in the night. "Sparkle," he said, stroking the side of her cheek before taking her to the door with him. "I have tickets for *The Phantom of the Opera*. I know you like that sorta thing—"

"That's wonderful—I'd love to go." She beamed, letting his hand go so he could put on his coat.

"We can go to Amalfi's for dinner before the play."

"When?"

"Next Saturday."

"Oh." She hid her disappointment at the week's wait.

"Pick you up at six."

"Did you make reservations?" She watched his eyebrows knit into a question, suspecting he had not. "It's all taken care of. So I'll see you tomorrow at Louie's." She wanted to ask him about later today. It was Sunday and they were both off.

"I enjoyed tonight," he said, taking her hands again.

"Me too."

He bent to kiss her again. His tongue set her body aflame. They tore themselves apart and he hoped he could walk. "Good morning," he said and tweaked that delicious indentation above her luscious, sweet lips. "I'll call you later." She watched him descend her steps until he was out of sight. She leaned against her closed door, letting the taste of him linger on her lips while the throbbing in her groin subsided. She smiled, and in the company of darkness, remembered that the last time she had felt like this, she was falling in love. Then, his name had been Joaquin Summer. He was a five-foot, eleven-inch powerhouse on the basketball team the first time she saw him. He was

Detroit's All-City, All-State and handsome; the color of shredded wheat with jet-black hair and a moustache to match. When she actually met him at the university, it was love at first sight for her. With all the women constantly around him, it took him longer to even notice Joi, but when the dust cleared, he chased her until he won her. By their junior year they were making wedding plans after graduation. He was going on to dental school and she shared her brother's sights on law school. They planned to celebrate those second degree graduations by having a baby: Joaquin Jr. if it was a boy, and Sky if it was a girl. Besides liking the alliteration of Sky Summer, they liked that when her teacher called her last name first, their daughter's name would be Summer Sky. The parents-to-be laughed in each other's arms with their serious-silly plans to spend the rest of their lives together. Folks always remarked on how lucky they were to have one another and how beautiful their children would be. The youthful innocence of it all, thinking that life was theirs for the taking, was unequaled.

The phone jangled Joi back to the present; she wondered who would be calling her at this hour. "Hello?"

"Hi." Joe Pride's velvet voice made her moist all over again. "I just wanted to say good morning, again."

"Good morning, again." She smiled into the phone.

"I hated leaving you."

"Then next time you'll have to stay."

"Oh, really?"

"Really."

"I accept," he said and Joi giggled. "So I guess the

quicker we go to sleep, the quicker time will fly by, and I'll
be there to pick you up for the play."

"Seems so," she said.

"Then good night and sweet dreams."

"Guaranteed."

∽◌∾

Every day they saw each other throughout the work
week, time became their enemy. Apt punishment for not
making love the previous Saturday, it seemed this Saturday
would never come. Finally, the night came and Pride eyed
the boa-clad bathrobe of Dante as he escorted Joi from her
apartment. In his fuzzy slippers Dante walked with them
past the stairs to his own apartment. "You guys have a
scrumptious time!" Dante said with a lilt.

"He's a good friend," Joi said before Pride could
comment.

"Don't bother me none. Could be worse," he said,
opening the front door for her. "Could be a platonic friend
I'd have to worry about." He thought about the Chris
Rock joke that a male-platonic friend is just a dick in a
glass—to be broken for emergencies. Pride chuckled to
himself but wouldn't dare share his thoughts with Joi. "I
don't have to worry," he said.

"But maybe *I* do," Joi teased as she sauntered ahead of
him toward the car.

"Believe me, you don't," he countered. "I'm one
hundred thousand percent male and proud of it."

"I just bet you are," she sassed. Her eyes glowed as she

lowered herself into the leather seat of his car.

"Oh, baby." He grinned like a Cheshire cat.

All of a sudden the nocturnal fantasy of seven nights ago was replaced by the sober reality of this night as the Pride party was led to a reserved booth at Amalfi Restaurant, nestled behind a flurry of ferns. Joi was both apprehensive and excited about the evening's prospects, remembering her brazen invitation for a private party after the play. She was so self-absorbed with her inner turmoil that she didn't immediately notice Pride's panic at seeing all the silverware, glasses, plates and bowls showcased against the backdrop of the pink linen tablecloth, awaiting his etiquette faux pas. Clearly he was in foreign territory. When the waiter ignited the candles and flapped the matching pink napkin into Pride's lap, he jumped at the gesture, obviously not wanting any man anywhere near his lap. It made Joi chuckle. Then he joined in, and the heavy tension was relieved by their laughter. When the waiter introduced himself with the cutesy name of Sean, Joi remembered her inner tirade regarding the luncheon-ladies at Louie's. By the time he finished reciting the specials of the evening, Joi was convulsed with laugh-crying so much so that Sean took offense and decided to give them a "few minutes to peruse the menu."

It was a great stress release for her, though Pride seemed a little confused. "I'm sorry," Joi said. She dabbed her tears and frowned at the little specks of mascara on her pink napkin, which Dante had talked her into wearing. "Well, *voila*! I'm a luncheon-lady!"

"I'm glad you're having such a good time," Pride

offered, perplexed by her proclamation. "Well, you're in such a good mood, maybe we'll skip the play." He chuckled and she didn't. "Maybe we put a little too much pressure on ourselves." Joi threw him an uneasy smile and, sensing her trepidation, he continued. "Maybe we'll just go with the flow and relax and enjoy the evening. As long as you tell me which forks to use."

She smiled. "Deal. Just start working your way from the outside in."

They selected a nice cabernet sauvignon and toasted "to friendship" before Joi got him to try escargot, not telling him they were snails until after he had said they "weren't bad." They talked, laughed and made up stories about other diners. Pride devoured his filet mignon—rare with baked potato—as Joi enjoyed her bouillabaisse. They shared a Caesar salad and mountains of crusty bread before settling on dessert: peach cobbler for him, and for her, chocolate decadence cake with white chocolate lava center and a spiral of whipped cream.

"Where do you put it all?" he asked, as they were served cappuccinos. They were about to go the distance with after dinner drinks when they realized that they barely had time to get to the play.

They dashed across town and settled into their red velvet seats during the overture.

Almost immediately, Pride was bored beyond belief. He couldn't relate to the screechy-singing of these white actors or the hokey plot: a phantom living in an opera house. He racked his brain for the last time he'd even been to a play; must have been when his mother took them to see *The Wiz* with Stephanie Mills, or *Guys And Dolls* with Robert Guillaume. He'd never been to a white play. But when he glanced over at Joi, he smiled. She was captivated by the music and the costumes. She was intensely absorbed by this spectacle. But then, she read *National Geographic* magazines, he thought. So he tried viewing the play through her eyes, and, in so doing, he began to understand and enjoy it. By the time the actors sang "All I Ask of You," Pride was looking past the irritating, high-pitched voices to the lyrics of the song, and he immediately saw the relevance. The words were going by him fast and furious, but the guy and girl were singing something about commitment—one love, one lifetime, being there to shelter and guide, anywhere she was going he wanted to go too.

Pride took Joi's hand as the heaven-sent song translated from the characters on-stage to the black couple in the eleventh row, center, just as the man and woman were promising that all they said was true.

The impact of the full orchestra crescendos swelled and filled every timber of the immense theater and thundered through the audience. Pride watched a tear spill from Joi's eye, journey down her brown cheek and fill her dimple with its sweet nectar. He offered his handkerchief, and she wiped her emotions away. At the song's end, Pride raised her hand to his lips and brushed them gently across her closed knuckles before kissing it. She looked lovingly at him, and her black eyes shone like polished onyx. He was happy he'd made her happy.

"I like that song, 'All I Ask of You,' " he critiqued as they walked hand and hand to the car. "But I'd like to hear

Jeffrey Osborne or Peabo Bryson do it. With their ranges they could put a hurtin' on it."

"It was beautiful, wasn't it? Thank you, Pride."

"Evening's not over yet. My buddy owns a jazz club. You want to go there for a night-cap?"

"No. I want to go home." Her eyes held his spellbound and, though no words were spoken, the meaning was not lost between them.

The door of her apartment whined open, announcing the arrival of a new beginning for the couple. Pride removed her coat and placed it on the hook next to his as she went in and flipped on the stereo. It was something slow, mellow, unrecognizable, but the title didn't matter because background music was not important here. He walked to her standing in the middle of the room, waiting for him. He approached her. Their arms slid comfortably around one another as if this had all been done before instead of the first time. His lips devoured her pouty perfect ones and they kissed in a never-ending explosion of exploration. Of longtime want and desire. She arched her back so that all of her body parts could touch every salient imperative part of his. The slow dance movement began, and the smell of faded cologne, of wine consumed long ago, commingled with a faint garlic chaser, and transported her to the earthiness of them. The naturalness of them. His granite-hard formation against her thigh let her know that, not only was the rhythm of their kissing in tune, but their mutual desire.

His hands slid down her body, caressing the fullness of her hips, then traveled back up past her small waist to her expansive back. He held her tenderly as they kissed. He held her like the prize she was: a black china doll, fragile and weary. He now held this elusive lady who had kept him company in his dreams for so many tortured nights, and in his thoughts by day. Now, in the wash of moonlight, all alone, he had her. He really held her, this woman for whom he had slowed his car down so that she and a shopkeeper were forced to stop their conversation and look at him. Pride had waved and Joi had looked dead at him and rolled her eyes in disgust, the unspoken word "Bama" hung between them. Now, he held this woman who wanted him as much as he wanted her. This woman who had joned on him for using texturizer in his hair. This woman who saw in him all that he could be, noticing the uniqueness of his bracelet. This woman who dared him to stretch and reach beyond his world. He now held her in his arms. He didn't want to rush her and risk losing her, but he felt her melting into him, thawing at his every touch. She moaned and moved with him.

Joi was pure liquid. Leaning into Pride was the only thing that kept her from falling. His touch had turned every pore to jelly, a viscous, malleable mass of want and need. When he broke the sweet suction their lips had created, she looked up at him.

"Sparkle," he said of her shining ebony eyes. "Are you ready?"

"No question," Joi sassed; a seductive smile danced across her sensuous pouty lips.

Pride removed his jacket tossing it on a nearby chair. It missed. Neither of them cared as he whipped both his knit

and T-shirts over his head, revealing such muscled definition that Joi felt both turned on and embarrassed by her
lack of matching chest pulchritude. Renegade rays of lunar
light played hide and seek in the chiseled recesses of his
lean, powerful body. He unbuckled his belt, then came to
her again and slid his hands around her waist. Their
tongues dueled; his became the wick that ignited her from
head to toe, like a fuse to dynamite—Whoosh! Her body
blazed with fierce passion as his hands deftly explored the
contours of her lithe brown form. He unzipped her dress;
she hunched her shoulders, allowing it to fall in a puddle
around her feet. He momentarily delighted in the smooth
feel of the silk chemise before he sent it to join the dress.
She had reciprocated by setting his pants free, and he lifted
her from her cloth puddle and stepped from his own
toward the sofa. He laid her on the clothed altar of the
couch in a stream of moonlight, then removed her bra and
savored the sight of her breasts free and firm before him.
He bent his head into the silver light and began anointing
her body with delicate, searing kisses. Her eyes shimmered
like polished obsidian.

"Sparkle," he whispered as he closed her eyelids with
tiny kisses and journeyed down her jaw, her neck, her
collarbone to the valley between her breasts. His slow-
hand-loving was driving her to a fever pitch; she felt as
though she was drowning in her own desire for him. She
fought against acting like a deprived sailor on shore leave
and accepted his tender loving for what it was: good,
strong and pure.

Pride drew one ripe nipple into the warm, moist cavern

of his mouth before flicking, teasing, taunting it, then leaving it to dry in the wind as his greedy lips closed around the other one, treating it to the same torturously delicious feel. Once he had spent ample time neglecting neither, he continued his southern odyssey with the sensuousness of his full lips, the tickle of his moustache and the length of his hot, serpentine tongue. He rested just above her triangle forest, and then slowly peeled her fuchsia panties from her rounded hips. The sight of her exposed womanhood glistened in his eyes, and if she'd had the strength of voice, she would have asked him, "who is Sparkle now?" His tongue continued its route down her left thigh, turning at her knee to venture back up the right side. Amid his auditory mantra of calling her name, Joi thought herself neglectful. He was pleasuring her in such a way that she had the desire, but not energy, to reciprocate. It was as if he had six hands, all expertly trained and patient. Joi clung to the jagged edges of this-world sanity as other-world ecstasy called to her. She thought she would explode prematurely. As if reading her mind, he stood in the lunar spotlight and removed his last defense, revealing an outstanding ability to pleasure her.

He genuflected before her again, beginning his odyssey anew. They kissed feverishly. Her hands glided across his sable-soft back, lightly consecrated with salty holy water, which shone metallic in the moonlight The air seemed thick and gelatinous as he filled all her senses—sight, sound, smell and taste. Her entire being was perched precariously on the edges of a perilous abyss where she had never been before. She was afraid to soar; she was afraid not to.

As he nibbled on her right thigh, the pungent, earthy perfume emitting from her secret garden taunted him with a sense of urgency he hadn't expected. With the promise of total satisfaction, his coiled tongue retraced its journey back to her lips, while his fingers deftly cajoled the passion-swollen flower that, like a sentinel, guarded the garden's entrance. Her moan, as sexy as the wail of a New Orleans' sax, matched his deep-throated growl—the sound of a predator anticipating entrance into Eden and basking in its full tropical lushness.

His need collided with her deprivation, and Pride used the secreted nectar to slide into paradise. They exploded together in rhythmic unison. Joi free-fell for miles before launching laughingly into heavens; she flew about the stars, cruised among the constellations. And when she came back, Pride was there waiting for her.

"Oh, my soul," Joi testified quietly. She was shocked by her winded, unladylike response to his loving. Her greedy inner-child cried out, *I want more, more, more!*

"Well, now," Pride panted. "I'd say that was worth waiting for." He eyed their glistening, intertwined nude bodies bathed in the moonlight on the slender sofa. "Next time we have to let this bad boy out." He patted the couch's cushions.

Joi looked up at him and giggled.

The second time, they opened the bed and used every inch of the covered mattress. The piety, pressure and pretension of the urgent first time was gone, freeing them to savor, linger and enjoy. This time Joi was more aware of his perfectly sculpted body—his Hershey-chocolate skin drizzled with silky licorice hair and inviting nipples. His loving of her was like a bright light which flowed into all the dark recesses of her neglected, overlooked body. He found places in her she never knew she had. When the visual images and physical sensations overloaded their senses, they exploded once again.

Although the remnants of his concern for them both were always there, Joi never once remembered Pride donning his latex cover, she realized as she drifted off to sleep. The man was good!

Pride was sexually satisfied but too excited to sleep. Despite her cool, sultry veneer, Joi was anything but, and the deliciousness of this surprise was an epiphany of discovery for him. Joi Martin had a child's heart with a woman's needs.

Pride was sure she'd awakened an hour or so later because she was aware of the unfamiliar feel of someone sharing her bed. She looked up at him and self-consciously wiped her divot and smoothed back the edges of her hair. He sensed that she was trying to pull away and reenter her aloof world, but Pride followed her, refusing to let her dilute the rarity of what they had just shared. At about three o'clock that morning, with a wipe of his hand along her bare thigh, he coaxed her into another ride to ecstasy before she lay in his arms.

This isn't right. This is all wrong, Joi thought, and then asked, "What are we doing?"

"Falling in love, I hope," he said, his head resting on her forehead. "Scratch that. I'm waiting for you to fall in love with me. I'm already—"

Joi silenced his lips with her finger. "Don't," her eyes implored. Love was not only a four-letter word to her but it was usually fatal. "Let's just take it slow," she said.

"The ball is in your court, my lady." He kissed her forehead and held her tightly.

❧

From the clock radio, the Queen of Soul woke Joi up at eleven. "Ugh!" Joi sighed, looking at the rain through the prism of her picture window. But Aretha belted out her sentiments as she sang about facing another day, being so tired and so uninspired.

"Ahh uumm!" Joi joined ReRe, then turned over and saw the place vacated by Pride. He had to go home, shower and change before work. At about five o'clock A.M., Joi vaguely remembered Pride leaning over her, his cheekbone to hers, and then fluttering his lush lashes with hers. Butterfly kisses, she thought. She knew he'd be excellent at it.

Joi sang out with ReRe this time, signifying how much Pride made her feel like a natural woman.

She rolled over and sprang out of bed, feeling delectably female after last night's tryst, and slinked to the bathroom mirror. She postured, smiled and grabbed the toothpaste like a microphone in time to join Aretha in talking about their men finding their respective souls in the lost and found and coming around to claim them.

Joi continued to back Aretha up as she stripped and

ran the shower water—hot, hard and steamy—over the physical remains of her lovemaking with Pride. She continued singing that prophetic song long after the shower was over and she was dressed and leaving her apartment. In the hallway, Dante's cat Beatrice eased up and rubbed around her legs. Joi looked toward her friend's ajar door.

"Have a nice day...you loud, *natural* woman," Dante decreed with a smirk.

CHAPTER 4

"Bingo!" Joi said, laughing as the spaghetti she threw stuck to the side of the refrigerator.

"Perfect. Al dente," Pride said. "Not Cajun like everything you burned."

"Hey," Joi protested, as her body swayed to the sensuous rhythms of Zack Fluellen's sax. "I got potential."

"You most certainly do." Pride joined her in the sexy dance and she fed him a string of pasta.

The music stopped and they remained intertwined.

"Well, we've had the horns of Coltrane and Davis and a little piano from Thelonious Monk. Who's next?" Joi asked. "We've had the masters, now it's time for the mistresses. Listen, I'm gonna introduce you to my dad's girls."

"Sarah Vaughn? I know her well."

They serenaded each other with "Someone to Watch Over Me" to a laughable end. "I am impressed," Pride said, kissing Joi's nose. "My dad loved Sarah, Selena Fluellen, Gloria Lynne and Dinah Washington."

"Mine too!" Joi exclaimed. It was good to hear them again from a man who revered them as much as her father. "Royce St. Marie was crazy about 'his girls.' He swore they were all born in New Orleans to sing just for him. He brought them to Detroit with him, though he didn't play much after that." The smile slid from Joi's face as she thought of Chip's death. "I guess you never get over losing a child. I never got over losing my brother."

"I hear you." Pride brushed hair back from her temples and pulled her closer to him. "Losing anybody you love is never easy."

Joi was eerily comforted by their shared losses. "Your parents and your brothers..."

"Hey, hey." He raised her chin forcing her eyes to his. "That was then, this is now. And we got each other."

"Yeah," she said quietly, tears brimming her eyes.

"We got spaghetti and the best homemade sauce in the world. Wine, garlic bread...a little salad."

"Yeah." His smile was contagious and melted her heart.

"And tomorrow—tacos!" They chatted and ate while "the girls" sang to them, finishing up with Dakota Staton.

"Whoa, look at the time. We'd better clean up. I've got work to do," Pride said.

"You cooked, so I clean up. Sand in My Shoes is going to want the full order of your jewelry by tomorrow morning."

"You sure?"

"Positive. You're a neat cook, there's not much to do."

"You'll come down when you finish?"

"Don't I always?"

"Yeah." He grinned, went over and kissed her nose before he went downstairs.

As Joi sank her hands into the sudsy water, she thought about how the man working in the basement had enriched her life. He was teaching her how to cook, to knead bread and monitor the ball stage of fudge. She had scorched her blouse as he taught her to iron. He had bought her three-pound weights and an exercise mat so she could work out with him. In showing her how to use them, he eased up behind her, and the demonstration turned into a calorie-burning, lovemaking session on his weight bench—ending up the same way the last pool demonstration, after sinking the eight ball, had. Pride had fired up the grill in the dead of winter because she had a taste for BBQ chicken, and he made the best. He'd enticed her to jog one morning—just one. Morning exercise was not her thing.

As Joi placed the dishes into the drainer, she remembered one Saturday morning, she had slept late and he went out for jambalaya makings; he returned and butterfly-kissed her awake, then showed off her white waitress shoes. Her run-over soles had been replaced by new ones, and he had bought her white shoe polish so they could shine their shoes together on Sunday nights. Joi tackled him onto the bed with gratitude and made love as the jambalaya fixings spilled across the floor.

As she dried the dishes and placed them in the cabinet, she reflected on how the love they made was beyond exquisite; it was honest, tender, sensitive and satisfying. All the cooking, cleaning and washing lessons always ended up with them half-dressed and answering the unrelenting demand their bodies had for each other. Sometimes Pride made her so happy, she would slip from his arms into the bathroom, look at her image in the mirror and cry with bliss before she returned to bed, wrapped her arms around Joe Pride and slept the sleep of angels.

As she wiped the stove, counter and table clean, Joi relished how they had settled into each other's lives like predestined lovers. *Deja vu*. It was all so natural, so easy, so right. His favorite thing to do was frequent the Blue Note Jazz Club, owned by his boyhood friend, Rudy. Her favorite thing to do was to cuddle up with him and an old movie on the couch. Pride had slowly introduced her to his friends in couples: Rudy and Jerona, Mike and Camryn, and Stan and Zanielle, before all six met at the Blue Note to catch Wil Downey and the Tony Rich Project. When it was their time to reciprocate, Pride did most of the cooking while deferring most of the credit to Joi as their guests played bid whist or pinochle. Joi liked his friends, and listened as they made summertime plans—the beach, dawn-cracking fishing trips and backyard BBQ's, which would include their children.

"Right now," Jerona had said, "I go out to get away from my little darlings."

Joi had noticed that Pride was especially close to Jerona whom he called Jer. Later, Pride had told her that Jer was his brother Ronnie's old girlfriend before he died. She was like a big sister to him.

Pride told her that Jerona had quietly taken notes of her own. She noticed the way Pride unconsciously slipped his hand around Joi's waist, or reached across the table to wipe away mustard nestled in the corner of her mouth. Jer told Pride that she had known him to be happy, but never this happy before. "It was good to see. Maybe this Joi was the one." Joi sighed remembering, and knew that Pride had caused her to rethink her position on him. She gave the kitchen one last look. "It is just a sexual relationship," she told herself and descended the basement steps.

She approached him working steadfastly at his bench.

She massaged his shoulders.

"Hummm…that feels good," he said, and leaned his head into her breasts. "So does this—best pillows in the universe."

"Get back to work," she ordered playfully. She looked at the pieces he had ready to go. "Oh, Pride, this one is beautiful." She fingered the metal.

"Yeah. I'm trying out the hammered brass motif."

"You are truly a talented man," she said absently.

He snatched her by surprise and she squealed. "I can take a break and show you just how talented." He nibbled at her laughing cheek. He let his hands roam over her body.

"Tell you what," she said. "You finish up here and we'll both display our talents."

"Deal. Leave me alone, woman, so I can work." He smiled and gave her a love-tap on the behind. She backed away, licking her lips. "I know what I want for dessert."

⊸❀⊱

Pride held Joi tightly and brushed his lips across her cheek as she slept contently in his arms. He hadn't had her for four days—Mother Nature had beaten him to the punch, but he didn't mind. He planned to outstay Mother Nature's range, planned to be there through as many pregnancies as Joi could stand, to have her when her hair grew gray at the roots, when wrinkles lined her pretty brown complexion. He was in for the duration. He'd been waiting for a woman like Joi all his life. She brought meaning and inspiration into his world. He was past the point where he just *wanted* Joi forever—he *needed* her, like the air he breathed. She had enhanced his existence in so many ways: When they went market shopping: trying the Portobello mushrooms in his spaghetti sauce. When she gave him the massages, replacing his baby oil with a fragrant citrus pear oil that teased and titillated his senses as much as she did. Her straddling his back, kneading out the weariness, and in the love. The feel of her delicate bud becoming engorged at the small of his back, as his manhood grew and then pressed into the mattress. He'd roll over, strip the strap of her lingerie, watch it fall, exposing the unmistakable invitation to feast on her ripe nipple. She said she loved the look in his eyes as he beheld her body. He loved the sight of her dimple appearing and disappearing as she traced kisses down his body, the feel of her in his hands, the taste of her in his mouth, the sound of her sultry whimpers giving way to the throaty calls of his name. He was so turned on by this woman. He could be sitting across from her at the Blue Note, catch a glimpse of the lush curve of her lips and get so aroused they'd have to leave. Whether she was a lady or racehorse wild when they made love, he loved it all—all she was and all she made him be.

His mother would have liked her, thought her too skinny and a trifle hinckty-acting, especially after she scrunched up her nose at the thought that she would put her feet into rented bowling shoes. But Bernadette Noble Pride would have gone shopping with Joi. Pride chuckled lightly, remembering the discussion his mom had had with Ronnie, his older brother, about Diana, the girl before Jerona. "Diana's a bona fide tramp. What kinda mother for your children would she make? Could you see me going shopping with her? I wouldn't take her to church, though Lord knows she needs it."

Joi stirred and momentarily blinked awake. "What's wrong?" she asked him sleepily, never fully waking up.

"My mom would have loved shopping with you." He brushed his lips against her cheek again.

"That's nice." Then she was deep asleep, leaving him alone again with his thoughts.

When he was in the tenth grade his mother went to the hospital for some "tests" and never came out. They pulled him out of algebra class and told him to wait in the front office for his father. James Pride picked up his son and drove to Mills Funeral Home. No explanation. Pride didn't have time to say good bye—his mother was gone for good. He remembered the feeling of abject terror and razor-sharp loneliness that followed. His father grieved by drowning his sorrows in the bottom of a bottle while Ronnie took to thrill-seeking—fast cars, mostly—and his younger brother, Tyrone, to drugs. Joe Pride just held on to the goodness of Bernadette N. Pride—the way she liked to cook, and her cleanliness. The house was never clean enough for her with three sons and a husband. But now he had a woman, Joi, who loved him and gave him permission to let some of the orderliness go. Joi showed him the comforts of having a lived-in house. Somehow he didn't think his mother would object, for Joi brought other pleasures and dimensions into her son's life. Yeah, she woulda liked Joi, he thought, not just for the person she is, but because of the vision she had for her son.

He'd had many women who were into clothes, cars, houses, clubbing and gambling trips to Ontario—women who just wanted him to round out or validate their existence. But Joi was a woman of substance. He'd dated his share of factory women, but Joi didn't need to party, hang out with a bunch of other women or profile—externals weren't her bag. Once, he saw her gather her ponytail in one hand and snip it off with the kitchen scissors with the other. He had watched in amazement as her hair coiled into itself and disappeared in the explosion of curls. She threw the offending hair in the trash, and when she caught him looking at her, remarked, "It was bothering my neck." He had dated women with wigs, weaves, fake nails and wrong-colored eyes, but Joi was natural. What God didn't give her, she just didn't need. Joi worked on the inside of her— knowledge and improvement. She had a confidence about herself. With her, he would be a partner, not just a sought-after statistic marked "husband."

He loved the way Joi liked to sit on the commode facing him, watching him shave or pick out and pat down his natural; the way she watched him making jewelry. Coming down from the kitchen with the teatowel still in hand, she'd perch on the stool opposite him, near his mother's bust, and it was as if the two of them were watching him create. She sat at his knees working a cross-word puzzle as he quietly strummed his guitar. He loved how she would crawl up between his legs as he watched a football game on TV, or just lay her head on his chest and take a nap. The way she would come up behind him as he dressed in the morning, slide her hands around his waist and marvel at their handsome images in the mirror. Armed with her own shoes, Joi had become a great bowler. She could now cook without making everything Cajun, and iron—if she really had to. He was a happy man and he intended to make Joi Martin as happy as she made him.

ᴥᴥᴥ

Pride jumped into the air and knocked the basketball toward his teammate, forcing himself off-balance and sliding backward on the polished court.

"Look at him slide. Slide, Joe Pride!" the woman in front of Joi rose and yelled.

"He could slide into me ev'ry day of the week. That Nadine is a lucky girl," the second woman said.

"Luck ran out on her. He cut her loose a good four months ago."

"Say wha? For why?"

"Wasn't 'special' enuf," she offered sarcastically.

"The woman got a new Caddy every year, owned a beauty shop, made boo coo bucks, and she wasn't 'special' enuf?"

"Pride gets his own new ride every two years. But that's the same excuse he gave for gettin' rid of the one fo' har,"

"The supervisor at the telephone company? She had a car and a house."

"Shorty say she wasn't 'special' enuf."

"Well, damn. What does he want?"

"Dating a waitress now."

"A waitress? You lie!"

"Just a waitress. Goldie say she's a looker."

"Keep what you got till you get what you want."

"Well, we know what that is. He's just biding his time with good looks and good sex until Miss Special comes along. Here come Maurice and his wife. Lookit." They stopped talking, then sang, "Hi, Maurice," in unison, greeting the couple with wide smiles until they were out of ear range.

"Po' wife ain't got a clue about Reese and Myrna down in shipping," one woman said. "Going on four years and wifey ain't got a clue. Myrna still thinks he's leaving his wife for her."

"They don't leave the wife—"

"Cheaper to keep her."

Joe Pride dunked the ball with fierceness and hung on to the rim before letting go. When he looked up to give Joi a victory wave and a wink, she was gone.

Joi rushed from the gym and sought the immediate refuge of her apartment. She eyed her image in the mirror. There was nothing special about her. She looked okay but her perfect caramel skin would be cracking soon and her soft brunette curls would thin and turn gray in time.

"Just a waitress" was what they had said, and they were right. No matter how much she read or dreamed about another life, she was just a waitress. Not a supervisor at the phone company, no beauty shop owner, no car, no house— no future. What did Joe Pride want—good sex and someone halfway decent to look at in the process?

Joi grabbed the crossword puzzle and sat on the sofa battling her natural inclination to fight an unseen enemy.

She was on her way to being somebody "special" but the kaleidoscope of fate had twisted her life into knots. Dr. Morton had told her how "the one, two, three strikes" had knocked out all of her reserves. Dr. Morton had warned Joi to guard against closing her fist around her heart—not letting any love in, or love out. The one time she takes Dr. Morton's suggestion and tries to open herself up just a little, love doesn't come in, but criticism from an outside source does, reminding Joi of her place—reminding her of her unspecialness.

Joi continued to work her puzzles and ignore the telephone that had been ringing all afternoon. The doorbell rang. He wouldn't come over unannounced, she thought. She peered through the peephole and was both relieved and pissed to see Ella.

"C'mon and go downtown with me to buy a pair of shoes. I been calling all day but got no answer." She followed Joi back to the couch and her crossword.

"I don't feel like downtown today," Joi said. The phone rang, and rang again. Ella reached for it. "Don't," Joi commanded.

"Good call. Probably your mama. Or maybe it's Joe..." she sang and then remembered. "Weren't you supposed to go to his game today?"

"I went," Joi said, trying to ignore the third volley of rings.

"Hello." Ella yanked up the phone before Joi could object. "Hey, Pride." Joi was violently shaking her head. "We're just fixin' to go downtown. She can't talk right now. Yeah, she's alright. Why wouldn't she be? Yeah, she'll give you a call when we get back. Later." Ella hung up the receiver. "You want to tell me what this is all about? Much as I want to go down and get them shoes. They're finally on sale. I've been watching them for weeks."

Joi was on the verge of tears.

"What is going on, girlfriend?" Ella asked as she sat beside her friend.

"Why me?" Joi said, looking up at the ceiling so a tear wouldn't spill down her cheek.

"Why you what? Oh Lawd, we're not going through this again. Girl, you rock my man Pride's world. It's as simple as that." She stood directly in front of her. "Don't make life so complicated. Who's to say who we fall in love with and who we don't? It's your time of the month, ain't it?" Joi nodded her head. "I knew it. Well, take some Midol, eat some chocolate and get over it. Put on some clothes and just be glad that this fine black man loves your dirty drawers." Ella shook her head, pulled Joi up from the couch and pointed her towards the bathroom. "Some sisters don't even know when they got it good. Got to analyze every little thing…"

As Joi went into the bathroom, Ella picked up the completed crossword puzzle, threw it back on the sofa and said, "Boy, yo' mama sure did a job on you."

⚬≈≈⚬

"What happened to you after the game?" Pride asked as Joi opened her apartment door for him.

"I went shopping with Ella," she answered weakly.

"Yeah, but I thought we'd get a bite to eat afterward."

"Sorry." She walked toward the living room and he followed.

"Joi, what's wrong?" He couldn't tell whether she had been crying or not. "Tell me."

"It's nothing, really."

"It's something. Tell me." His brown eyes implored.

"It was just some women at the game," she began and was instantly regretful. She hated whining in others, and now she felt she was guilty of the same thing. But she knew Pride wouldn't give up until he cleared it up.

"About what?" He bent down trying to engage her eyes with his. "Me?" Joi looked at him but didn't reply. "Joi, I told you that I've never been a saint, and some of those people have known me since I was a teenager. They've seen it all; I've done it all." He slid his one arm around her waist and lifted her chin to him with the other. "That's how I know what I want now. I know what I have and I will do anything necessary to keep you. I love you." Joi sucked in her breath at the sound of his revelation and was immediately unnerved.

"And nobody else. I don't know what it is that keeps you from loving me, but I understand that because of certain things that went down in your past, you can't say it to me right now. That's cool. Because I don't want you telling me because I tell you. I want you to feel it enough to say it. And when you do." His handsome face split into a smile. "It's gonna rock your world, the way loving you has rocked mine." He hugged her. "So it doesn't matter what anybody does or doesn't say about us. They can't see what we have. All that matters is you and me." He looked at her again. "I am a patient man, which is easy when there's no place else I'd rather be than with you. Besides." He rubbed the back of his fingers against her cheek. "I know you love me. How could you not? I am the man. I am your man—and that's what that counts."

"You got some ego, Joe Pride," Joi teased, thankful for the playful mood. "Pretty sure of yourself."

"Most definitely." He let his hands drift down and cradle her derriere. "Make me feel like paradise."

CHAPTER 5

After lovemaking, Joi lay in Pride's arms. The setting sun escaped through the blinds, painting perfectly symmetrical chevrons on his glistening mahogany skin. "What do you want to do for Thanksgiving?" Joi asked. Her question seemingly surprised him.

"I thought you'd be spending it with your mother," he said.

"Fortunately for us, she spends Thanksgiving in Atlanta with my sister. We're not gonna be so lucky for Christmas."

"I thought it was just you and your mother? You were all she had."

"The mantra of Jacquleen St. Marie. Translated, it means 'you're the only one I have left to worry about.' My younger sister, Noel, has a degree, a husband, two-point-five children, a house, two cars and a dog. I'm the loose end of the tidy St. Marie package. As soon as she gets me properly squared away, she's free to relax and enjoy life."

"Umm. Well, we'll do anything your heart desires. You want to go away for the long weekend? Over to Ontario and hit a casino or two?"

"Is that what you do with all your old chippies?"

" 'Chippies?' " He laughed. "Is that another one of those New Orleans words?"

"I just imagine you and Canada have seen a few of your women, and I don't care to be part of the old Pride love-tour." She cut her eyes playfully at him then rolled them back around to gaze into his soft browns.

"Sparkle, we could go and stay in the very hotel, in the exact same bed…and it would be like the first time for me." He kissed her and she ran her hand slowly up his back. "Still, I want to go someplace you've never been with any other female before."

"We've already been there. I go there every time we make love." He ran his lips tenderly across her hand. "In fact, I'm there right now."

"You ever been to the Poconos?" Joi changed the subject quickly. She had already heard those three words once, outside the love-making venue and she didn't want to hear them again. Despite what he said, she did feel a subtle pressure to reciprocate.

"The Poconos?" he asked.

"They have heart-shaped tubs and meals that go on for days."

"That will take some planning—"

"I got nothing but time." She encircled him in her arms and he beamed. "Meanwhile, you, me and Tom Turkey will do just fine."

࿏

For once, Pride broke tradition and didn't join Rudy and Jerona Hampton and their family for his Thanksgiving meal. He and Joi celebrated at his home. After they ate, Uncle Joe made his appearance at the Hampton home, introducing Joi to the children, two sets of grandparents and a cast of aunts, uncles and cousins. Joi watched the interaction of this loving extended family and realized how much she had missed in her own childhood. She saw what she wanted for her own children—if she was ever so blessed. This is what families are all about, generational love and affection, she thought wistfully.

Christmas without Pride was another story. Shopping for the jock had been easy enough, but spending the holiday without him was torturous. While he was no doubt enjoying himself at Rudy's and Jer's with the same Thanksgiving cast of characters, tradition forced Joi to escort her mother to the home of her best friend, and recent widow, Hazel Barnes. Joi had spent countless, uneventful Christmases with the Barnes family, which included their children, grandchildren and assorted relatives. The house which once appeared roomy was now crowded with people and over-decorated. Jacquleen and Hazel had become friends because they shared similar ideology on upward mobility; but Joi had never been close to the Barnes children—they were of different ages and educational accomplishments. Joi looked at these holiday get-togethers as opportunities for the Barnes children to spout their latest professional achievements, since they seemingly only saw each other during the Yuletide season. Joi could never figure out what she was doing here except to play the role of Jacquleen's "beautiful," underachieving daughter.

After Hazel's brothers favored the crowd with their ritual rendition of that holiday classic, "Ole' Man River," they passed out in front of the TV during the football game. As things quieted down, Joi took her usual refuge upstairs sitting among the overflow of coats in front of the bedroom television. For once, *It's a Wonderful Life* wasn't on. As she channel surfed with the remote, a blur of black folks caught her attention. She immediately recognized Ethel Waters in Cabin in the Sky. Joi chuckled when she heard the actress singing something about happiness being just a thing called Joe.

"You ain't said nothing but a word," Joi said, pushing the coats aside and sitting on the edge of the bed.

Joe Pride was so good to her and for her; his name said it all: an eponym of what he exuded and instilled in others. He had forced her from the periphery of life to jump right into its center and become the core of it. Her love life had been like a ten car crash, leaving her love-shy and not at all anxious to try again. But Pride had lulled her into the security of him. He challenged her, dared her, freed her and supported her. She was important to him; her name an eponym of all she'd given him. "You are the center of my joy," he'd said one Sunday after a gospel group had just finished their song. Her embalmed love life had been a sad refrain; now, with Pride, it was the hallelujah chorus.

Joi cradled a throw pillow in her arms and drove her thumbnail between her front teeth, thinking of him. So much of who she was had been shaped by what she didn't have, but Pride celebrated what she did have. This is it, she thought. She was finally somebody's somebody. She had finally found the man who made her feel complete, the man she wanted to share her life with. She was reminded of Dante's words right after his California trip to Big Sur. He had said he thought of her as he watched the huge granite rocks of the shoreline that would never experience the freedom of being taken out to sea. He'd told her to "let the shoreline go, Joi. Free yourself to enjoy the wild abandon of the sea." Joi had been glad she hadn't followed her friend's advice with Dr. Geoff or the two men that preceded him. But with Pride, she finally understood what Dante meant. With Pride, she was willing to let the shore go. With his patience and tenderness, he was slowly prying her fingers loose from the security of the anchored rocks, coaxing her, seducing her into the swirl of the nearby waves before reaching the smooth-sailing tranquility of the ocean's horizon of forever.

She smiled, realizing that she *trusted* Pride. She hadn't really trusted a man with her heart since Joaquin. With Pride, she shared an intimacy and understated majesty she had never felt before. She and Pride were together every waking moment when they were not at work. She thought of them shopping for food, for Christmas gifts, trying ice skating until they fell and laughingly decided that that sport wasn't in their genes. She recalled their going to Symphony Hall for a classical music concert and how the concertos relaxed them both to sleep. They each took turns elbowing the other awake until they gave up and went for coffee. She thought of him carrying her piggyback up the steps because her toenails were wet with newly applied polish, and then ruining them and his sheets anyway as they made love. They enjoyed the simplest of tasks as long as they were together. Pride made her want to stop smoking, stop biting her nails, let her hair grow, buy new lingerie, paint her toes ruby red and get refitted for a diaphragm. He made her feel sixteen and in love for the first time again. Like the Stylistics said, he made her feel "brand new." Of course he wasn't perfect—she didn't know what that foot massager as a Christmas gift was all about. But he had surprised her with deliveries: the philodendron plant and a CD of Barbra Streisand's "All I Ask of You" from their first play, *The Phantom of the Opera*. The card had read that her apartment needed some greenery to spruce it up when he wasn't around, and she couldn't kill this plant if she tried. Of the CD he'd said, "It's not Peabo or Jeffery, but Babs does a pretty good job for a white chick." The second plant, a schefflera, had come accompanied with "I Believe in You and Me" by the Four Tops with Levi Stubbs, superbly expressing Pride's sentiments. The card had read, *This is an umbrella plant. I want it to protect you from the rain and storms when I'm not with you. It's the least I could do for someone who gives me sunshine every day.*

So, Joi thought, there was hope for him in the gift department. She chuckled as she squeezed the throw pillow and watched the movie credits roll. She sighed at the thought of her life before Joe Pride. Time had seemed to gobble up space in seasonal clumps: summers, springs, falls, winters and Christmases. This was the seventh or eighth year she'd never planned to spend in Detroit. Finally, a winter in Detroit seemed like summer. Maybe Pride was God's way of rewarding her for giving the married Dr. Geoff the boot. Or maybe Pride was God's way of saying He was sorry. All the pain was intended for someone else all along, and to show you I am good, I'm sending you Joe Pride…forever.

Joi laughed, tossed the pillow aside, picked up the phone and dialed the familiar number. "You're there!" Joi said. "I thought you'd still be with Rudy and Jerona."

"Too much family, not my own." Pride stopped, then said, "Merry Christmas."

"And to you."

"Coming over?"

"No. Jacquleen's still holding court downstairs. I think they pulled out a deck of cards."

"I love you, Joi."

She froze. There was something almost urgent, palpable in the way he said it. Then she smiled, and said, "I love you too." It was a rush, a release, it was orgasmic to finally admit her feelings, not only to him, but to herself. With this revelation, Joi then realized how much she loved him. A single tear broke from her eye and slid down her cheek.

"I'm gonna want that in writing," he said.

"How about just in person?"

"The perfect gift," he said, and Joi could feel his understated happiness through the phone.

Neither of them spoke, each wanting to savor the admission of true love not driven by the passion of heated bodies.

"Well." Joi filled in the silence. "I'll see you tomorrow."

"No question. Call me when you get in, doesn't matter what time."

"Okay."

During the ride home, Jacquleen chatted on incessantly about nothing Joi cared about, and she practically jumped from the car when her mother let her out. She was still floating, not only from Pride's words—she knew he loved her—but from the absolute freedom of telling the one she loved how she felt, especially when it was an emotion she never thought she'd ever feel again. It should have been more romantic over a candlelit dinner, she thought. But it happened when it happened—unscripted, spontaneous, direct from the wellsprings of deep feelings and glad hearts.

Joi climbed the steps of her walkway. Footsteps fell in behind her, yanking her from her lofty perch and putting her on guard. Her eyes quickly scanned her quiet building and she casually glanced over her shoulder and increased her speed. If someone were following her, the problem was going to be at the security door, so she got her keys out, ready to stick them into the lock or the person following her. When she neared the door she swung around, but saw no one. She turned quickly and stuck the key into the lock, then was grabbed from behind. Her scream was muffled by a hand as she fought violently until he swung her around.

"Wild woman!" Pride said with a boyish smile.

"What the hell are you doing?" Joi seethed. "That's not funny!" Her heart was still racing; she wouldn't accept his "I'm sorrys" or attempts to hold her as she kept pacing.

"I just wanted to surprise you!"

"It's four o'clock in the friggin' morning, and I hate surprises!"

"Hey, what's going on down there?" a man shouted from his window.

"Mind your own damn business!" Joi shouted back.

"Joi! C'mon, calm down. Let's go inside."

"I got a better idea. Why don't you go home and I go inside." As she turned her key and walked inside her building, it was clear it wasn't a question.

The next day Joi's apology to Pride was tempered with her explanation that woman were raped and assaulted all over the nation in record numbers, and some things were simply not funny. Pride countered by telling her he had waited for her in his cold car for well over an hour because he just wanted to see and surprise her. He ended the telephone call with the balance of his Christmas gift to her, hoping she didn't mind one more surprise—a trip to Sleepy Hollow Inn in the Poconos.

The weekend after ringing the new year in, they set out on the Poconos adventure ensconced in the LTD, which they left at the airport. Joi boarded a plane for the first time in her life. She had been a zillion places in her mind, but she had never flown before. She sat near the window as Pride folded his tall frame into the bulkhead seat and held her hand for the duration of the flight. The exhilaration of taking off reminded her of making love with him. They rented a car at the airport and Joi studied the map to the Sleepy Hollow Inn while Pride complained about the smallness of the car, the snowy roads and poorly marked signs.

Once Joi saw his classic sign of agitation, the tensing and releasing of his jaw, she tried reassuring him that the resort was just ahead. She slid over near him, nibbled on his ear and ran her newly manicured fingernails up his tight thigh.

"All right, Joi, don't start nothing you can't finish," he said with a playful chuckle, never removing his eyes from the winding road. "Who says?" she teased as she drew his earlobe between her teeth, and her hand disappeared under his coat.

He was responding to her despite himself. They rounded the bend. "Sleepy Hollow," Pride decreed with relief and excitement as he turned into the lodge area. "Now, we will finish this when we get to the cabin."

Sleepy Hollow wasn't the small, quaint-sounding hide-away its name proclaimed. The huge lodge, which had a few rooms, was mostly the hub of all the activities including the dining and entertainment. But Pride had secured the most remote, deluxe cottage available and they drove past all the others which dotted the many acres which formed the Sleepy Hollow enclave.

"These look like slave cabins;' he remarked as the tires of the car crunched to a halt in the snow. He parked and they walked to the door.

Huh," Joi exclaimed as she eyed the cabin's interior. "Slaves never lived like this!"

As rustic as the cabin appeared on the outside, inside was a modern wonderland. There was a roaring fire blazing, welcoming their arrival, around which sumptuous couches and love seats were arranged toward the left. Dead ahead was a circular bed which seemed to be free-floating on a magic carpet in the middle of the room. To the right were floor to ceiling mirrors reflecting a heart-shaped tub surrounded by a riot of sealed bubble baths and oils with labels reading, "Welcome, Pride Party!"

Tucked in the wall behind the bed and adjacent to the tub was a vanity with miles of neatly arranged towels and two fluffy bathrobes. "Well, how long do we have again?" Joi teased, turning to a smiling Pride.

"Five days."

"Well, let's get started." Joi shed her coat and tackled Pride onto the round bed.

"You a wicked woman, Joi Martin," he said gleefully, while he allowed her to plant happy kisses all over his face. They had made quick love and napped before breaking the seal on the bubble bath and trying out the heart-shaped tub for size. From the piped-in music channels, they alternated between an R&B or jazz station. They luxuriated easily in one another's arms, taking turns washing each other with the velvet-soft cloths, then Joi sat on Pride's lap, rested her back against his inviting chest and laid her head on his shoulder. She pointed her big toe, then placed it into the gold-colored spigot.

"Is that a invitation?" Pride spoke softly into her ear.

"Do we need an invitation?" She felt his hands, buoyant and beautiful, tickle her womanhood and she moaned. "I'm at a disadvantage," she managed.

"You just relax and enjoy." And they made love that would make Neptune blush.

They dressed in their fluffy robes as the water drained from the tub. They were still discovering things about the cottage. An inconspicuous refrigerator packed with champagne, assorted cold cuts, and fresh fruit was hidden to the left of the bed near the closet. They had been so ravenous for each other that they hadn't realized how hungry they were for food until they came upon it. They picnicked in front of the ever-roaring fire. They drifted into slumber again, rejuvenating themselves to the soothing sounds of Kenny G. Pride awoke to the titillating sensation of Joi's probing hands.

"Oh, you're awake?" she teased. "Time for a massage."

"You first. I always get gypped," he said. "The one who goes first gets great loving, but not a full massage; the one who goes second gets both."

Pride positioned Joi's nude body facedown on a towel centered in the mammoth round bed. He poured the warm peach blossom oil into his palm and let it drizzle in long, languorous streams from his closed hands down the small of her back.

Joi's spine rejoiced at the river of warmth, and when Pride's hands spread the oil with a thumb-palm motion, moving rhythmically down her back to encompass her buttocks, Joi moaned loudly.

"That feel good?" he asked.

"Exceptional."

"Keep your eyes closed," he directed. He methodically kneaded the meat of her derriere, then moved down her thighs and her calves, then back up again. "I like the feel of your meaty flesh in my hands."

Pride looked at the glistening oil as he slid his hands up and down Joi's lithe body. He stroked it, possessed it; it was his, and he became aroused.

"Turn over," he commanded huskily. She did so without further prompting. Her eyes opened and she saw his desire-swollen nature rising magnificently from the tangle of his silken black hair. She reached for him, but he redirected her hands to her side, closing her eyes with his long fingers. He let the warm oil pour from his hands again and watched it seep from her collarbone down the valley of her breast. Her nipples stood erect and demanded to be suckled.

In a prayer mode, his hands followed behind the oil before opening and spreading across her even-toned caramel skin. He stood over her and let his hands glide down the center of her body to her bikini line and back up again. On the trip back he encompassed the sides of her, purposely skimming over her breasts but ignoring her demanding nipples. He repeated this sensuous teasing exercise four times, five times, until finally he delved past her bikini line into the forest of his desire, down to her thighs, then up again, bypassing the plump, floral swell just as he had her nipples. He then let his thumbs brush the ripe bud, ever so lightly, almost imperceptibly, like the whisper of the night wind on a deserted stretch of beach.

Joi couldn't tell whether the sensation was actual contact or just her ache for him to touch her there. Finally, there was no mistaking his firm-soft caress. She smiled just as he simultaneously massaged her throbbing center and lowered his warm mouth to feast on her nipple. The tactile sensation caused her to explode, and Pride delighted in watching the rhythmic spasms jolt her gorgeous body.

"Always the gentle man," Joi finally oozed with a closed-eyed smile. "I can't believe you went first and got a full massage," Pride said as Joi rolled over.

"Not just any massage—a magnificent one." She raised up on her elbows. "Besides, I have more control."

"Oh? Is that a challenge? Like I can't make it through without gettin' it on, huh?"

"Precisely."

"Up," he said, grabbing her hands to help her up. She positioned his splendid, muscle-hard body on the bed. "Mango oil please."

Pride almost received his full body massage. It delighted Joi when his urgency caused the super-cool Pride to impale her on his manhood. "You're not going to let me live that down are you?" he asked her, forehead to forehead, when they both caught their breaths again.

"Not in a million years." She climbed from him and snuggled beneath his chin, resting her head on his chest.

He heard the familiar cadence of her sleeping breath, but he was too happy to join her. For all he may have done wrong, he must have done something right to get Joi in his life. He thanked the Lord every night for her, and he still couldn't believe that someone like her loved him. She was his dream come true; she brought springtime to his winter. He loved her, but love was such a feeble, inept, weak word to describe how powerfully he felt about her; the way she consumed him and elevated him. In the introspective, confessional conversations that lovers share, they had treated one another to their childhoods, their hopes, dreams and other relationships. Pride had been relieved to discover that someone as gorgeous as she had limited male companionship. He liked that Joi was moral—a characteristic difficult to find in today's society, especially in such a striking package.

Joi was not only bright and beautiful, but she had such a strong sense of right and wrong. She believed a person should return phone calls, pay her bills every month and keep her appointments on time, whether doctors or repairmen. She believed that drunk drivers should have their license revoked after one offense, and that convicted rapists and child molesters should be castrated, since they apparently don't know what to do with what God gave them. She believed that ten items or less in the checkout line meant just that, and cars should last until a person decided to get rid of them. She believed in freedom of choice. That tobacco companies should not be liable for lung cancer deaths anymore than bartenders should be responsible for keeping track of grown folks drinking at a bar. She believed that marriage should be "until death do you part" and last forever.

Pride felt the heat from her body as she slept and thought that Joi's staunch beliefs were probably fostered by her Catholic upbringing—that black and white, no gray, thinking, although she could change her mind if more facts were brought to light. He recalled her thought processes regarding the dogs across the street from his house on Phoebus. Joi had witnessed the supposedly pedigreed dogs being set out in the yard from six o'clock in the morning until six in the evening by purportedly caring masters while they went to work. The dogs whined or barked all day long at each other, at neighbors minding their own business, at the wind—at their own neglect. "They certainly destroy the peace of the neighborhood," she had remarked. Initially, she blamed the dogs for their incessant and unreasonable barking, but then, as a teacher who was challenged by a recalcitrant child looks to the parent for clues to bad behavior, Joi looked to the dogs' masters. In the dog-loving community around Phoebus Road, she noticed that no other neighbors left their pets outside, unprotected, all day long. She then watched the dogs get drenched by sudden rains, frightened by thunderstorms, shiver with plunging wind-chills, frozen to the core by surprise blizzards, and, she imagined, roasted in the summer's sweltering heat. "Yahoos," she had called their owners. Then she began to notice things about the owners' lack of consciousness: planting a willow tree so close to the property line that it wept allover the house of another neighbor, or ratty bamboo that tore up yet another neighbor's driveway. Pride had told her when Mrs. Wright asked them about the control and damage caused by the bamboo runners, the yahoos said it was "not our problem." Joi had said, "They are not neighbors, they are residents. Mrs. Wright should have saved her breath trying to reason with needlessly nasty folks who aren't worth the spit it takes to tell them off. Just because you can afford a neighborhood, doesn't mean you belong." He grinned remembering. Of the yahoos, Joi had concluded," Actions speak louder than words. You don't love your pets and treat them like junkyard dogs. They lie. And no one likes their lies pointed out to them." She had been right about them; Joi had called them yahoos, most folks around Phoebus called them the Clampetts—no one called them neighbors.

Pride chuckled aloud at her thorough thought processes and smiled at her sleeping, angelic face. Black-and-white thinking, he thought She clearly hated lies and liars. The secret he had wasn't a lie. Perhaps fraud but not a lie. He stroked her brow tenderly. In her assessment, she had been kind to man's best friend. He hoped she would be as forgiving to man himself. He hadn't lied to her. He just hadn't told her everything about himself. There was nothing between them but this secret. He had to tell her. He had meant to tell her before now, but it had been both his secret and shame for so long, it was hard for him to confide in even her. He had to be positive that they had a future together before he would disclose it. It was probably the best-kept secret in Detroit; no one else, living or dead, knew. But he was tired of being its hostage. It walled him off from the world, confined him in a tight little space, preventing him from expanding, moving, dreaming. It sniped at him, pecked at him, abused him and laughingly vanished until its sudden appearance the next time. It came and went in cycles; the more he advanced at work, the greater the shame. He couldn't outrun it or outlive it. It was always there, mocking him, waiting for the next opportunity to demonize him.

Joi stirred dreamily and hugged him tightly before drifting back to sleep.

He'd tell her and not feel judged, and pray her love for him wouldn't change. He had never told a soul, but he'd never loved anyone the way he loved Joi, never trusted anyone the way he did her. She deserved to know. He couldn't keep it from her any more than he could keep it from himself.

❦

"Oooh, lalalalalala," Joi joined Gloria Estefan in singing "All I Want to Do Is Love You," as she pushed Pride back down on the bed.

Joi hiked her half-slip up over her breasts so that it barely grazed her upper thighs; when she danced, Pride was treated to interrupted views of her hairy cove, which was directly affecting his manhood.

All those childhood New Orleans dance lessons paid off as she pranced with aplomb to the Afro-Cuban beat of the song. She snatched the fringed afghan from the couch and provocatively tied it to one side over her hips as she did slide steps and hunched her shoulders. As her hips swayed rhythmically, enticingly, Pride anticipated a brown thigh intermittently jumping out at him while her beautiful bouncing breasts, with chocolate-drop nipples, strained just beneath the slip's elastic. At the song's end she ripped off the fringed afghan and seductively approached him. They made their last love in the Sleepy Hollow Inn.

"Thank you, Pride. I hope we can do this again real soon."

"Yeah, sure. You're welcome. Maybe once or twice a year." He didn't want to think about expenses now.

Just as they were leaving, Levi Stubbs reminded the couple of how much he believed in them both. In the tender winter sun they slow dragged and made silent promises with their hearts. Joi had given Pride summer, there in the frigid mountains, and time had flown like the wind. Their time was up and their ticket for return to the real world had been punched. He kissed her gently on the lips and then, cheekbone to cheekbone, they fluttered their long lashes in unison and laughed. She sauntered on ahead of him into the bright day and he watched her walk appreciatively.

He still hadn't told her…but he would.

The next day, the delivery man rang Joi's bell. Attached to a bouquet of colorful balloons was a forty-five record complete with the yellow plastic disc converter. The record was the one they had discovered at Sleepy Hollow, the Fantastic Four, and the card began with a paraphrased line:

You are the Joi that makes life so grand. I had fun in the Poconos. Thanks for coming, and coming and coming…

Love, Pride XXOO

"You are so bad," Joi said with a blushing smile as she slid the record on the turntable. "How did you find this so quick?" she asked him in absentia. The voices filled her apartment the way Pride filled her life, telling her they shared treasures more precious than diamonds or gold.

She went over to the balloons and laughed. She loved this man. She hoped they lasted—just like this—forever.

CHAPTER 6

"Heard some noise over here; thought it was a prowler," Dante teased as he followed Joi into her apartment. He threw a tendril from his boa-clad robe around his neck. "Come to water your plants?"

"I've been otherwise engaged," Joi said with a wicked smile.

"I can see that. Your skin is clear and you're in a good mood. Whatever—it's done you good."

"You can say that again." She was emptying her suitcase of clothes and packing more.

"Well—a new innkeeper?"

"Dante, I'm having a good time."

"And you deserve it, Lovey. I'm happy for you. That Pride is a scrumptious-looking man. That body—is he as good as he looks?"

"Better. The best I ever had." They slapped five and howled with laughter. "My life is a four-leaf clover."

"So," Dante began, "is this it? Has he caused you to abandon all your goals of marrying well?"

"Don't bring me down, Dante." Joi eyed him suspiciously.

"Lovey, do you know what you're doing? Men like Pride have a way of making a girl—and a guy for that matter— forget their purpose in life."

"I am not an adolescent."

"Who you tellin'. You are long in the tooth!"

"Bitch," Joi said playfully.

"Oooh thank you. I rarely get compliments so early in the

morning." He threw up his hands. "But seriously, Lovey, about your grand plans. Does this mean Pride has caused you to kick your old plans to the curb? 'Cause you know a person without a plan becomes the tool by which others accomplish their plans."

"Is it Sunday, Reverend Dante?" Joi mocked. "Pride's a good man." She looked into her friend's eyes.

"No argument. But he's not rich. So does this mean you finally know what is most important in life?"

Joi stopped packing. She really didn't want to get into this with Dante because she was having a hard enough time dealing with it herself. She had alternating bouts of clarity and conflict when dealing with her relationship with Pride; the former when she was away from him, and the latter when she was with him.

"I've gone Hollywood," Joi said insouciantly. "I'm going to do like the stars do, live and love for five or ten years until it gets old and then call it quits."

"Sounds like rationalization to me. So, he's good enough to screw but not to marry?"

"Must you be so crass?" she sighed.

"I just don't want you to get hurt."

"How? He loves me," Joi said flippantly.

"That's obvious to anyone who has two eyes. Do you love him?"

"I think so," she lied. She was just able to admit it to Pride, she couldn't discuss it with Dante.

"So when's the wedding?"

"Nothing's changed. I made a pact with myself. I keep my own place and, of course, no children. So when someone perfect comes along, I'll pull up stakes and go."

"Uh-huh," Dante said skeptically, raising one perfectly arched eyebrow. "Sure you will."

"C'mon, Dante. Don't ruin this for me. Finally, I'm having fun! Right now, Pride is the man in my life. I'm content."

"I guess so. The man cooks for you. There's no better foreplay than a man toiling over a hot, steamy stove for you."

"Or kneeling down to build you a fire," Joi said wistfully.

"Oh, the caveman fantasy. Showing his cute little tushie."

"There's nothing little about Pride."

"Brag, brag, brag." He flipped his boa. "I am happy for you both. Truly. I just don't want you to get in so deep you can't pull out when your knight in shining armor rides into Louie's on his white horse."

"I prefer a black stallion."

"You already got him!"

"Yes, I do."

"Just be happy, Joi. Whatever." He sashayed toward the door. "And if you need me, just holler,"

"Thanks." She watched Dante leave.

Finally, the kaleidoscope turned in her favor, all its stones surrounding Pride—the best man she'd had since Joaquin. Pride was good enough to her and for her—but not for her children.

Clearly she wouldn't be having any anytime soon.

∽✵∾

Pride and Joi caught Diane Reaves at Rudy's club, so

called by the "in crowd" for its owner. Everyone else called it the Blue Note for the single, neon-lit note in the window. Even that name had evolved from 225, pronounced Deuce and a Quarter, after Rudy's all-time favorite car. Not only did folks not call it right, they kept confusing the name with the address, so to simplify it for everybody, Rudy renamed his club the Blue Note. After the show, Pride and Joi ended up at her house for a change. They fell asleep without making love, but Pride kissed her into wakefulness in the morning and they made hot, passionate love in the stream of cold sunshine. On this lazy Sunday, they ate breakfast, then returned to bed. Pride snoozed in Joi's lap to the muted sounds of a gladiator movie while she devoured the paper.

When he stirred she commanded, "Here, read this" before he could refuse.

"What I want is not in that paper." He tossed it aside and, in one playful swoop, pulled her down under him. They giggled and awakened each other's bodies for more afternoon delight. The doorbell rang, interrupting their frolicking.

"Joie?"

"Aw, damn, it's my mother!"

"Tell her to come in. I'd like to meet her." Pride threw back the covers, exposing his most manly feature, which stood at full attention ready for whatever introduction Pride wanted to make.

"Joie?! Are you home?" Her mother continued ringing and knocking.

"Pride!" Joi whisper-yelled, covering him back up and jumping up to stare down the door. Her thumbnail lodged between her two front teeth; she wished her mother would disappear as quickly as she came.

"Joi, how old are you?" he said, seeing how upset she was. "Calm down." He grabbed her hand and brought her back to the bed. "Does she have a key?"

"No!" Joi snapped. "What would be the point to that?"

"Then relax. That knock's a request for entry, not a guarantee,' he said soothingly. She climbed in next to him. "Besides, you're not here. Joie."

"Don't call me that."

"Sparkle. Like that better?" He carved a small trail of kisses on her cheek past her dimple. "C'mere, I'm taking you back to paradise." He kissed her and she fought to stay focused on his arduous advances.

Her mother finally shoved a note under the door. Joi went to retrieve it. It read, "I was here, Mother." Like a schoolgirl, Joi began giggling at the ease of it all, letting her mother knock and not responding. She half covered herself with a sheet, looked out the window and she watched her mother get into her car.

"She's gone!" Joi rejoiced and laughed into Pride's arms. "You know she wants to meet the man I've been spending so much time with." She traced his lips with her fingers.

"That's easy. I'll have you two to dinner on Saturday."

"Uh—" The girlishness drained from her face at the thought.

"Too short a notice?" he asked.

"No." Joi was trying to keep them apart and now they both wanted to meet one another. Maybe she should just get it over with.

"Should I call to invite her?"

"No," she answered quickly. "I'll do it."

"Ooh, meeting moms. This thing must be getting serious." He tackled and tickled her. She laughed uproariously outside, but inside—she died.

∞∞∞

The next weekend, Joi escorted Uncle Joe Pride to the Annual School Carnival where RJ, Rudy Jr., threw balls at the target, trying to release the hitch that would dunk his father into a vat of water. Joi had helped Jerona by making seemingly thousands of cupcakes to sell as well as lending some arts and crafts aid to Camryn and Zanielle for the handicrafts booth. Joi bought cotton candy while she and a crowd of boys and girls followed Pride around the circumference of the indoor fair, watching him display his athletic prowess and his generosity in giving the prizes away. This black Pied Piper had won gifts for all of his entourage. He then hoisted a little boy on his shoulders and patiently instructed others on how to throw and score for themselves. Joi noticed that he was excellent with children. *Why was she surprised?* she wondered, *Pride was good at everything he did.* She also watched women watch Pride and she felt totally secure—which was new for her. *He's mine, ladies,* she told them mentally, *at least for the time being.* She remembered her promise to her unborn children—the bottom line of her existence; her children would never have to worry about money like she did and still does. Her father had given her emotional and financial support until his death, and then both were seriously compromised. If he had left her money, she would be in a different place now. Any children she had with Pride would still be a death away from financial security, from poverty. She could have a long life with Pride and no children, but she was sure he would want children. He had such a hunger for life and living.

Pride and Joi had come full circle and were back at the beginning of the fair by the cotton candy stand. She bought a lilac puff of confection this time and they joined the adults, devouring fried chicken, potato salad and corn on the cob. They tried to engage in conversation as the indoor carnival grew louder by the second. Pride and Joi said their good-byes.

"Quiet," Joi proclaimed as she sat in the cushioned environment of his car.

"Kids can keep up some noise, can't they?"

"Heat, please!"

"Coming right up," Pride said, as he pushed the vent full force and tuned in the music. The car sped along the river.

"That was fun," Joi said in a contented, relaxed voice. She sat with a bouquet of cotton candy in her lap and watched the tall masts of the sailboats pierce the frigid sky as they passed the marina.

"You ever want a boat?" she asked absently.

"Never thought about it. We use Mike's for fishing. It's nothing like these, though."

He looked over at her and smiled; she reciprocated. He was going to tell her now, while she was held captive in the car. Now was a good time while they were in a neutral, non-sexual place. Now, while he could see her expression, and she had nowhere to run.

"You ever think Detroit will warm up?" she asked.

"Maybe in July." He chuckled.

"They're playing our song," Joi said and turned up the volume as Marvin Gaye sang their namesake. They sang to its predictable end. "I love you, Pride," Joi said simply. His grin was bright enough to light the dismal gray skies and wide enough to wet his ears. He beamed and threw his right arm around her shoulder. He loved to hear her say those three little words. It always left him proud and speechless.

"I know—as black as you are—you're not trying to blush," she teased, then kissed him before resting her head against his shoulder. She loved his response to her declarations of love almost as much as she enjoyed it whenever they were beginning to make love, and she'd catch the first look of her nude body in the reflection of his eyes.

As the LTD cruised along the river's edge, Pride imagined that none of the other vehicles knew that the occupants of this car were blissful. That never, in either of their lives, had they ever been so happy. That they had been looking for something undefined—something beyond love. Something that still had no name, but they'd found it in one another. Whatever this indescribable entity was for which they'd searched all their lives, they were lucky enough to have found it in one another. Whatever it was—it was lusciously intoxicating and oh so satisfying.

I'll tell her later, he thought. Life was just too perfect right now.

≈≈≈

Pride awakened not at all surprised not to find Joi in his embrace. She would start out that way, but when she was seriously asleep, she didn't like to be touched. But he was surprised to find her completely out of his reassuring reach. He heard the rustle of plastic.

"I know Dante wouldn't live in a building that had mice," he spoke into the moon-infused darkness. "So it must mean my Sparkle is into the cotton candy again." He rolled over on his side just in time to catch her leaping towards him. "Umph!"

"Busted," she admitted, as she straddled him and the moon caressed her left cheek, highlighting her dimple. "Want some?" She fed him a mouthful of the spun sugar before he could answer.

"Nothing to it," he said as it melted the moment it touched his tongue. "I like something I can get a hold of." He sat halfway up and kissed her neck. "Like caramel."

Joi nibbled on the candy as Pride nibbled on her, soon forsaking the airy puff for the substance of his lips, the feel of his tongue dancing with hers. She loved the sensation of his big hands situating her more comfortably in his lap and running across her back.

"Ummmm," she moaned. The cotton candy began to melt from their body heat. It dribbled seductively down her body, coating her caramel skin with a gooey sugar that made her body glisten in the silver light. As if he were following a road map, everywhere the confection dripped, Pride coiled then whipped his tongue to savor the sticky sweetness. Her nipples, the well of her navel. His espresso-dark fingers disappeared between her cappuccino thighs.

With relish, Joi watched his tall ship rise thick, full and majestic from the hairy jungle of his constant need for her. She slid beneath him as his throbbing cargo sought then launched into her fleshy lagoon, releasing and billowing its sails of rapture, and the sound of love's fury resonated, then shook her body with a raw and tender ecstasy. She loved to watch him, watch her, watch him, watch her…

Life was good and oh, so sweet!

❦

The new year had begun with such promise, but now, two weeks later, three people—Pride, Joi and Mrs. St. Marie—sat at the kitchen table the host had moved it into the living room and covered it with a spring linen table-cloth. The delectable feast ringed the fresh flower center-piece. Beside each plate, two forks stood ready, crowned with two glasses, one for wine the other for water, both of which Mrs. St. Marie declined as she spun her tale of New Orleans lineage.

"Joie," her mother intentionally exaggerated the French pronunciation (Zhwa) of her daughter's name, "has chosen to chop off and change her name from St. Marie to Martin to make it easy for everyone else. But that's Joie for you. Never wanting to hurt anyone's feelings regardless of sacri-ficing her given name. She can be too accommodating."

"I just got tired of folks messing it up, Ma," she said, toying with her peas. "St. Marie sounded too pretentious for a waitress. I shortened to Joi Marie, and folks always waited for a last name. So Martin does just fine by me."

Her appetite had been stolen from her ever since this fiasco had been planned. Pride's home she so loved seemed sparse and inadequate when seen through her mother's eyes.

They had discussed all the polite topics—the weather, some politics, sports. But they had danced all around the subject of Pride's people. "So, Joie tells me you went to Eastern High School. What year did you graduate?" Mrs. St. Marie asked.

Joi knew her mother was leading up to his nonexistent college credentials and her stomach churned. She just wanted to hold him. She just wanted him to hold her.

"I didn't," he said, wiping his lips free of gravy. Joi stopped breathing.

"I beg your pardon?" Mrs. St. Marie stammered, her eyes darting from him to Joi for some clarification.

"I didn't graduate. My mother died and my father was overwhelmed with raising three teenage boys, so I went to work in the factory and, with the exception of a stint in the Army, I never looked back," he concluded without apology.

"I see." Mrs. St. Marie pursed her mouth, basking in the awkward silence she had just created. Joi looked at her mother's self-satisfied smile. She picked at the food so lovingly prepared by Pride. "This meat is very tender, Joe," Mrs. St. Marie said after a lethally long minute.

Joi felt the life seep from her body. This dinner was a mistake.

⤜⧉⤛

"Well, that was a very interesting dinner," Mrs. St.

Marie finally said after she and Joi had driven three blocks in silence. "Did you know he hadn't graduated from—"

Here it comes, Joi thought, and said, "No! Alright? No, I didn't! I need a cigarette. Got any?" She began searching through her mother's glove compartment.

"You know I don't smoke. What a filthy habit."

"I haven't needed a smoke since I've been with Pride."

"Goodness' sake, Joie, that's no reason to date somebody. You can get a patch for that."

"*Mon Dieu, Maman*," Joi said, slipping back into native patois the way people slipped and cursed without meaning to. "Your judgment in men isn't great. You liked Geoff, and look what happened!"

"I never liked him after I found out he was married. I told you to drop him like a hot potato. It was your doing to keep that adulterous affair going. They never leave their wives."

Joi was sorry she'd brought up his name. "He did— eventually. The month after I called it quits, he left his wife to take up with, and later marry, another doctor."

"And he'll leave her as well, one day. Once a leaver, always a leaver. It's just a matter of when. But the wife got a house, a car and the summer place in—"

"Things! That's all you ever care about, what people have! Geoff was short, bowling-ball-black, with nappy hair. But you liked him because he was a doctor and could get me things! And now I have a beautiful, milk-chocolate black man who can give me a decent life—"

"Decent? Without a high school diploma? How do you go from dating a doctor to dating a black factory worker?

Who gives you a cotton candy machine and a foot massager? No class."

"There you go." Joi shook her head in resignation, ignoring her mother's comments on Pride's gift-giving, but picking up on the way her mother had said "black."

"Which is it, Ma, the fact that Pride is two shades darker than me or that he's got no future? Pick one, Mother."

"If you persist with this relationship…and I don't know why for the life of me you would—"

"Cheeze, I need a cigarette!" she screamed as her mother pushed right on.

"Your children with Geoff wouldn't have been that attractive, but, with his money, you could have improved their looks accordingly. But dark and poor, their self-esteem—"

"Then they would be like their maternal grandmother. Right, Ma? Dark and poor." Mrs. St. Marie screwed her mouth into a tight little knot as Joi continued, "You always saw yourself a few shades lighter than you really are. It doesn't matter to me, it doesn't matter to most folks, but you want to be light so badly and you're not, Ma. Okay? You are not. Dad was the redbone, you are not. You cannot become light by association."

There, she'd said it; her mother was hurt into silence. She knew her mother wished Joi had been the beneficiary of the biscuit-brown hue. Her mother had decreed that "it makes it so much easier in polite New Orleans society for the girl to be light-skinned." Joi was creamed caramel instead. "But at least Joi got the 'good hair,' if she'd stop chopping it off," she'd overheard her mother say to her friends on numerous occasions.

Her brother Chip had tried to explain their mother to her. That she was a woman ahead of her time—a beautiful, pitch-black, dark woman with keen features. But the times caught up with her, and Jacquleen never got over being just ordinary.

They rode in silence for one mile before her mother spoke. "Is it wrong for me to want more for my child than I had or could give?"

"Are we talking things or color now, Ma? I can't keep up?" Joi asked contemptuously without looking at her.

"You can be so cruel, Joie."

"Uh-huh," Joi sighed, bracing herself for the old commercial and nursing a headache.

"Every generation is supposed to improve their lot. No grandchild of mine should have to drop out of college and get a job because his father was shot in a robbery. I don't want to have to worry about another generation not making it. It's just as easy falling in love with a rich man as it is a poor—"

"So many of them come into Louie's diner, Ma. Many on white horses," she mocked, folding her arms in disgust and looked out the side window. "Pride is far from poor—"

"One accident, Joie, one mishap, like an untimely death—"

"Dad was shot, Ma. He didn't plan to die."

"And you'll be strapped."

"I don't know what you're worried about. We haven't discussed marriage," she snapped. "In case you haven't noticed, I'm no spring chicken. Relax. Marriage is not in the cards for us. Okay?"

But Mrs. St. Marie knew the look of love all too well and she saw it in his eyes for her daughter. And the few times when Joi wasn't fiddling with her peas or staring at the pattern on the tablecloth—when she managed to raise her gaze to look at him—she saw it there too. You can live on love alone when you're young and the uncharted future lies wide and open ahead, but at this stage, security is of the utmost importance.

"Joie, do you ever think of Joaquin, how things would have been different?" Jacquleen knew how to calm her daughter.

"Not much, Ma. That was a long time ago."

Mr. and Mrs. Joaquin Summer—that dream had ended for Joi one bright October day. She had waited for him at the campus Punch Out and he had been late. Joaquin was never late. He was handsome, dependable and all hers. There had been a lot of commotion around campus, to which Joi had paid no attention. But as it grew later, she had allowed snippets of words from passing students like "tragedy" into her consciousness, until the full realization had approached her in the form of her best friend, Iris. Joaquin had fallen dead on the basketball court during practice. No sickness, no signs—but heart failure at twenty-one years of age had been the cause.

Life's kaleidoscope had turned and taken three of the most important men in her life: her brother, her father and then her fiancé. Her father had been there to help her past Chip's death, and Joaquin had helped her survive her father's—who would help her past his? Yeah, she remembered Joaquin and how she was left to deal with his dying all on her own. It had taken its toll on her…on her life.

"We're all we got left, Joie. Each other. Let's not fight. Huh?" Jacquleen said as she dropped her daughter off at home, and watched her climb the apartment steps.

Jacquleen sighed heavily as she opened the door of her house. She looked around at all her worldly possessions and thought she'd give them all away and live in a box if she could just get Joi suitably married. She removed her hat and gloves and walked to the mantel, looking at the old family pictures of her handsome husband, Royce, Xavier their son, nicknamed Chip, and their daughters, Joie and Noel. Is it wrong to want the best for her? she thought.

Missing from the collection of family pictures were grandparents from either side: one side by force, the other by choice. The St. Maries were ashamed that they had raised their grandson Royce to make such a poor choice in a wife. The wife, who ironically shared the St. Maries' ashamedness, wanted to show Royce and his family that he hadn't ruined his life by marrying her. But Jacquleen had little to show for it, and those St. Maries with all their wealth and power live on and well in New Orleans. It wasn't fair to make Royce choose, but he had chosen Jacquleen, and the St. Marie door to access, privilege, wealth and influence had slammed tightly behind them. It was absurd that a St. Marie would ever take a cab, much less drive one for a living. It ultimately had become his coffin.

Jacquleen sighed and went into the kitchen, putting water on for tea. She was still steeped in remembrances that she seldom allowed. Her Royche Xavier St. Marie had been born into a family who had fought in the War of 1812. They couldn't remember the black folks who had made them Creole. An unspoken but staunchly observed tradition dictated that they never marry anyone darker than a half-done biscuit, no one whose hair required heat, or anyone who would not further enhance their sociopolitical standing.

Jacquleen recalled her first introduction to the St. Marie legacy. As she swept up the fluffy black hair at her mother's beauty shop, she heard of these people who never used a hot comb to render their hair straight; a family of women who seldom ventured out to get their hair coifed. They had Michellene of her mother's shop go to their mansion instead. They were New Orleans royalty, whose century-old lineage held a cadre of *gens libre de color*—their sons, grandsons and great-grandsons had studied at the Sorbonne in Paris while most blacks were still in slavery. In fact, between their two households, the St. Maries owned about thirty house slaves. Their Mardi Gras floats threw off the best baubles and their in-town mansions were rivaled by their summer house on the Bayou Teche, where they fled to escape the heat and tourists. The St. Maries were a study in inclusion and exclusion, and the grand dame, Au Claire de Beaucharnais St. Marie-St. Marie, sat at the helm. Like her 17th century namesake, Au Claire De saxi de Veygoux St. Marie-St. Marie, was also double St. Marie having married a third cousin and, thereby, closed the family's wealth and influence around the revered St. Marie name.

Au Claire loved her cousin, Francois Honore Vauban

St. Marie, and when he died no one thought she would remarry. But Au Claire married Edouard Toussaint Bienville de Maupassant, who was too good a prospect to pass up. After six months, when it turned out that his name and heritage were much larger than his estimated wealth, Au Claire divorced him on the grounds of fraud, and took not only his chateau in France, but his New Orleans sugar refinery and seafood fleet in the settlement. Having reduced the entire de Maupassant family to a mere middle class existence, Edouard returned to France to begin from scratch, but he was never heard from again. Rumors circulated that Au Claire had arranged for him to take a permanent cruise in the labyrinth of bayous and become the snack of hungry crocs. Au Claire then had her marriage to him annulled by the Catholic Church, thus reverting her name to the widow St. Marie. She dressed herself permanently in black, her signature color, and busied herself in running and ruling the St. Marie fortune ,and New Orleans with an iron hand and will. Her amusement was said to be the buying, selling and swapping of secrets for favors; thus, she owned everyone from priests to public officials to seamen.

It was into this grandiose empire that she took her great-grandson Royche at the age of nine after his ne'er-do-well father, Maurice Lafitte, had been shot on the docks after a lucrative but unconventional business deal. Nine years later, Royche walked into the front parlor of the St. Marie mansion with Jacquleen Brioche, just before the senior prom. The Grand Dame had the girl wait in the front parlor like a common beggar trolling for a handout.

She summoned her great-grandson to her, purposely leaving the richly carved pocket doors ajar.

"Have you taken leave of your senses and your God-given place in society?" She assaulted Royche without apology. Jacquleen could only hear Royce's muted defenses, but the booming retorts of his great-grandmother were quite clear.

"Trash!" She banged her imported cane on the polished floor. "Your family predates the Americans, and this girl doesn't even know who her father is! Oh, I've checked. Her mother was born Jewel Benett, and she decided to rename herself Salome Brioche. Lyrical as it sounds, it means nothing. Because they are nothing. I guess we should be thankful she didn't choose the name croissant. The mother followed some man down here from Cincinnati, then had four children, and none have the same father. And that one you're defiling our family's name with today is named "Jacquleen." She enunciated the name with relish, then continued. "Misspelled, because the illiterate mother didn't have a clue of its correct pronunciation or spelling. These people are clearly beneath us."

The kettle whistled loudly, bringing Jacquleen back to the present. She poured the steaming water over the infuser and watched the clear water stain dark, the irony of it piercing. She could remember the tormented feeling of exclusion and not being rich. Her mother had worked hard and owned her own beauty shop. Truth was that Madame Au Clair St. Marie knew more about her family than she ever had. She thought that she and one of her sisters had had the same father. One thing for sure was that she had loved Royce from the first time she had seen him—before she even knew what a St. Marie was. He was everything she wasn't—light skin, hazel eyes, straight blondish hair—and he thought she was the most exotic black girl he'd ever seen. The attraction was immediate, intense and mutual.

As Jacquleen poured sweetness into her cup, she thought of the venom of the St. Marie family, conspiring to break them up by sending Royce off to Fisk University. That second year, she and Royce had married, and the St. Maries had cut him off.

The note Au Claire had sent to Royce had read: *One does not reward unacceptable behavior. Do not expect any further finances from this family until you come to your senses. When you do, we will be there for you.*

Royce never "came to his senses;" he struggled to finish college while working, but two years later, Xavier St. Marie was born and the real world crashed in on the couple. Royce loved that boy—"a chip off the old block," he decreed. So the family of three moved back to New Orleans and Royce carved out an honest masonry business. After suffering a number of miscarriages, Jacquleen was blessed again, nine years later, with Joie, so named by her father, and then, two years later on Christmas day, *Noël.*

But Xavier was a special child and young man. Jacquleen hated his classmates calling him "X," because he was anything but an algebraic unknown. He was a born leader, confident, and could successfully negotiate with a vendor on the street or an insurance man at the door. He was smart, athletic, handsome—a true St. Marie, although he was never acknowledged by the prestigious clan. By the time he was in junior high, folks had taken to calling him Senator because of his verbal prowess and unflinching courage. That is what the police called him when they brought the gruesome news to her on that hot August day.

"The Senator is dead," the policeman began. "He was trying to break up a fight and took a bullet in the back."

She knew immediately that Nitro had something to do with it. She knew, in the way only a mother knew, that some friends meant her children no good.

Jacquleen drank a gulp of the hot tea, hardly feeling the scalding water fill her mouth and spill a blazing path down her throat.

That suave Italian boy had been slinking around her son sinces he could remember. They had been friends since grade school, when his name evolved from Antoni De Niro to Nitro to reflect his unpredictable, explosive temper. The split between her son and Nitro had been prophetic as he went the way of high times, big money and a low life expectancy, while Chip was at Tulane majoring in political science with an eye on law school. Jacquleen never worried about Nitro negatively influencing her son; he knew what he wanted and how to get it. Then, one day, she saw Nitro leering at an eight-year-old Joi while she jumped double-dutch, and it turned her stomach. Chip called Nitro on it, and Jacquleen overheard him tell Chip "she's a fox who ain't gonna be young forever. When she grows up, I'll be waiting for her."

The police confirmed that Nitro had been the one for whom the bullet had been intended. Weeks later, when Joi was let out of Nitro's car after accepting a ride from dance class, Jacquleen had verbally assaulted him and kicked the car he was driving. Most folks chalked the incident up to grief, but the glare between her and Nitro blazed pure hate. Shortly thereafter, the St. Marie family of four moved to Detroit, away from all the past bad memories and the future threats. Nitro had claimed one St. Marie life. They were determined that he wasn't going to get another. She had to get Joi away before her uncertain fear about Nitro had turned to adolescent fascination for her spirited and curious daughter, and any parental warnings concerning the slick hoodlum were discarded by her as unwarranted nuisances.

Jacquleen knew Nitro's type too well: big money, small mind and perverted sexual appetites. Her own sisters had been caught by his type, had babies by his type, and were abandoned and put on welfare by his type, undoing everything her poor mama had worked so hard to prevent. Maybe Au Claire had been right. "You cannot rise above the quicksand of your origins. Someone will always be there to drag you back down again."

Jacquleen could still hear the eerie threat as Nitro said good-bye to Joi. "If you ever need anything, darling. Anything at all—you just ask."

"She doesn't need your drug and blood money!" Jacquleen spat, while her husband loaded the car.

Nitro motioned his boys back from the woman and sent his cold, black eyes to cut into Mrs. St. Marie's. "I'm going to let that slide out of respect for the Senator," he had said. He turned back to Joi and smiled. "You remember what I said, Sweetness. Anything you need. I'll be easy to find in the Big Easy." He winked at Joi as she obeyed her father and got into the car.

The teacup handle broke in Jacquleen's hand. She would do anything to protect her children. She recalled going back home for her mother's funeral; Nitro had the audacity to attend. She had not brought Joi, but there was an exact replica of her draped over Nitro's body. He smiled his slow, sick smile and tipped his cap. Jacquleen seethed. She hadn't been to New Orleans since. No reason, the same way she had never seen Au Claire before or since that day in her parlor. The Grand Dame never left the fortress of her world; there was no need, when the world came to her. She wielded and manipulated all the power from her plush and stately environs.

Jacquleen wiped up the spilled tea and threw the cup into the trash. She had never received any response from any of the birth announcements she had sent her children's great-great-grandmother. She recalled receiving an outrageously beautiful spray of flowers after Chip's death. The accompanying card with the raised engraving and elegant St. Marie seal had one word scrawled across the expensive vellum in black ink: Pity. Jacquleen was furious at the old woman's insensitivity, and happy that Royce hadn't been home when they arrived. She drove to Lake Pontchartrain and dumped them in. She watched them float in the murky water, all the while knowing that Au Claire credited her side of the family with the low-life death of their son.

Jacquleen stopped staring down at the broken cup in her trash bin and went back into the living room. She wanted so much to show that old bat how wonderful her children really were. She had expected and received no response from Noel's wedding announcement. Her children's future was not damaged by the tainted Brioche blood. But now…Jacquleen shook her head and clung to the newel post of her stair. Now her daughter was dating a high school drop-out factory worker.

"Good grief," she said aloud. "When will the sins of the father and mother stop revisiting this innocent child?" She went upstairs to nap her headache away.

CHAPTER 7

Joi wrapped her robe around herself and settled in on her couch with a spoon and pint of deep dark chocolate ice cream. The talk with Pride and the hot shower had helped some, but she hated fighting with her mother. Sometimes Jacquleen could be so anal, so suffocating, so wrong. Pride had worked hard to have a nice dinner for them and all her mother could do was rant and criticize. Money. Money. Money, the end-all, be-all panacea for a dreary life. It was all Jacquleen Brioche St. Marie understood, respected—craved.

Joi spotted a browned tip on her *Dracena marginata*, the fourth plant Pride had sent her. She filled her watering can and, pouring the nectar of life on the Pride Forest, she thought of how much the greenery around the picture window had added brightness to her bleak apartment. How Pride had said to her that she could do anything she set her mind to, including caring for these plants despite her brown thumb. He had kissed her thumb, then her open palm, then his lips had traveled up her arms…the water splashed on the floor from the overflow tray. Why couldn't her mother see how much depth and dimension he added to her life? How he was the healing elixir for her amputated spirit. She had been waiting all her life for the love he was giving her.

Joi sank back onto the sofa and held her ice cream, dabbing the spoon around the melted edges, and thinking of how different her life would have been had the three men who mattered most lived. If her brother had lived, then her father would still be alive, but she would have never come to Detroit and met Joaquin. She had struggled through his traumatic death alone as well as the remainder of her junior year in college but had lost both battles heroically. Her mother's encouragement had evolved into nagging and Joi had moved out into a small efficiency near campus, the way she and Joaquin had planned. Her concentration gone, she had lost her scholarship, had been ineligible for work-study and had refused her mother's offer to refinance her house again. Joi knew that after taking out a second mortgage to finance Noel's education, Jacquleen would probably be denied a loan approval; her mother's part-time salary as a receptionist was no collateral. After reminding her mother of Nitro's, Chip's old friend, invitation to call on him if they ever needed anything, Jacquleen had gone insanely ballistic. So, that summer, Joi had taken a job as a bank teller at the same institution that had denied her a loan. Her intention had been to attend classes after three o'clock. But by fall, she hadn't been able to find a better paying nine-to-five job to support herself or the evening classes she needed to advance her field of study. Then she had taken a department store job where she could work evenings and attend classes during the day. Not only had this job eaten up her income with its wardrobe requirements, but it had left little time for studying. Next she had found a job at an upscale, downtown restaurant but, with the number of folks working and her lack of seniority, there had been no regular work schedule, which had been left to the whim of the assigning supervisor. The tips had been excellent and Joi had decided to work one semester, then go to school the next. It would take her longer, and the degree in law was becoming a distant dream, but maybe elementary education or a degree in literature was within reach. She had worked at the restaurant for three years before answering an ad for Louie's. She told herself she would have fewer stations, more study time, and she wouldn't be serving people who were going places that she was not.

Again, time proved no friend. It hurriedly turned its pages while her life stalled. The onset of her thirtieth birthday and the clamoring sound of her biological clock had sent her into the vulturous arms of Dr. Geoffrey Rollins. Joi laughed as she spooned ice cream into her mouth.

She had recently seen him downtown and he was old, fat and balding badly.

Pain and sorrow roamed free in the universe and Joi may have gotten more than her fair share. Now God sent her Pride and said, "Joi, be happy." And she was sure going to do God's will.

Pride and Joi had survived the dinner with her mother, being away for their first extended vacation, and returned to normal. The only difference is that now Joi cooked for him.

~≈≈~

Selena Fluellen's satin-smooth voice wafted from the living room's stereo as Joi adjusted the burner under the boiling potatoes.

" 'The King Is Dead,' " Pride read the *Detroit News* headlines in passing, heading for milk in the refrigerator.

"Oh, read that to me," she said as she shook more seasoned chicken into the floured paper bag.

"Same-o, same-o." He came up behind her, smelling of fresh sweat from his workout. He nuzzled her ear.

"C'mon, I'm busy. Read to me. A little reciprocity—I always read to you." She slid the white-coated poultry into the crackling hot skillet of fat. "C'mon." She bumped him away playfully with her rear.

"You'll see it on the news," he said and sat down in a chair with his glass of milk.

He glanced at the paper before she turned around. "Read it! You can read, can't you?" she said laughingly, waving the long fork at him like a magic wand.

His soft, soulful brown eyes beneath his thick curly lashes turned hard and cold and held hers. Her playful question hung between them, dangling like the reins on a loose racehorse. When she noticed the agitated tension and release of his jaw, the smile faded from her face. All she could hear was the spitting grease in the loud quiet. It sounded like rousing applause of a final act.

"Now you know," he said. He rose quietly from the table and went to her. The hardness of his eyes turned soft again, as if the revelation alone lifted his heavy heart. "Now you know all my secrets, Joi," he said, as if reading her mind and her questioning eyes.

She wondered how much more she didn't know about him. "But…how is that possible?" She grappled to make sense of this revelation, as he turned from her and went into the living room. She followed him. "You're articulate, you drive, get promotions at work, you count money—"

"Which has nothing to do with reading." He turned toward her abruptly, causing her to stop her approach. "I read enough to get by. I listen to the commentators on radio, TV, just like the foreigners. I do a lot of delegating and report-back-to-me, at work." He hunched his shoulders and moved toward her, his soft eyes pleading, crying without tears. "Joi, I've never told anyone before, so I've never asked anyone before, but I'm asking you. Will you help me?"

Tears welled up in Joi's eyes then trickled down her cheeks.

"Will you help me learn to read?" His eyes implored hers.

Her mouth was open but nothing was coming out. Finally she said, "Sure." She went to him and held him, batting back more tears. "Sure, Pride. It's never too late."

Joi now understood his unfounded tenseness at the airport and driving through unfamiliar territory toward the Sleepy Hollow Inn. He must have memorized the road signs just to cover it up—the way he'd give his order directly to the waiter while laying the menu down. How a man this fine, this intelligent was able to slip through the cracks without learning to read was incomprehensible to her.

So Joi set about teaching this man—who was marvel, mystery and gift to her—how to read. She began with the alphabet and, with her untrained assessment, guesstimated that he had about a third or fourth grade reading level. She bought him workbooks, and after dinner they worked on phonics. Before they went to sleep, Pride read from children's books and then graduated to reading the paper and magazines. The more he read, the more he wanted to, and in two weeks Joi was competing with the printed word for his attention. Often, after making love, he would read her to sleep, and after breakfast they'd return to bed, make love, and do the crossword puzzle. She had never known a man with such a thirst to learn.

∽◈∾

Joi's eyes flew open from habit the way they always did in that slit of time between late night and early morning. But this time it wasn't the urgency of her bladder, or the storm forming, or being rest-broken from her last shift, or the realization that her life was going nowhere near the plans she'd made for it. This time she lay in the commingled stream of moonlight and street lamp which shone though her picture window. The fresh air from the open window skimmed her cheek, but she wasn't chilled. The night enveloped her. She could smell the tang of the coming rain and hear the rumble of distant thunder. She lay in peace, so contented, so happy that a single tear leaked from one eye. Everything was so right. Everything was so wrong.

She wiped the wet from her cheek without disturbing Pride. He slept on his side facing her, his body fining into the contours of her own. His heavy arm lay across her waist. The rise and fall of his breathing was a comforting lullaby in her ear—the beginning of a snore to come in a few years, she supposed. She was supremely happy. She smiled into the moonlight as it was obliterated by passing clouds, laced her fingers into his and kissed his fingertips. He did not stir. He slept the sleep of an innocent man—not a perfect man; a man who, in his younger days, preferred laughing with the sinners to praying with the saints—nothing illegal or outside the bounds of the commandments, just mischievous. But he had paid his penance, made his retribution and moved on with only faded remnants left, like that scar hidden in his thick right eyebrow. A man at peace with himself, a man who never intentionally hurt another human being. An honest man who didn't lie, cheat or steal. He had no need. For that, the angels visited him every night, bestowing a deep, cleansing sleep to rejuvenate this extraordinary human with the unselfish spirit. A good man was Joe Pride, and Joi had been waiting all her life for him. He was happy with her and she didn't know what she did to deserve him.

The thick rain came and fell like silver needles from the dark brooding sky. Joi sighed as she tightened her grip of his hand. The hands that he let her manicure, finding shoe polish, not dirt, embedded there. Macho Pride reluctantly allowed her to buff his nails, but she couldn't use any of that "sissy," clear polish.

Yet in a world where the measure of a man was his education, his job and the things he had acquired and accomplished were paramount, this beautiful black man paled in the eyes of others. Kingdoms, empires and presidencies are built on pairing of compatibilities not in personas, but in things: in bloodlines, lineages, combined wealth, guaranteed futures—the love inconsequential. Her own mother had thought she could "do better." No one, not Mrs. St. Marie or Joe Pride's boys had any idea how much he gave to Joi, the specialness of this uncomplicated man who needed no second-guessing or questioned motives; this man who personified security. None of them cared that he was her dream come true. She could put her hands in his and never look back. Outsiders never peeled through his layers of being because they dismissed him at the education/job level. Joi had known many educated, well-positioned men who weren't good enough to clean Joe Pride's shoes.

Another tear fell for the sadness of the world which forced the happy to be unhappy, and the educated to think they were gods just by being. These differences, which had been pounded into her since childhood, painfully separated from the embodiment of Joi. The kaleidoscope of time turned again and all its colorful stones fell away from Joe Pride. She was not confused, for it was clear—she reminded herself again—she could never marry this man.

❧

On Valentine's Day, Joi ascended her steps to find a box of flowers, with a big red bow, propped against her door. When she got inside, she pulled out the card, which read, *Joi, I love you. This is the first of many Valentine's Days. —Pride.* She unboxed the roses as she listened to her messages: her mother, Ella saying good-bye, gloating over her new man-friend who was whisking her to Las Vegas for a few days, and Pride. Twice.

"Umph!" she said as she spread out the red roses, popped a Lean Cuisine into the microwave, turned on Alex Trebeck and shed her uniform. This routine was all tirelessly familiar; only Pride's calls were different—calls, flowers, balloons, but not him.

"The next year that will be written in only four Roman numerals?" Alex asked the Final *Jeopardy* question as the familiar tune ticked away the seconds.

"MM," Joi answered as she switched her dinner from the microwave to a plate. "The year 2000," Joi told Alex before the contestants put down their writing pens.

Pride was planning some "big surprise" and had asked her to be patient. That had been weeks ago. First, he had slowed down, then had stopped coming by the diner for lunch or dinner. She was seeing him less and then not at all, even on the weekends without explanation, except this "surprise" bit. Her understanding had turned to impatience then suspicion. Why would he suddenly not have a need for her—physically, socially, companion-wise? He had opened up the rusted floodgates of her passion, and then left. Maybe he had found someone "special enuf," and hadn't bothered to tell her. Maybe he was keeping her on the back burner while he found out how this new woman played out, before dumping Joi altogether. Maybe he was letting her down easy, hoping she would call it quits. But then, why the calls at all hours of the night? "I just wanted to hear your voice, Joi. You sleep?"

"Hell, yes—it's 3:15 A.M.!"

"Sorry, but I love and miss you so much."

"Then what the hell is going on, Pride?" she longed to ask him, but didn't; she wasn't sure whether she was ready for his answer.

Then more of the balloons, flowers and cryptic, loving messages on her answering machine. Words, just empty words, Joi thought. She started erasing some of his messages without listening to them. They were all the same old excuses of being busy and not being able to see her. He set up an occasional date only to cancel it later. She wasn't going to ride this emotional roller coaster with Pride at the helm much longer. Was he lying to her? and why? She remembered Dante's words, "You know how you can tell if a man is lying? His lips are moving." She hadn't seen Pride's lips in weeks. Joi longed to talk with Dante about it, but he was in Barbados for his usual February Caribbean jaunt. Joi wouldn't dare call the wives of Pride's friends, Jerona, Camryn or Zanielle. She couldn't talk to the lunch-guys from the factory about Pride either; they'd probably be close-lipped, though she didn't believe he would tell them any more than he had told her. It was Ella who had first connected Pride's absence with Joi's surly mood. "Hell, ask him! Ask him why he made and then canceled two dates," she had ordered her right before she left for Vegas.

The doorbell stole her attention from television.

"Chantel!" Joi said, surprised to see her at her door at this hour and without her son. "Where's Jabari?"

"At my sister's. Can I come in?"

"Sure. Well." Joi didn't know what else to say. They weren't friends, they were coworkers. Their mutual friend was Ella, and when Chantel and Jabari were in the mix, Joi usually bailed out. Chasing after the rambunctious four-year-old was not the way Joi wanted to spend her off hours. "Can I get you something?"

"How 'bout a drink?" Chantel asked and Joi remembered their single-girl-night-out visits to the Hot Spot. "Well, maybe no drink," Chantal said reluctantly. "I think I'm pregnant."

"Oooh." Joi was shocked that, in this day and age, anyone would get pregnant without being married.

"With Ella out of town, I didn't know where else to go."

Joi tried to remain nonjudgmental, but she couldn't fathom pregnancy in the '90s unless a woman truly didn't care about herself or her future—birth control failure notwithstanding.

She wondered what Chantel wanted from her.

"I've decided to have an abortion," Chantel said. "I can't bring another child into this world without messing up mine and Jabari's. He shouldn't have to pay for my mistake. I will not go on welfare, but I wanted to know if you would take care of Jabari that day."

"What day?"

"Whatever day you have off."

Joi was not an avid lover of children, mainly because she had never been around them. Chantel had all the sisters in the world. Joi hesitated.

Chantel said, "I don't want my sisters to know. If I ask them to keep him all day, there'll be all sorts of questions, and I don't want to go through all that hassle. You know I wouldn't ask unless I had to."

"What about the father of the baby?"

"Let's just say he's not available." Chantel's brave veneer crumpled and she began to cry." Nothing worse than an old fool who should know better." She sobbed and vented.

Joi listened to Chantel and how she had arrived at her decision. She thought of how hard it must have been to come to such a resolution, but how at least women have an option, a safe choice. She wondered what would happen if she were to get pregnant with Pride's child—now, while he was "not available." She could no more raise a child alone than the man in the moon. The two women talked late into the night before deciding on Friday as the day to bring Jabari.

The sleeping boy was dropped off at 6 A.M. Baby-sitting was easy until he woke up with a full blast of energy, and Joi felt immediately inept. If Dante were here he'd come to her rescue; so she tried to think like him and set about tiring out the four-year-old. They colored with the crayons and books from his satchel, then went out to eat and to the playground. They napped until six that evening. Jabari got his second wind just as Jacquleen came over for a visit.

"Isn't he just the cutest little thing," Jacquleen gushed, sticking her face into his and eyeing her daughter. Joi answered the ringing telephone and spoke to Chantel for a few minutes.

"Here Jabari, it's your mom," Joi said, handing him the receiver.

"Think I'll ever have any grandsons?" Jacquleen asked wistfully, watching him talk to his mother.

"Maybe Noel will oblige. Three girls—fourth one's the

charm, Grandma." Jacquleen didn't smile. "I have Jabari for another day," Joi went on quickly. "You can play grandma to a boy if you like. We're going to the movies. Wanna come?"

Although Jacquleen wasn't quite up for the movie, she volunteered to drive them and have them over for dinner afterward. Joi ran down the steps behind Jabari just as her answering machine clicked on. Jacquleen hesitated since she thought it might be Chantel calling back. She heard Pride's voice. His apology at not seeing Joi lately made Jacquleen smile. His saying that, with the long weekend, they needed to take some time and catch up, made Jacquleen frown. She yanked up the receiver from the machine.

"Hello, Joe. How are you?" she asked, keeping her eye on the door. "No, she is not here." Just then Joi appeared and motioned to her mother that she would be downstairs. Jacquleen nodded her head as she listened to Pride. "Yes, I'm still here. So you haven't been seeing too much of each other lately, huh, Joe?"

"We've been communicating by phone."

"Just why is that, Joe?"

"Would you just give her the message that I called and to call me back as soon as she gets in—"

"Oh, well, I'm so sorry you missed her. She went away for the long weekend. I guess she's celebrating President's Day someplace else. I certainly don't want you waiting around all weekend for her to call when she's out of town."

"Where did she go?"

"Well now, Joe, that wouldn't be proper for me to tell

you, but I'll give her your message and tell her to call you as soon as she gets back. Alright? Good-bye, Joe." She hung up unceremoniously.

Well, a fishing expedition that paid off, Jacquleen thought. Her daughter certainly hadn't told her of his inattention. What was he up to? Joi was too good for him, and he was treating her shabbily? God was finally answering her prayers, clearing the deck of Joe so that someone truly marvelous could come into her daughter's life. Things were looking up. She eyed the machine, making sure no part of his call had registered, picked up her purse, adjusted her hat and pulled the apartment door closed.

❦

On Tuesday, Joi returned to the diner in a foul mood. Not one call from him over the entire long President's weekend. Ella and Chantel watched their friend keep to herself all day, chain smoke, bite her cuticles and spit them clear of her *National Geographics* during her breaks.

"Your boyfriend sent you this," Chantel said, presenting her with a piece of construction paper with a crayon heart with *Joi* scribbled inside.

"Ah, he's sweet," Joi said. "Jabari's a regular little Picasso. Tell him thanks."

"He's got quite a crush on you. He wants to know when he's going to see you again."

"Glad somebody's interested," Joi said. She jerked a quick, sad smile and took a long drag on her cigarette.

"Chantel!" Louie barked. When she scurried back to

her customers, Ella slid over to finish the conversation.

"Haven't heard from Pride yet?"

"Not a peep. Not this entire, long weekend. Maybe he had other plans." She glanced out at the setting sun. This romantic limbo, as confusing as the concept of white chocolate or a white girl sporting cornrows, was killing her.

"I have a mind to go over there, jack him up and ask what kind of game he's playing," Ella said.

"No," Joi said, looking straight into Ella's eyes. "Let me. Can I borrow your car?" Without hesitation, Ella reached into her pocket and presented her with the keys. "Thanks."

Joi turned onto Phoebus Road and saw the porch light illuminating Pride's walkway and steps, meaning he was home and expecting someone.

"If it's not working, just be man enough to let me know so we can both get on with our lives," she rehearsed. "No need to drag it out."

She blew out the last of the smoke and crushed her cigarette in the ashtray. When she slowed down and looked up at the house, Joi saw Pride's body silhouetted against the amber glow of his porch light. His dazzling smile, usually reserved just for her, was thrown at the figure of a woman climbing the three steps from the sidewalk to his yard. Joi's heart raced uncontrollably, and her eyes blurred in disbelief. As she drove the car past the house, Pride and the woman—clad in high heels and a feathered hat—disappeared through his front door. Joi's heart jumped into her throat, squashing an unintelligible gasp.

As the car rolled on, seemingly on its own, her voice returned. "Son of a bitch!"

Involuntary tears of anger and betrayal clouded her eyes; it was all crystal clear now. Pride had found someone else; Joi had been replaced. Her heart ached, her eyes shed water and her mind yelled at her, "You fool!" She could barely steer the car she was so shaken. If she had a gun she would have gone back and blown both their brains out.

"How could he?" she asked the stop sign. "Why would he?"

"Just a waitress," spoken by the woman at the basketball game, spanned time to ring in her ear.

"Maybe the sister in her hat and heels was special enuf," she said aloud. "Bastard!" she raged. "You stupid fool," she chastised herself again. Her mind struggled through a labyrinth of clashing emotions. She was mad-angry; mad at him for turning out to be a typical male, and mad at herself for believing him to be different. Falling for him, trusting him. When would she be able to judge character in a man? "What a fool," she repeated. Then she remembered the old Chinese proverb, "Realizing you're a fool is the first step to wisdom."

Well, she thought as she sorted through her emotions with quicksilver accuracy. Two can play this game. She'd be cool and circumspect. When Pride finally told her that this relationship wasn't working out, that it was him, not her, or that he found somebody else more "special," she would respond with a shrug of the shoulders and a simple "Okay." She'd relish the confusion or surprise in his eyes. If he continued to follow the typical male route, he'd want her back as soon as she didn't want him. He'd go into the "I was a fool, it was you all the time, I made a mistake, she meant nothing to me, I'm sorry take me back" routine.

"Yeah, right," Joi savored saying aloud. She, of course, wouldn't relent. And thereby, emerge with her dignity restored victoriously over this sham of a relationship. That's what she would do. Be cool, lie in wait for his declaration and then—zap!—rip her fingernails across his tender heart and fragile ego. Hurt him the way he had just hurt her. Hurt me once, shame on you; hurt me twice, shame on me, she thought.

She laughed at herself with cynical pity. "A surprise," she said. "Well, we'll see who gets the surprise."

Her inner soliloquy kept her company as she returned the car to Ella and asked Louie if she could be excused. Both Ella and Chantel noticed her distress and volunteered to take the overflow, leaving Louie nothing to do but give her permission.

She called in sick for the next two days, wanting to be alone despite the recently-tanned Dante's attempts to comfort her, and despite hearing Pride's routine calls on her machine. "I was falling in love and now I'm falling apart. This is no good," she lamented to herself.

She set about minimizing the effect of his betrayal on her. He had held her love in the palm of his hand and he'd crushed her in and closed her out. He'd sent her butt crashing to earth—not hell; hell would be having a terminal illness. He was just a man who'd done her wrong, stomped on her heart and fed it to the wolves. Why should she have expected more? He was just a man, like millions of other men who did this to women every day of the week. She'd get over it and him. She'd done it before.

Joi was uncharacteristically cool and allowed him play his hand out. Pride had had the audacity to call her the same night, only a few hours after, after she had seen Miss Hat and Heels enter his house—late, of course, since he had been entertaining earlier. Maybe the woman had left early. Maybe she was in the shower or upstairs in his bed. Upon hearing his voice, low and soft, Joi had picked up the receiver and let it drop back down into the cradle, disconnecting him and not recording his message. He had called back again. She had repeated the exercise. On the third call she had decided to let it play out.

"You need to check your machine, Joi," he had said. "It keeps cutting me off. I hope everything's all right with you. This seems to be the only way we're communicating lately. I'd hoped to spend some time with you over the long President's weekend, but well…I miss you."

She had sucked slow and hard on her cigarette.

"It's March and things are really picking up—" he went on.

"I just bet they are." She couldn't resist.

"At work and…otherwise. My time is really crazy—it gets away from me. Sometimes I think it's just not worth it, and then I call you and I get inspired."

"Blah, blah, blah," she said. She went to the bathroom and drank water straight from the spigot. When she came back, he was still talking. "Cheeze, man."

"Where are you at this hour, anyway? On a date?" he said jokingly.

Joi flipped off the volume. "Like you, you loser! I can date, too." She went into her kitchen and looked in the refrigerator. When the call was finished, Joi took Ben and Jerry over to the machine and erased the tape without listening to the rest of his one-man oration. Maybe Miss Hat and Heels had come back into the room, wearing nothing. Joi fought the image of Pride's taut manhood rising and waiting on anyone but her. She remembered the way his hands slid around her waist, the way he cupped her buttocks in his fevered palms before he groaned and inched his long fingers up to her breasts, where he would offer her engorged nipples to his luscious hot mouth. Tasting, tugging, licking—

"Stop!" she said aloud in the darkness. She took a deep breath but it didn't stop the flowing of her bodily juices. "Damn you, Joe Pride!" She jerked her terry robe around her like armor and fell into a chair. She reached for her melting chocolate ice cream. Without warning, she began to cry. For him…for them. It hurt to think that her best hadn't been good enough. "Well, to hell with you," she muttered.

CHAPTER 8

"Who are the suits?" Joi asked Ella, eyeing the four well-dressed men seated at a center table.

"You are really out of it," Ella answered. "They started coming in last week. They're some engineers inspecting the factory to bring it up to code or set some codes or something. The cute one's name is Claude Jeeter."

Joi glanced up from her order pad to see who Ella was referring to. "He's too young for you."

"That's what you think." Ella winked and popped her gum.

"First luncheon-ladies and now luncheon-men," Joi muttered as she slapped the order on the counter for Louie. Joi walked past the table and this Jeeter guy smiled at her. She was annoyed.

"Drives that black Porsche out there." Ella sidled up to her and continued her commentary on the man.

"Figures," Joi said as she handed a customer extra napkins.

While serving a nearby booth, Joi noticed his designer specs perched on a tapered nose which was set in smooth cafe-au-lait skin and framed by a neatly-coifed natural. The overcoat draped over a vacant chair was cashmere; his loafers Italian, his nails manicured. On his right hand a diamond ring, on his third finger left—a college class ring.

"No wedding band," Ella said, circling on Joi's left. "May be your knight on a white horse."

"No thanks. Men aren't worth the trouble." She had

compromised her hopes and dreams of getting her degree and marrying well once to date a factory worker, which resulted in maltreatment. It served her right—she should have known better. Her judgment was off. "I'm swearing off men," she told Ella.

"We all say that. If we're lucky—we're proven liars."

Joi stood at the back station pouring cheap catsup into half-empty bottles. Louie could afford a brand name, she thought, but he used the cut-rate condiments. After dark, the diner turned into a bar and he made money hand over fist. The revenue from selling the drinks alone had sent three of his four children though college, and that had been years ago. Louie was rich; he didn't wear it, didn't live in it and didn't drive it—his car was twelve years old. Ever since she started working here, all he'd been talking about was retiring to Florida.

"Bye, Joi," a man's voice pierced her thoughts.

Joi looked up to see Claude Jeeter in his cashmere coat at the door bidding her good night. "Bye," Joi said, stunned and self-conscious by his attention. From across the diner, Ella's eyes bugged out in surprise, like a minstrel show caricature. Joi just hunched her shoulders in wonderment and went back to filling her bottles.

❧

"Haven't seen that much cheese since the government gave it away." Ella ranked on Joi's atypical demeanor as she grinned and talked to customers. Ella had noticed how her friend's resignation was disguised beneath a false gaiety. "I guess you hope some of this gets back to Pride?"

"You wanted me to chit-chat with customers," Joi said, balancing a BLT and blue plate special. "So I am."

Ella eyed Claude Jeeter. "What's he doing back here anyway?" she asked, "The inspection at the factory was over a week ago and he should be gone."

"Why don't you ask him if you're so interested?" Joi said, pouring coffee into a customer's empty cup at the counter.

"Maybe he sees something he likes," Louie said, putting in his two cents. Both women rolled their eyes at his intrusion.

"So," Ella continued, "how's Pride? What's this 'big surprise?' "

"I dunno. With me taking Chantel's late shift, him working late hours every day and this 'surprise,' I don't see much of him." Joi assumed a casual, "no-biggie" posture. "Oh, really?" Ella said, plucking her pencil from her hair. "Still calls every night?"

"Every night, but we don't talk long. A real puzzle ain't it?" Joi asked flippantly.

"He's pulling away from you and you don't mind?"

"He pulls away, and I'm not running after him. I guess the bough breaks, huh?" Joi pulled out a cigarette from her apron pocket. "Probably just as well. I don't need a Mack truck to run me over to get the message."

Joi went out back, leaned up against the cold cement wall and lit up. She recalled how Pride's recent calls had sounded duty-bound, with little to say. He seemed remote, distracted; she couldn't remember when she'd last seen his face. Guess Miss Hat and Heels is getting the best of him now, she thought. She could feel herself reverting to a numb indifference regarding him. The wall he'd torn down with his love, she was slowly reconstructing. She flicked off her cigarette and walked back inside.

"Joi, we still on for the dinner and movie?" Claude asked. "I get to pick the movie this time."

"Sure, why not," Joi said with a hunch of her shoulders and a quick smile.

Unlike her relationship with Pride, Joi knew this one with Claude Bryant Jeeter was going nowhere from jump. What would this handsome, college-graduated, owner of his own engineering firm, Jeeter and Morris, and driver of a black Porsche want from her but companionship and sex? Joi was willing to give him the former, but when he asked for the latter, she would cut him loose. Meanwhile, they could enjoy movie and dinner dates peppered with lively intellectual discussions. The bonus was she wasn't home to hear Pride's messages click on and off her machine. She wondered how long Pride intended to perpetuate this charade and come clean: "I've found someone else, Joi. I thought it was you, but it's Hat and Heels instead." Ending it seemed so easy to her.

At least Pride had pushed her out into the dating scene again, and for that she was thankful. Claude was pompous but palatable to Joi. This was their second date and she would enjoy his company as long as the ride lasted. She had time to fill and nothing to lose with Claude. In fact, he was just what she needed to get over the neglect and ultimate demise of Pride and Joi.

"Joi, what are you doing?" Shorty stopped her at the

diner door and eyed the Porsche waiting for her at the curb. "Excuse me?" Joi's almond-shaped eyes rounded wide with contempt at the nerve of him questioning her.

"What about the 'surprise?' "

"Does everyone know about the 'surprise' but me?" she said, swinging her bag over her shoulder. "Better watch it. The surprise might be on Pride." As she pushed the diner door open and moved into the setting sunshine, the car door slid open from the inside.

"Hey, good lookin'," Claude said.

"Hey, yourself."

As much as she tried putting Pride out of her thoughts, he crept in, uninvited. She had always prided herself on picking definitive men—wrong men, but at least definitive. She had only heard about relationships that limped to an end because some weak-ass man couldn't say, "It was great, but it's over." She had thought Pride was a man like that; instead, he was taking the wimp's way out.

"You okay, Joi?" Claude asked as he steered the car through rush-hour traffic.

"Sure. What movie are we going to see?"

Claude had never met a woman like Joi. She appealed to the controlled renegade side of him. Women of grace and grit, like Joi, didn't travel in his circles. He was used to intelligent women but not independent. His usual women acquiesced to shopping sprees, travels abroad, standing spa dates and golf club tee times. Joi was into none of that. Her natural beauty had captivated him the first time he'd walked into Louie's. Her striking, exotic features were set in flawless pecan skin. Her hair was an amazing mass of short explosive curls. He couldn't wait to see how her body panned out beneath that ugly uniform. After seeing her in regular clothes on their first date last week, she did not disappoint. She had clad her shapely legs in blue denim and the jeans fit her curves with precision; her breasts rounded alluringly under a turtleneck sweater. And her mind was always engaged, analytical and articulate. She was so unpretentious; he was wholly bewitched by her. Ah, and wouldn't they have beautiful children? he thought.

She would round out his life perfectly. What was left for him to conquer? His firm had been featured in *Black Enterprise*, three times on the cover and numerous times inside. His red BMW had been replaced by this black Porsche to indicate his growth and maturity. At thirty-five, he was ready to settle down, and she was what he needed to complete the idyllic picture. He could fix her flaws, mainly her lack of a college degree and overall polish. Nothing designer frocks and an expensive car wouldn't cure. He planned to find out how those gorgeous lips felt tonight; he'd wait until later to feel them all over his body. She had to be fantastic in bed. The passion she felt about human rights had to spill into the bedroom. He hadn't felt this alive about a woman since Laurel, but she had blown it with her obsessive penchant for the material. But Joi Martin Jeeter sounded good to him, and JMJ would look good on the vanity plates of her sports BMW that he'd get her for an engagement gift. He had a few more inquiries to pursue before making her his.

∽≈∼

Shorty stopped by Pride's office four times before finding him in. They had talked while Pride was pouring over books. "Man, maybe you better tell her something or at least get over to see her," Shorty said.

"If I see her, I'll tell her. Then I'll want to be with her, I'll lose focus and ruin the surprise," Pride said.

"Man, somebody's beating your time. She's out on a date. She's gone to the movies."

"Is that all?"

"That's how it starts. Man, I don't like this, Pride."

"It's not much longer. I got it all under control." He rose from his desk. "Your ego is out of whack, man."

"Who's she out with? You know him?"

"You do, too. That engineer who did the inspection a few weeks back."

"That Jeeter guy?" Relief washed Pride's face and he laughed. "He's not Joi's type. I am."

"You young pups got all the answers, huh?" Shorty went to the door. "Always talking about 'communication,' but not doing it."

"I know my woman, alright?" Pride teased. "She loved my last surprise." Pride thought of the Sleepy Hollow Inn in the Poconos. "This one is going to knock her socks off."

"Like my granddaughter said to her big brother, 'You better recognize.' " Shorty turned the doorknob. "Well, I did my do. It's all on you. Later, man."

Pride returned to his desk, sat down, picked up his pencil and opened his reading comprehension workbook again. He had been fortunate enough to have grasped the math quickly, but the English composition and writing was kicking his butt. The GED examination was given the second Saturday of every month and he had targeted the date he was going to take it. There was an increase of twenty points from his two practice tests, but he still had a long way to go. Working ten hour days, studying through lunch and after work before going to classes five days a week, was finally taking a toll on him. After class he'd grab a bite to eat and resume studying. When he didn't feel focused or was getting sleepy, sometimes, he'd go to the computer lab at school that was open twenty-four hours a day. As if work and school hadn't been enough, Sand in My Shoes was demanding more of his jewelry, and he had been foolish enough to add the Afrique Boutique to his client list. He often popped a VHS tape on a GED subject matter while he worked on his pieces, listening to mathematical equations as he fashioned metal and stones into his exotic Nubian Pride jewelry. He was overworked, but his mission was clear—to get his GED so he could advance more quickly at his job and, when he retired from the Ford factory, get a good position in the private sector. He was doing it for himself, but more importantly, he was doing it for Joi.

Pride reared back in his chair and thought about her. His life was fine before her, but she showed him that it could be exceptional. She wanted it all. She deserved it all, and he wanted to be the one to give it to her: frequent trips, fancy restaurants and a car of her own. She wanted to finish college herself and, of course, there would be college for their children. He'd have to attend college himself just to keep up with his family—and the first step was this GED.

He would further surprise Joi after the OED graduation ceremony. He would fix all their favorite foods and then propose to her. He toyed with the idea of putting a diamond ring on layaway, but felt a one-of-a-kind Pride original ring of hammered gold would be more special. He had it at home and looked at it and her picture for strength when times got challenging.

Pride twirled his pencil above his workbook. "So, no," he answered Shorty in his mind. "I am not worried about this Jeeter guy." No man on this earth could love Joi more than him. In only a few more weeks, it would all be over and he could give her the surprise of a lifetime. They would laugh and talk about it with their children for years to come. He'd tell their children how hard it was working, going to school and doing jewelry, and when he thought it would all come apart, he would just call their mama up. His Joi. Just to hear her voice, sometimes at three or four o'clock in the morning. Then he would remember why he was doing it— for her and for them—the children they were to have.

Pride smiled, then opened his workbook. He worked one problem, then stumbled through the next three. He couldn't tell her now, just in case he failed and didn't pass the GED exam. He finally admitted to himself that he didn't want her to think of him as a failure. How would that look? She had almost graduated from college and he couldn't get a GED. He had promised himself that if he failed the test, he would at least tell her what he was doing. But he didn't want to see the pity in her eyes, the way he had seen it in his teachers' eyes as they socially promoted to the eleventh grade.

Pride shook his head free of negative thoughts and moved to question number four. He got it right and relaxed. He glanced at his watch and realized he had just enough time to make it to class.

⋘⋙

Claude walked Joi to her door after the movie. "Mind if I come in?" He moved in closer and then tried to kiss her.

Joi stepped back. "Listen, Claude," Joi began. "You're a nice guy but I am just not interested in a relationship. Friendship is all I can handle, right now. So, if you're after more you've got the wrong—"

"Hey, a guy can always use another friend. Right?" He backed away. "Of course, I can't remember when I've ever been refused by a woman. Probably never." He held her hand and kissed it good night. "Certainly, none as beautiful as you."

"Now if this is going to be a problem for you, then we can just say our good-byes now."

"Ouch! You are a hard woman. But I like that."

Joi gave him a wary look.

"Friends."

"Good-night, Claude." Joi opened her door and went inside.

The answering machine winked red in the darkness and Joi played her messages. Pride had called twice telling her he loved her but showing her nothing. "Just cut the crap already," she said, stabbing the machine void of his voice.

⋘⋙

"Oh Claude!" Jacquleen's ultra-feminine voice lilted over the other patrons of Aloutte's, Detroit's most expensive French restaurant.

Jacquleen's preening and fawning was embarrassing to Joi, who thought she should leave Claude and her mother alone so they could get a room. Joi could tell her mother was in love…with Claude Jeeter. Joi sipped the Dom Perignon and viewed the pair over the rim of her crystal flute. It was as if Claude and her mother were conspiring in some secret deal and she was the unwilling prize.

Joi wasn't sure what Claude's angle was; maybe he thought he was doing some bizarre community service or amusing himself by slumming with the common folk, but it was clear that Jacquleen St. Marie thought she had hit the golden cow, not only for her daughter but for herself.

Bored with the bend of conversation, Joi let her eyes roam the posh, five star restaurant before she took another sip of champagne. She surveyed the patrons full circle and sighed with disappointment; it seemed the only entertainment was the couple who sat at her own table. She eavesdropped on their conversation and watched how engrossed her mother was in every word that sprang from Claude's lips. Her mother seemed captivated by Claude's pedantic recitations of his regal parentage, his childhood complete with nanny, maids, prep-schools, skiing in St. Moritz, summers abroad or at his family's summer home in Sag Harbor. She was enthralled by constipated stories of his college and fraternity days where he had bucked the three-generational Howard/Harvard University tradition of his family by going to Princeton instead. Dollar signs seemed to bloom in Jacquleen's eyes as he spoke of his cars, his annual Parisian shopping sprees and his boat, "Exce$$," moored at the marina. And when he spoke of returning to his native Chicago to throw his hat into the political ring, she thought her mother would faint.

"Detroit is a little too blue-collar for this blue blood," Claude quipped.

"Oh, politics," Jacquleen gushed. "The White House?"

"I'll start with mayor first, then governor, then we'll see."

Since Jacquleen was too old for the boy, Joi knew she was trying to assess just how to make her baby girl part of this great scenario. Relax, she mentally spoke to her mother, it ain't gonna happen. "I'm starved. Can we order now?" Joi interrupted their clandestine conversation and flipped open the menu with no prices.

Once the tuxedoed waiter had taken their orders, the two players reverted to their private drama. To amuse herself, Joi decided to look at this alliance through her mother's eyes. If Joi married Claude, then Jacquleen would not have to worry about her again, and she would certainly outdo her sister, Noel.

As Joi tore off a piece of bread, an officious waiter appeared from nowhere to rush to her side and whisk away the crumbs with his little broom set. It seemed ironic that a penguinesque waiter would be waiting on a waitress from Louie's. Then she realized that she was in the company of luncheon-ladies, who were now out to dinner. After their husbands left their foreign cars with the valet and checked their furs, they were escorted to their tables. Their designer gowns hung on their spa-induced curves and their diamonds danced in the glow of the candlelight; classical music accessorized their perusal of the priceless menus of exotic cuisine and combustible desserts. Those whose children accompanied them looked as suitably bored as was Joi, but they instinctively used the correct forks, bread plates and napkin corners to wipe away pheasant gravy.

This world was as foreign to her as those she read about in *National Geographic*, but attainable for the right money, the right ticket. Your money and ticket is Claude Jeeter, her mind spoke her mother's words. With Pride she had dined among the luncheon-ladies; but with Claude Bryant Jeeter, she would *be* one. There was no other way here on this earth she could jump the wide chasm between her world and this one. There was no way she could reconcile the material with the spiritual, for her heart and body shouted, "Joe Pride!" Just then, a man of his stature, color and build swiped her attention, and Joi's nerves rocked at the thought it could be him. Maybe Miss Hat and Heels had money and class. She turned around to see that it was not him. Her sudden movement caused both Claude and Jacquleen to stop talking and look at her. When she returned her gaze to the table, their eyes waited and searched her.

Before Claude could say anything Jacquleen piped up. "Did you hear what Claude said?" She seemed to know immediately what and about whom her daughter was thinking. "Wouldn't that be fantastic?"

"Sure would," Joi answered, not even interested enough to ask what they were talking about.

At the meal's end she learned that she had inadvertently agreed to take a nightcap at Claude's condo. The doorman opened the car door for the ladies, then opened the lobby door before going back to park Claude's Porsche in the garage.

"Close your mouth, Mother," Joi said to her mother's awe as they walked through the cavernous lobby to the cushioned elevators—a sentiment she repeated with her eyes as the door opened onto Claude's marble foyer which was crowned by a crystal chandelier. Jacquleen went and stood in the sunken, high-tech living room with a balcony overlooking the river.

"Oh, my, this is wonderful!" Jacquleen gushed as Claude turned on his state-of-the-art electronic equipment. Soft jazz filtered over the leather and glass decor.

When Claude disappeared behind the bar, Joi stood directly in front of her mother and said, "Get a grip! None of this belongs to us!" Jacquleen left Joi and went to the bar where Claude was pouring brandy into crystal snifters and swirling it around the generous bowl. He inhaled the bouquet of the amber liquid. "This is good stuff, Mrs. St. Marie. You'll enjoy it."

"I told you to call me Jacquleen," Her mother said in exaggerated French. Joi cut her eyes at both of them.

After a tour of the condo and another twenty minutes of polite chit-chat, Jacquleen said, "Well, I've had a delightful evening, young man, but I must be getting home."

"Yep, all good things must come to an end," Joi said sarcastically. "But I have to get up early, too."

"Why?" Jacquleen challenged, taking Joi by surprise.

"I'm a working girl, Ma."

"No, no, no. You kids stay and finish out the evening.

The night is young—and so are you."

"I'll take you home," Claude said, going to the telephone to call for his car.

"No, no, you're not listening," Jacquleen said, teetering to the door on her high heels.

"At least let me call you a cab," Claude offered.

Jacquleen seemed anxious to leave. "That's what that doorman downstairs is for, am I right?" she teased.

"I was raised better than that, Jacquleen." He turned to Joi. "I'll be right back."

"Good night," Jacquleen sang to her daughter.

"Why not just sell me for a price?" Joi said sotto voce as she closed the door on the pair.

She looked around the condo at the expensive leather furniture, the glass and brass accouterments, the electronic equipment, the big screen television and the twinkling lights of a nocturnal Detroit seen through the balcony balustrades. She gulped the brandy down and poured herself more from the heavy crystal decanter.

She heard the click of the door.

"Easy on that. The good stuff slips up on you," Claude said.

"Mom—"

"Got her off okay. Imagine she didn't want me paying for the cab."

"Imagine," Joi said, and swirled her body in his direction. Her head was on delay and she swayed.

"Let's sit shall we?"

She was high. She knew it. It was time for her to go. Claude brushed his lips across hers. "What are you doing?"

she asked.

"Escalating our relationship. It's time for renegotiating."

"Who says?" She sounded weak even to herself, but alcohol had a way of playing tricks on your mind. It was an indiscriminate liquid because her body began to respond. "So, you think you are entitled to some sort of payment for the last three weeks of dates? For feeding my mother?"

"Not at all. It's just the natural progression of things. Relax," Claude breathed into her ear.

She tried to. Closing her eyes she felt his lips graze hers. She accepted the sensation of someone wanting her. Someone whose breath charged with every touch of their lips. Someone whose fevered tongue explored hers with a jumbled energy as his hands slid down her back.

"Stop!" she yelled and jumped up. "I can't do this. I'm not ready. This isn't right. I just can't."

Claude was shocked speechless at the abruptness of her action. Both of his heads—the one above, and the one below his belt—were stiff and erect, and pivoted in her direction. Only the top head spoke. "Ah, what happened here?"

"Sorry." She was readjusting herself. "I told you just friends. I'm not ready for a relationship. You are moving too fast. I just can't," all tumbled out of her mouth as she scurried to the foyer closet for her coat.

"Well, we can talk about it—later. I can see you are determined to go home. I'll take you," he said, still stupefied but unable to get up; his lower head was still keeping hope alive.

"No. I'll get a cab," she said as she pulled on her coat and opened the door in one swift movement. The light from the hall flashed a perfect blade across his almost satisfied body, then vanished with the closing of the door.

In all his years, this had never happened to him. Not as a fifteen-year-old virgin with a seventeen-year-old "experienced" girl. Not with the subsequent virgins he indoctrinated into the world of lovemaking.

Not in his college years, not in his early career years and certainly not since he had attained wealth independent of family money.

He chuckled and went to the bar to pour himself a short brandy. He toasted the door through which Joi had just disappeared. Once again, Joi Martin had gifted him with an experience he had never known. He thought he'd done it all, including a ménage à trois which had immediately satisfied and humiliated him. Like that Earth, Wind and Fire song, his "reasons had no pride." Certainly neither his father nor his other ancestors had ever engaged in such a lewd and disgusting act unworthy of a Jeeter. Even back then, he thought of how damaging this discovery would be for his political career.

He gulped a healthy swallow of brandy to wash away the remnants of that unsavory tryst, the way a person would if they stole something needlessly at ten, or took advantage of a willing girl who was more drunk than amorous. Now, at this stage of his life when all of his encounters fell into the "been there, done that" category, Joi had given him a wholeheartedly new experience.

Claude savored the last sip and thought of her. She was surely no virgin. No one that fine who lived that long could escape the passions of the flesh. Not the way she just responded to him—the smoldering before the ignition—then those ridiculous words: "I can't do this. I'm not ready." Women were always ready for him. He had to slow them down. They were always anxious to claim him, to become part of him and his money.

He laughed aloud. Joi made him feel sixteen and unsure again, like a teenager trying to score. He hadn't felt this invigorated in years! Alive, stimulated—teased. She had reduced him to the living embodiment of that old song standard, "Bewitched, Bothered and Bewildered." She was crafty. She intended to make him work for it. It was retro in approach, nostalgic; she was conjuring up old-fashioned values and morals in this too ready, too willing and able world, where freakiness was the rule instead of the exception.

Of course, Claude felt the presence of another man, but Claude Jeeter was never afraid of a little healthy competition. He hadn't accomplished all he had without a winning attitude. It was the Jeeter way. That made the prize all the more worth having. And Joi was worth having. He was on a crusade and she was his Holy Grail. He'd treat her that way—like a religious icon.

He set his crystal snifter on the polished bar. Sex was nothing nowadays, just a means to an end. Women used their bodies like a commodity, to get what and who they wanted. He would wait until Joi was ready. He would keep her chaste and pure until their honeymoon—provided it was a short engagement. He laughed boldly at the prospect. He could tell his children he waited until they were married to consummate their love. What a hoot, he thought. How novel. Surely none of his friends could dare say they waited until their honeymoons. But he could. Like those boyhood dreams of marrying a virgin and schooling her. To get a real virgin these days he'd have to date the classmates of his ten-year-old niece, he thought. He'd be the first on his block, in his circle of friends, to proclaim this victory. New adventures were harder to come by the older he got; he'd never not slept with a girlfriend before. What a distinction! A feather in his already lauded cap.

He would make Joi his after he saw how she interacted with his friends and associates at the upcoming party hosted by Jonathan Morris and his wife. Claude was positive that Joi was the woman worthy of the title—Mrs. Claude Jeeter. He was seldom wrong. He would propose to her and then wait until the honeymoon to consummate their union. Even if she proved to be a temptress and wanted to make love, he would not. He would be victorious, but what else was new?

∽◈∾

"I'm sorry, I pushed you too fast," Claude said as Joi continued to wait on her customers.

"I'm just not ready for a sexual relationship," she whispered. "It was a mistake."

"Mistake? Jeeters don't make mistakes!"

"Keep your voice down," Joi ordered as she eyed Ella, Chantel and Pride's boys.

"Joi, I think I'm falling—"

"Oh, God no!" She grabbed her head in disbelief and

began massaging her temples. "This cannot be happening again. I can't handle—"

"Okay, okay! I'll back off, but you still have to go to Vivian and Jonathan's with me. Remember? My business partner and his wife? You promised last week and they are expecting us."

"I don't think it's a good idea—" Joi began. Louie shot her an impatient look.

"Wear the Armani cocktail suit I sent—"

"About that. I cannot accept that suit—"

"Why not? No strings attached. I just want you to look as gorgeous as I know you can."

"It's not right—"

"For friends to give friends gifts? Oh, come now, Joi. You have never taken a gift from a friend?"

"Not that expensive."

"I have the money—think of it as a five dollar T-shirt if it makes it easier for you. Just wear it tomorrow. I'm not leaving here until you agree. I'll call your mama on you," he threatened playfully.

"Okay," Joi said, feeling trapped and self-conscious. She wiped sweat from the divot above her lips and brushed hair away from her face.

"Pick you up at seven." He surprised her by giving her a peck on the cheek. Ella, Chantel, Shorty and the boys looked at her, then looked away.

∞≈∞

"Sounds like playing two ends against the middle to

me," Dante said to Joi as Mrs. St. Marie entered the apartment.

"Dante," Joi's mother acknowledged dismissively.

"The Queen Mother. My cue to leave," he said to Joi. "Mrs. St. Marie, aren't we looking positively—radiant!" he said brightly, cutting his eyes at his friend.

"Dante's leaving tomorrow for three weeks in Aruba and Curacao!" Joi said to her mother.

Jacquleen's face remained unimpressed. "Didn't you just get back from somewhere?"

"Well, how nice of you to care," he said sarcastically. "I go Caribbeaning at least three times a year—in season. This is the season! Ta-ta, Joi. Have loads of fun tonight!"

"Bon voyage to you." Joi waved him out the door.

Mrs. St. Marie turned toward her daughter with an accusing look. "Why is he always hanging around here? Claude hasn't met him yet, has he?"

Joi shot her a weary, cut-the-crap look, and Jacquleen continued. "This purse goes perfectly with that dress. What's that around your eyes? Mascara? It's smudged. You look like a raccoon."

"That's Dante's doing. That's why I don't wear this mess. It's coming off." Joi disappeared into the bathroom just as the phone rang. Jacquleen thought it might be Claude so she slid the volume up. Instead, she heard the voice of Joe Pride on the machine.

"Joi, it's me, your loving man, Pride," he said. "Pick up." Jacquleen hurriedly turned the volume down. "I decided to take some time off. It's time for you and me to reacquaint our bodies. The reunion of a lifetime."

Jacquleen gagged and cut her eyes, then checked the bathroom door, wishing he'd just spit it out and hang up. "Joi? Give me a call when you get in. I've got some cotton candy mix and some of your other favorites simmering—the best of it is me. I'm hot for your bod. Call me soon. I miss you."

"Hang up already!" Jacquleen snapped through his absurd kissing noises, keeping her eyes glued on the bathroom door. When he finally hung up, she snatched the phone from the receiver so the call would not register. "You low-life loser."

"Was that the phone?" Joi asked, returning to the room.

"Phone? I didn't hear a phone. Ah, you are a vision, *ma petite*. You'll throw all those bourgie babes for a loop."

"Whatever, Ma. This will probably be my swan song with Claude anyway."

"What?" The doorbell rang. Panic flitted across her mother's face at the thought that Joi would dump Claude. Joi opened the door. Claude stood on the threshold with an explosion of spring flowers in his arms.

"Wow, you look great," he said.

"Thanks," Joi said, and continued putting on her earrings.

"Jacquleen," he acknowledged her mother, bowing slightly at the waist.

"Hello, Claude. How very handsome you look."

Claude eyed the roses in the vase. "Ah, you already have some," he said, with a note of disappointment in his voice.

"Those old things are on their way out," Jacquleen said. She unceremoniously took Pride's flowers and dumped them in the kitchen waste basket, then quickly rinsed and refilled the vase with water before accepting Claude's expensive bouquet from him. "My, how exotic. Bird-of-paradise aren't they?"

"Yes. You know your flowers, Jacquleen." Claude eyed Joi again. "Wow, you really look like a million bucks."

"From your lips to God's ear," Jacquleen said quietly. She had already been doing weekly novenas for this union. God had to be on her side because she had been here to intercept yet another of Pride's calls.

"Ready?" Claude asked.

"I am. Ma?" Joi stood at the door waiting for her mother to join them. She never left her nosy mother alone in her apartment.

Jacquleen looked around, glaring at the answering machine whose red eye was constant. She wished Joe Pride would just die. Joi disappeared into the highly polished sports car. Its reflection caught an enraptured Jacquleen contemplating the potential of her daughter's prospects. As she climbed into her own car and snapped her seat belt, the golden couple tooted their horn as they spirited off.

Like the magic coach in Cinderella, Jacquleen thought. Finally, her Joi was aptly paired with someone deserving of her. Maybe Joi would redeem the St. Marie name. The Jeeter money could never compare to the old-line St. Maries, but Jacquleen would relish sending the old, too-mean-to-die Au Claire Joi's wedding announcement followed by all the magazine and newspaper coverage this union was sure to garner. If the old bat could hang on for another few years, Jacquleen would messenger her Mr. and Mrs. Claude Jeeter's campaign agenda and all his activities as he spun toward being the first black president of the United States. That would show all of those uppity-aristo-cratic St. Maries. She'd have the President and his First Lady send them White House Christmas cards. Maybe even invite them to 1600 Pennsylvania Avenue for a state dinner, then—at the last minute—rescind the invitation and never invite them again. Jacquleen laughed out loud, then choked herself quiet and thought, I hope Joi doesn't mess up this chance of a lifetime.

❧

As the sleek black car sped through the streets toward suburbia with the soothing backdrop of a Grover Washington Jr. CD, Joi thought of how Claude's attitude had become less pompous when it was just the two of them—but more possessive since her rejection of his sexual advances. Patience and waiting until she was ready was all he could talk about.

Surprisingly, Joi didn't feel guilty about the neglectful Pride. Like when Noel had left her expensive bike out in the rain and someone had stolen it. Although she had cried and wailed for days, Joi hadn't had any sympathy for her sister, either. Noel should have treated it better; Pride should have treated her better. For over three years she had corralled all her love and feelings, locked them up and thrown away the key. Along came Pride who had liberally applied lubricant and exquisitely rubbed open the corral lock without a key, releasing her long buried desires. And then he'd walked away as if his mission were accomplished.

He'd left her alone to re-harness what he had set free. She wasn't guilty; she was angry and still confused. The future she thought she had with him had become her past.

Claude glanced at her and downshifted. "Joi? Where are you? Don't be nervous. You've already met Jonathan and Vivian and everybody else will be more of the same." He patted her hand and smiled.

Joi didn't tell him that her somber mood had nothing to do with this party or the over-friendly Jonathan Morris and his pretentious wife, Vivian. She couldn't care less about the lot of them. Being here with him tonight was about void-filling; going out with Claude beat spending another Pride-less Saturday night. This would be her last date with Claude and his friends, anyway. She had no intention of sleeping with him—ever. It wasn't fair to keep this thing going when there was no future to it. It was too late for the spring session, but to fill her upcoming summer nights, she'd decided to take a class at the university.

Joi was treated to the usual introductions once inside the Morris home. She grew increasingly weary of the conversation, which spanned topics from politics to cat food. Joi moved with ease among the elegantly chic and self-impressed crowd. Ease, not because she was equally as appointed—Claude had seen to that—but because she didn't really care about any of them and never planned to see them beyond tonight. They were the type who would see you, yet not see you, in a store. She could be just as gracious and aloof as them, who didn't know that their days were numbered in her book.

As Claude accepted a drink from the tray of a roaming

waiter, he watched Joi from across the room. Insouciance personified, he defined her: the rare combination of effortless grace and earthiness, with the bearing of a king's firstborn. A woman of understated elegance, outrageous beauty, and unlimited potential. The Armani suit he had given her as a surprise was tastefully sculpted to her luscious curves and showcased her pecan skin. Both men and women watched her cool confidence from afar. Sometimes she was too self-sufficient for him, but that was part of her allure. He was used to women throwing themselves at him, trying to snag one of the most eligible black bachelors in America—the guy with the old money, family pedigree and nationally-renowned reputation. Joi wasn't impressed. It seemed the harder he tried, the less interested she was. Women will never understand that men liked challenges, like sports, he thought. There is no sport to easy women, and no prize to attain like Joi Martin, the New Orleans beauty. She would be perfect on his arm as he negotiated the political/business world; poised, fluent in two languages, and she could speak on any subject from the Giza's pyramids to world trade. She would be an asset to him and he to her. While he stoked his political machine, she would finish up her degree; for graduation, he'd start her on one of their three beautiful children. The way she made his stomach do flips when she neared him guaranteed that Joi had to be sexually satisfying. To start his volcano erupting, all he needed was to see her nude body, which, like the rest of her, had to be the color of iced tea standing in a ray of sunshine; just as cool and inviting.

He felt his manhood straining against its silk encasement and was happy for his generously-pleated designer pants. Yep, he thought, as he let the expensive golden liquid slide down his throat with the sight of her, the perfect First Lady of Chicago; a union made in the boardroom of heaven and assured success, once he stopped her from smoking and got her away from Detroit. He knew the other man, for whatever reason, was on his way out. Clearly this cat wasn't Jacquleen's favorite, and Claude doubted that this dude could give Joi what he could. So, as in all tactical maneuvers, he planned to use his advantages to close the deal. Once he had Joi in a marriage for two or three years, she wouldn't even remember this cat or the original circumstances; all she'd know would be the benefits of being Mrs. Claude Jeeter, He sauntered over to her side.

"So, Claude tells me you are into cuisine management at a downtown bistro?" A curious luncheon-lady broke the ice with Joi as she spooned beluga caviar onto a toast point.

"I'm a waitress," Joi clarified and sipped champagne from a Lalique flute.

"Who's going to the university in September." Claude spoke up as Joi's eyes flashed angrily at him.

"Oh? What will you study?" the luncheon-lady asked.

Claude responded before Joi could reply. "French Literature." Joi acidly stared at him.

"*Parlez vous français?*" the woman's husband asked.

"*Oui.*" Joi answered and conversed in fluent French as Claude stood proudly by her side.

After more inane conversation, eating and drinking, Joi glanced at her watch. It was midnight, Sunday morning, and she was ready to go home and send Claude packing back from whence he had come.

As they walked down the long driveway of the Morris home, Claude tried to take Joi's arm. She jerked away. He opened the car door for her and closed it. She had snapped her seat belt by the time Claude eased into the driver's seat.

She lit into him. "Don't you ever apologize for what I do, or answer for me—do you hear me? I am not your show dog. And waitresses are some of the most decent people I know."

"No doubt, a noble lot," he said politely, turning toward her, "but you deserve so much better."

She offered him her profile, her lips pursed in total disgust.

"Let me be the guy who takes you away from all that."

"Yeah, sure. You got a cigarette?" Her eyes met his and she wondered why he hadn't started the car.

"Joi, will you marry me?"

"What?" she asked, stunned, as he took her hand in his. "This isn't funny. Just take me home."

"It's not a joke. My friends love you. You're not only beautiful, but smart—"

"So is this what that was? An audition? I had to pass inspection. You inspect my mother and your friends inspect me? You got some nerve."

"Not at all. I have all kinds of women after me—"

"Aw, cheeze! I don't want to hear this crap."

"Joi, we'd be so good together," he continued, disregarding her remark. He eased closer to her; his expensive cologne wafted across her nose. "We are good together. We'll be great together."

"How would you know that? Claude the all-knowing," she said sarcastically.

"I know the potential of what we have."

"What are you talking about?"

"I know there's someone else. The flowers, the way you resist me. I know for whatever reason, it's not working with him. I know that I could give you the world. Can he do that? I can give you *this* world with a single 'yes.' "

Joi was slapped silent.

Is this what adult love is? she thought. Bargaining for the best deal, who could give or do the most for you? "You have got to be kidding me." Disbelief was in her voice and eyes.

"No, I am not." He looked at her pleadingly as he rubbed the side of her dimpled cheek with the back of his hand.

She stared at him, then looked outside the car, seeking escape from the incredulity of it. Reality smacked her back. The gargantuan Morris home was lit; its floodlights cascaded over the two-door entrance way, across the bonsai-clipped shrubbery and down the cobblestone driveway. And from nowhere came the voice over the years saying, You could live like this. You could have a house in this neighborhood.

Joi then realized she could have a cleaning lady, and a cook, and throw lavish parties with shaved salmon offered by strolling waiters. Her children could have a bus from their private school pick them up daily. They could go to college, any college, straight through. They could take exotic vacations, plucked from the pages of *National*

Geographic, three times a year—like the Morris family. If she said yes, the quality of her life would immediately change. She could move into a high-tech apartment, drive a Porsche and cruise on the yacht "EXCE$$" on the weekends. Would she be a fool to pass this up?

"Joi?" Claude nudged her back from her mental survey.

"Why…why me?"

"You deserve me, and I deserve you. We'll have such gorgeous, smart children." He smiled. "C'mon, Joi. I love you—"

"How can you say that?"

"Why? How? Because it's only been a month? There's no time schedule to love. You know when you know." Joi thought about Pride and how quickly their love had blossomed…then wilted and was soon to die. She had fallen too fast, too hard.

"Besides," Claude continued, "I'm a mover, a shaker and a deal maker. I can size up the right and wrong of something in a snap. It's what I do for a living." She was still staring at him blankly. "When you get to be my age and my sophistication, you know what you're looking for. And when you find it, you grab it." She sighed and he continued. "I know you may not feel the same way about me now, but you will, especially when this other cat is history." In her eyes, he saw the first glimmer of a reaction. "With all I plan to do for you, you *will* love me. And neither of us is getting any younger."

Her eyes fixed on his without blinking, and she thought, somehow, he was right. They did deserve each other. He wanted his children to look a certain way, and she wanted her children to never want for anything. Even if it didn't work out and they divorced, their children would be safe and their futures secured. He was probably physically satisfying, though he could never make her feel like Pride did; never make her heart skip or her body jump and sing like Pride...used to do. And probably would never do again. Claude was a nice guy—just not the right guy. He deserved more, but he was still willing to settle for less. What did she have to lose? It was a win/win proposition. She and Claude were the same side of the same coin, only he was fourth-generation college graduate and she had never finished. They could successfully perpetuate the American Dream as well as the next couple.

Joi saw that same kaleidoscope of time clicking again, taking her brother, her father, Joaquin and even Pride. The colorful stones surrounded Claude like a halo, like compensation, second chances and peace. She swore she heard God's warning, *If you don't take this one, Joi Martin, then you can't ever complain or pray to me about not having a decent man again.*

"Can I have a fireplace in the bedroom and back stairs to the kitchen?" she asked dreamily, still staring through the front windshield.

Claude beamed. "Baby, you can have whatever you want. I'll give you a Beamer for an engagement gift, a Jag when you graduate and a Benz-wagon when the kiddies start coming."

And her children would have everything. They'd be born to it. Used to the fine house, the pool, the clowns and rented ponies for birthday parties; the dance, music and karate lessons. There was only one answer. She'd have to start on her heirs soon. She didn't want to have kids in her forties, parent teenagers in her fifties and sixties, and be an embarrassment to them in her seventies at their college graduation when classmates mistook her for their "grand-mother."

"You understand that I don't love you now like I should?" she clarified.

"You will. Sometimes you have to help fate along. Without it, we'd be lost. Without it, I wouldn't have come to Louie's for lunch." He chuckled as he flicked one of her curls.

After another pensive pause, Joi finally took the bird in the hand. "Okay, Claude, I'll marry you." Her practical self answered "yes" to the promise of an idyllic life for her and her yet unborn children.

After all, she reasoned, Princess Grace of Monaco had had to pass a fertility test before Prince Ranier would marry her, and Jackie Kennedy had married Aristotle Onassis to protect her children. Marital contracts of immense wealth were made every day; the practical over the romantic— decisions of the mind, not the heart. White woman did it all the time. Well, now it was this black woman's turn for some carpe diem—time for her to seize the day with this black man. An opportunity like this didn't knock often for a thirty-three-year-old black waitress. The only other prospect she had had was a recently distant, drop-out factory worker who did jewelry on the side. Pride didn't compare with a Howard and Princeton University graduate whose firm and family graced the covers of financial magazines. She and her children, with her new lifestyle and a husband in politics, could end up on the pages of *Ebony* and *Life* and be interviewed by CNN.

"You've made me so happy!" He was kissing her. "We'll honeymoon in Europe. You pick the itinerary. Then you'll finish college at Loyola or the University of Chicago and graduate. And we'll buy a huge house and fill it with pretty babies…" he was saying as Joi watched another sepia couple laughingly stroll down the Morris driveway and disappear into their Rolls-Royce.

CHAPTER 9

"Surprise!" the crowd shouted at Joi as Claude escorted her into his foyer. The light from the chandelier illuminated the faces of Jacquleen, Jonathan, Vivian and a cadre of others Joi had met at their home.

"What is this?" Joi exclaimed. Claude took her coat and handed it to the butler.

"Our engagement party," he whispered in her ear.

"And the fairytale begins," Joi said to her mother as she smiled at the guests.

Joi talked, danced, sipped champagne, nibbled on colorful hors d'oeuvres, delighting in her role as the belle of the ball. Claude cut the music. "Will you join me, my love?" He held out his hand to Joi and she strolled into his embrace. He kissed her and the crowd Ooooh-ed. "Well, most of you have known me for some time. Many of you have wondered, indiscreetly, when I was going to settle down. I had my own agenda, my own windmills to tilt and quests to conquer. I didn't have time to consider a love life—until now. This lady has changed all that. I was floored the very first time I saw her. Isn't she gorgeous?" Joi blushed from embarrassment; her looks were the least of her.

"It's not just her drop-dead good looks, but she's intelligent and has those old-fashioned values that many of us discarded on our way to making millions. She reminds me of the best of who I am. This is the kind of wife I want for me, and the kind of mother I want for my children. So…"

He fished in his pocket, snagged the small blue box from Tiffany's and sank to one knee. "In front of all these people, I am asking you if you'd join me in holy matrimony. I already asked your mother and she said yes."

"Yes," Joi said simply, uncomfortable with this type of attention.

"Let's seal our deal with this ring." He removed it from its velvet pillow, held it up so everyone could see it, then slid it on her finger. He then sprang to his feet and planted a movie star kiss on her. The crowd applauded. He held up her hand. "It's only a two-carat pear-shaped diamond. I wanted three but Joi thought that would be too ostentatious. I plan to cure her of that malady in the years to come—along with turning her party affiliation from Democrat to Republican." He draped his hand around her shoulders.

Joi extended her hand so she could see her ring at a distance. "It's beautiful, Claude. Thank you."

"It's only the beginning, my love." He kissed her cheek.

She couldn't believe that she had this superlative ring and a man who promised to make all her dreams come true. She was supremely happy. She was relieved. Finally, at thirty-three, she could relax and enjoy life instead of worrying about it—fighting it. She not only snatched the brass ring, she got the entire carousel.

"Congratulations, Joi." Her teary-eyed mother smiled and bear-hugged her daughter. "I am so happy for you. This is what you deserve."

"Thanks, Ma."

Other guests rushed the couple forming an impromptu

receiving line and asking when the big day was. "Soon," Claude said. "The sooner the better."

"It's almost April. Your mother'll die at having to plan a wedding quickly," Vivian overlooked Joi to say to Claude.

"My mother has been waiting ten years to plan my wedding! She'll be delighted. She's used to planning grand affairs."

Joi looked at Jacquleen, mother of the bride, and could see both hurt and relief danced on her keen features. She seemed to understand that her input into her daughter's upcoming nuptials would be minimal.

"Send the gifts either here or to Chicago," Claude said. "If you send them to Joi's they might get stolen." He chuckled with the crowd.

Joi's smile froze on her face; the snide remark was unnecessary.

"What's the matter, babe?" Claude asked, noticing her expression.

Was she being too sensitive? Joi thought.

"For presents," Claude continued, caught up in the excitement. "We accept cash in denominations over one thousand dollars—any less just donate it to your favorite charities in our name." They all laughed.

Joi and her mother exchanged half-smiles. "He's excited and happy is all, Joie," Jacquleen said in defense of her future son-in-law. "Every woman alive has had to put up with a husband who makes stupid statements sometimes. In fact, it's a wife's duty to show her husband how to be more sensitive. He means well."

The show was over, the applause had been sweet, but

the final curtain had dropped and the audience had gone home. As Claude settled up with the caterers and bartender, Joi admired her ring, watching it shimmer in the moonlight escaping through the sliding glass doors. Joi wanted to share her happiness with her friends, Ella and Chantel, but they were not here. She knew Jerona, Camryn and Zanielle would get a kick out of it, but they were friends of Pride's friends. Dante would howl, but he was still in Aruba—even if he were here, Claude would not have invited him either. Joi supposed the folks who just left—the clients, colleagues and business associates who passed as friends—would be the nexus of her new social circle. She wanted into this group, and Claude had parted the waters for her and escorted her to the immediate center of these society folks.

Claude walked toward Joi and hugged her. "Happy?"

"How could I not be?" She welcomed his warm embrace, feeling fulfilled and as giddy as someone who got exactly what she wanted for Christmas. It was wonderful being loved and adored. She hoped that she could feel the same way about her future husband.

He cut off the last lamp and they slow-dragged to the music from the stereo. She closed her eyes as their bodies meshed. "Humm. You feel good to me," he said, nipping at her ear, pressing his aroused manhood against her. "I can't wait until our honeymoon." He squeezed her body tightly and his hands roamed across her back.

Joi shuddered at the feel of this strange man's hands exploring her. She expected these little twinges of longing for Pride, fueled by the regret of what will never be. She had told herself that it was understandable that her feelings would overlap when she started on this new romance. She hadn't completely discarded her feelings for the old relationship yet. She needed closure with Pride, before she could free herself, to turn the like and admiration for Claude into love. She thought of her allies, Princess Grace and Jackie O.; their practicality led the way to love. Didn't it?

"Humm." Claude's moan brought her back. "I could make love to you right now. Throw you on that couch and ravish you like you have never been ravished before," he said huskily.

Joi laughed nervously. Was she ready for this tonight? "Well, I am your fiancée. It's official."

"Didn't I tell you?" He reared back and looked into her eyes. "I decided that we will not make love until our honeymoon."

"*You* decided?"

"No one I know can make that claim." He held her again.

"Competition right to the end?" she muttered. *Truth is stranger than fiction*, she thought.

"Besides, that will give you time to want me as much as I want you. I will drive you crazy. It's just a few months. I couldn't stand more than that." He ground his love-muscle into her pelvis. "Humm. It's late. Why don't you stay the night?"

It was Joi's turn to rear back and look into his eyes.

"Oh, don't worry. Once I decide something—it's decided. You can stay in the den."

"*I* can stay in the den?"

"Oh, well. I'll sleep in the den, you can have my bed."

"Maybe I'd better go home and not tempt fate."

"You're not listening. Once Claude Jeeter sets his mind to something—it's done. It's the Jeeter way." He kissed her cheek. "I just don't feel like driving you home. And I don't want you in a cab."

∽∾

"C'mon, Joi, you've got to go," Shorty pleaded as she served beef stew to a customer. "I know Chantel's back, so you'll be off today in time to attend."

"Why, Shorty?" Joi asked as she swung to take her tip from another table.

"Ruby's getting an award and she wants you to come. You want us to pick you up?"

"No." She took the last piece of peach pie and gave it to a customer. "What time?" She wanted him off her back. "This is no late April's Fool joke is it?"

"No joke. 7:00 sharp at Eastern High School auditorium."

At 6:55, Joi got off the bus in front of the auditorium. She ran up the steps placing her change back in her purse. She meant to checkout the sign posted on the outside marquee so she would know what type of award Ruby would be receiving. She went in and took a seat in the nearly empty hall. Shorty and Ruby waved her over to come and sit by them, but Joi gestured that she'd stay by the door. Whatever this was, she wasn't staying long. She was tired and planned to leave right after Ruby's acceptance speech. Then she wondered why Ruby was sitting with Shorty if she was being honored.

As the ceremony began, an usher handed her a program. Eastern High School's GED Graduation. She searched for Ruby's name—and then she saw it. Joseph Pride. Joi's heart soared then sank. Oh, God, she thought, Oh, no—this is the surprise. She wanted to leave—she wanted to stay. While she battled with her inner demons, the procession began. Pride looked so proud—so happy— so good. He gave her a wave as the class proceeded to their seats. Then, seated in the first row on the left side, she recognized the feathered chapeau of Ms. Hat and Heels. Joi's insides froze. I suppose Pride invited her himself, she thought. Me, I get a second-hand invite from Shorty.

She retrieved her engagement ring from her purse and slid it on her finger. The diner wasn't the place for a two-carat diamond and, despite everything, she wanted to tell Pride herself. It shouldn't be relayed secondhand like the invitation to this ceremony. But now, it was payback time for his cheating ways. After the ceremony, she would saunter up front and force an introduction to Ms. Hat and Heels from Pride; the passing of the love baton, intro-ducing his old woman to his new woman. Then she would casually flash her pear-shaped diamond so the light would blind them both, and she'd mention her upcoming marriage and move to Chicago. Somehow she'd let it slip that she wished her BMW were ready, but she and her fiancé were going to pick it up this weekend. She would tell them that Claude was trying to get Luther Vandross to sing "Here and Now" at their nuptials and that her fiancé didn't want a house in Highland Park where Michael Jordan lived because they were new houses for new money. They were going to buy a house in his old neighborhood, where he'd grown up and his family still lived.

Throughout the brief ceremony, Joi never sat back in her chair; she was poised to flee, but couldn't. Despite his lying, she wanted to see him receive his reward for all his hard work. She stopped her inner soliloquy when Pride went up onstage and received his diploma. What it must have taken for him to achieve this, she thought. The hours of study and struggle. She was proud of him, and sad that she wouldn't be the one sharing his private victory party.

After all the awards were given, the master of ceremonies ended with: "There is one special award we are giving tonight. Ms. Chetwynd." He motioned for someone in the audience. "This is Ms. Minerva Chetwynd, who has been running this program for over thirty years."

Joi watched the feather in the hat quiver as the woman beneath it rose from her seat and walked up onstage.

"Oh, no," Joi groaned aloud. Horror gripped her heart as it plummeted to the depths of destruction. Amid thunderous applause from the graduates, Joi could see that Ms. Hat and Heels was old enough to be the students' grandmother. There was no way Pride had betrayed her with this woman; but she had betrayed him with Claude.

"Never in our many years of officiating this program," the master of ceremonies continued as Ms. Chetwynd joined him onstage, "have we ever run across a man so motivated, so dedicated to complete the course and pass all five areas of the exam with flying colors as the man to whom I'm about to give this special award. Because he entered the program late, he could not qualify as valedictorian, but no man worked harder and longer to achieve his goal. We all agreed, there is no man better equipped to meet the world than Joe Pride. Joe!"

Joi watched Pride's solid frame rise in the cap and gown, the tassel dancing beside his handsome cheek. As he walked with confidence, she could feel Shorty's and Ruby's eyes on her, but she refused to acknowledge them. She hadn't seen Pride in weeks and she wasn't prepared for what his glorious image would do to her. His smile filled the auditorium as he accepted the award, shook the man's hand, kissed Ms. Chetwynd on the cheek and stepped to the mike. He cradled the polished plaque in his arms, and the crowd quieted as he leaned into the podium.

"This just goes to show you that anything is possible as long as you believe it can happen," he said, his deep voice reverberating in the hall. Then, aiming his soft brown eyes directly at Joi, he continued. "I have two special people of my own to thank. As Dean Richardson said, I entered late and had a passel of homework to catch up on before I could even get to the level of you guys. I was working full-time and couldn't get to the library many times because of my late hours. But Ms. Minerva, as we call her, would come by my house sometimes and bring me the books and tapes." The crowd interrupted him with their applause in praise of Ms. Chetwynd. She smiled with pleasure.

Oh, cheeze! Joi thought as she wiped her face with her hands, then lodged her thumbnail between her teeth. This couldn't be happening to her. How could she have been so wrong about Pride?

"So I have something for Ms. Minerva." He reached into his pocket and pulled out a small box. "It's just a token of my appreciation. I could have never done it without your dedication."

Ms. Minerva opened the box, then gasped at the sight of the pin—a Pride original. She showed it to the crowd, then asked Pride, off mike, how he found the time to make this exquisite pin. She kissed him gratefully on the cheek before blushing her way offstage. Pride aimed his eyes directly at Joi again. "And to the other woman in my life," he said. "You changed my life. I owe you one, Joi, and it's the sweetest debt I'll ever have to pay. I intend to spend my lifetime trying." He threw her a kiss. "Thank you."

Joi sat there with tears streaming down her face, trying to regain her composure. Her emotions collided—she was sad, angry, happy and confused. When she saw the battle was lost, she ran from the auditorium and hailed a cab.

She blew her nose continuously in the cab, thinking of her life as a runaway train ever since Pride had embarked on his "surprise" without her. But that train crashed tonight in Eastern's auditorium. The flood of tears was never-ending; tears for the mess she had made of her life, happy tears for Pride reaching his goal, tears of regret for a marital contract she wished she could get out of. But it had all gone too far. It was too late to rectify any of this. She cried tears for tears' sake.

She slowly walked up into her courtyard, her mind still on overdrive. Her thoughts rattled around in her head like broken china, and she wondered if she could ever order the mental chaos. She fought to sort out her feelings. She just couldn't bear to hear Pride's voice tonight. She couldn't bear to see him—up close, in the flesh and personal. She climbed the six flights of steps, opened her door, hung her coat on its hook and went to put cold water on her swollen face. She looked a mess, but she felt even worse. She knew Pride would be wondering what had happened to her after the ceremony. If he came over she just wouldn't answer the door. She'd see him tomorrow after a good night's rest. She'd have herself together by then.

The best defense is an offense, she thought as she picked up her telephone and dialed his number. She thanked God in a silent prayer when his answering machine clicked on. "Hello, Pride. It's Joi. You did it. I am so very, very proud of you." Tears ran down her cheeks. "That's one helluva surprise. I had a pre-arranged emergency with my mother—" She stopped and chastised herself, "a prearranged emergency?" Good grief, she said to herself and continued. "And I had to leave, but we need to talk. I have a surprise of my own…" Her voice trailed off. "I'm at my mother's until very late tonight, so just call and leave a time when we can get together on my machine. I have the early shift, so the evening would be good." A few seconds passed. Joi didn't want to break this last connection with him, but finally did. "Bye." Joi hung up and fresh tears sprang to her eyes.

The doorbell rang. She cursed. Please don't let it be him, she prayed as she tiptoed to the door and was about to peer through the peephole. With a cleansing relief she heard, "It's me, Lovey! I'm back!"

"Dante!" She flung open the door and looked at her friend. He was tanned to a rich, sun-kissed brown. "You're beautiful!"

"You're not," he quipped. He entered the apartment and handed her a souvenir cover-up from Aruba. "You let yourself go when I'm not around?" He took his usual seat at the dinette. "Or is it the two men in your life?" He crossed his legs elegantly as he reached for a jar of peanut butter. "So how is the middle, and which end is winning? Pride or Claude?"

"So how was your trip?" Joi knew how to get him off the subject; like any man, he loved talking about himself. She surely wasn't ready to discuss her predicament until she had decided just how to handle it.

"Going away 'in season' is the only way to go, but being with a man, even Paul, 24/7 is too much togetherness. I need space, and lots of it." He popped open an ornate, imported fan and put it to work. Joi plunged her finger into the gooey substance. "Hold the phone! Hold the phone!" Dante screeched, catching sight of the ring. "Let me see that rock!" He lunged for her hand. "Holy Moses! Pride musta mortgaged his house for this diamond." He grabbed her hand and inspected it. "Platinum setting—did he sell his car, too?"

"I'm getting married," Joi announced. "To Claude."

"Say what? Lovey, my money was not on him."

"Well, he gets the prize."

"C'mon with the details."

"It was you who said love unattended dies."

"Don't piss on my shoes and tell me it's raining. Give

me the straight dope 'cause I know you love Pride."

"Well, it got complicated."

Dante slipped into the vernacular of some of his younger patrons. "First he was sweatin' ya and now he's forgettin' ya—wuz up?" Joi had to chuckle at her erudite, ultra-articulate friend's bilingual prowess. "I have a mind to go over there and see just what his problem is."

"It's been done. I found him with another woman."

"Pride? How could I have been so wrong? I know men," he declared. "Well, it's either on, or it's over." Dante punctuated his statement with a fierce snap of his French-manicured fingers.

"Over." In the little time Joi had to assess her feelings, she decided that letting Pride be the scapegoat was a way to keep Dante at bay.

"End of chapter, end of verse," Dante decreed.

"Besides, Claude is growing on me," Joi said bravely.

"Yeah, from the fungus oil in that rock, third finger left hand." Dante watched his friend wipe her finger along the side of the jar and stick the mound in her mouth. "Let me give you another pearl of wisdom from these not so innocent lips. Make a bed with the devil and Satan will get his due." He looked directly into her eyes. "Does the word rebound sound familiar? I think you're going into this 'marriage' with your eyes wide shut."

"You have never met him."

"And if he has his way, I never will. Lovey, I've met all types of men during my stellar years on this earth—the good, the bad and the ugly. Claude strikes me as one of the ugly."

"He's a good man."

"Spoken like a girl who has just bagged the golden fleece."

"What do you want from me? I'm making the deal of a century."

"How European," he said drolly.

"Oh, and Paul's money had nothing to do with you and him?"

"I have been with Paul for fifteen years. I love him and I would stay with him even if his wife and kiddies left him without a dime. Can you say the same about Claude? Would you marry him without his money?"

"It's different. Claude knows I don't love him the way he does me, and he accepts it."

"How romantic," he said mockingly. "This relationship has 'success' written all over it. It's a shame to belong to one man when the right...bank account comes along." He rolled his eyes. "They say when God wants to punish you, He answers your prayers. But Lovey, you should start off in love even if it doesn't end up that way."

"Look, I had to work it out the best I could while you were gallivanting allover the Caribbean."

"And this is what you come up with? Marrying one man while you're in love with another?"

"Happens all the time."

"Now, we're cliché." He looked at Joi. "I suppose you are not open to discussing it beyond mentioning that some folks are especially happy. Speaking of Mumsy, she must be wetting her panties over this impending nuptial charade."

"She's pleased."

"As a whore at a rodeo. Well," he said, snapping his fan closed. "I'm tired. I'm going for a nap. Just wanted to pop in and give you your gift. I had no idea I'd be treated to a Shakespearean drama—a tragedy of epic proportions." Joi shot him an acid look. "Sorry." He lifted one elegantly bejeweled hand in his defense. "Congrats, Joi. If this is what you really want—I'm happy for you. Tah, tah. Oh." He stopped by the door. "One thing. How did Pride react to all of this? I see you're still in one piece, so I gather he took it well?"

"I'm going to tell him tomorrow," she said with obvious dread. "It's the decent thing to do."

"Ah, yes. Decency." He raised his arched eyebrow. "It is the decent thing to do." He swirled out of the room.

Her answering machine clicked on. "Joi!" Pride's voice echoed in the efficiency. "I hope your mom is okay. I just realized that I don't have her number. Anyway, I was really hoping we could celebrate in fine fashion tonight and take off tomorrow. You know, so you could congratulate me all…day…long." He chuckled seductively. "But since that's not cool, come on by for dinner after your shift—my place, my GED, my body, your body. Have mercy. If you want me to pick you up just call and I'll come get you. Joi, I love you. Now we can resume our lives as usual with no more separations, ever. I can't wait to see you." The sound of his kisses filled her bleak apartment and he hung up.

"Damn," Joi said, as she saved his message.

⤜⥱⤛

Joi parked her new, fully-loaded red BMW convertible by the bus stop—that place on which she stood and depended upon public transportation for over five years. Rain, heat or snow, it was her and that black projectile spearing from the cement that flagged down her way home. Now she had a car, an engagement gift that cost more than her five years salary at Louie's.

Joi entered the diner and headed for the Employees Only section.

"Haven't seen you much since you cut back your hours," Chantel said.

"Hey, Chantel," Joi said without stopping.

"Well, if it isn't the princess bride," Ella said sarcastically.

"You said more than a word," Joi quipped, removing her sweater and shoving her locker door shut. Joi raised her hand.

"Good googa mooga! Look at this!" Ella spotted Joi's ring, grabbed her hand and then her in a bear hug. "Girl, I am so happy for you. You and Joe? Oh, honey, was that the surprise?"

"Wrong. It's not Pride," Joi said, unable to meet Ella's gaze. She removed her ring and stuffed it into her pocket. She didn't want Pride to find out from anyone but her.

"Then who, Joi?" Ella challenged, her hands on hips.

"Claude," Joi said, mustering enough courage to look in her friend's eyes.

"Damn, Joi—"

"Just be happy for me."

"Happy that you're ruining your life?" Ella shot as

Chantel slipped from the room to avoid the brewing argument.

"It's a great opportunity—" Joi began.

"Opportunity! Since when is marriage considered an 'opportunity?' "

"Maybe it should be. Then folks would stay married."

"It's not a job—"

Joi stared directly into Ella's eyes. "It's the biggest job there is. What you do for a living and who you marry can make or break your entire life. This particular gig has benefits, a pension plan and security. And Ella, at this time in my life, I need security." Ella cut her eyes in disgust. "You're always talking to us about common sense. Well, this is it. Tell me you wouldn't jump at the chance if this was to happen to you?" Joi's eyes devoured Ella's.

"I'm old enough to know better. I listen to my heart…not my mama," Ella sniped, her eyes resting on the huge pear-shaped diamond. "Tsk. This is no more than prostitu—"

"No. This is no one night stand. I'm talking longevity, commitment, children—the whole nine yards. And I do care for Claude."

"You 'care' for him?" She scoffed and folded her arms across her chest. "Well, ain't that nice."

"He'll be good for me." Joi ignored her inference. "You can come visit, swim in my pool." Joi smiled.

Ella didn't. "You're really dreamin' if you think he's gonna let us stay friends. I betcha he's got a list of everything you supposed to do and become. For starters, you gotta have a degree before you can have babies. No child of his is gonna be born to a woman with no college degree. You gonna be bargaining with him for the rest of your life. He's Professor Higgins to your Liza Doolittle, but you ain't no fair lady." When Joi opened her mouth to retort, Ella pressed on. "What about Pride? He know yet?"

"I'm meeting him for dinner tonight. I'll tell him then."

"Betcha he's cookin' for you, huh?" She shook her head in disbelief. "I sure hope you know what you're doin'." Ella left Joi to herself and her decision.

"So do I," Joi said sotto voce.

CHAPTER 10

When Pride opened the door for her, Joi walked into the bungalow on Phoebus Road and saw the table set immediately in front of her. "You like?" Pride asked indicating the linen tablecloth, fresh-cut spring flowers, candles and wineglasses.

Joi smelled something delicious coming from the kitchen. "Table looks nice," she said.

"Thanks," he said, as she visually scanned the room. His GED diploma was proudly displayed next to his special award and trophies on the mantel. The plants in front of his window almost obliterated the last of the sun's setting rays. She let him remove her jacket.

"Nice speech last night." She tried not to look at him. She wasn't prepared for the sight of him and what it would do to her. Like a Pavlovian response, she immediately began salivating from every orifice of her body.

He stripped her nude with his long-lashed gaze. "I meant every word." He kissed her cheek and she flinched. "I hope you don't mind me asking Shorty to invite you, but I knew if I spoke to you directly I'd blow the whole thing. I figured we lasted that long, might as well keep it going one more night. You want something to drink?" He disappeared into the kitchen and continued speaking. "How's your mom?"

"Fine," she said, amazed that he actually thought they could just pick up where they'd left off, well over six weeks ago. Men were clueless, she thought. He reentered the room carrying a piping hot dish of macaroni and cheese—as hot and delicious as he appeared to her. "Joe?"

"Joe?" He set down the bubbling casserole on a trivet. She had never called him that before. "Just plain ordinary, everyday 'Joe?' " He walked toward her. The heat from his body leapt to hers, seeking to soothe the ache being so near him brought. "Well, you won't ever call me that again. Not after my Nefertiti is completed for the Detroit Museum."

"What?"

"That's my other surprise. When Dedra, the buyer from Sand in My Shoes, came by to check out my larger pieces…seems the bigger the better for Nubian Pride jewelry. That's what I call the line. Anyway, when she came by she saw my bust of Moms and she told her friend from the museum. From that contact I got commissioned to do Nefertiti for an exhibition. Then a Masai warrior after that!" He grabbed and kissed her quickly before bear-hugging her. "Oh Joi, this is it. It's starting for us. I can just feel it. Two other mail-order catalogs want my Nubian Pride line of jewelry, but I just don't want to spend any more time away from you."

Joi held on to him, unbelievingly, while her constant craving for him sprang to every pore, clamoring for the missed nourishment his body gave hers.

"I have to thank you for your understanding and patience over the past few months," he said. "I was working long, crazy hours, going to class five nights a week, studying nights and all day on the weekends and still doing the jewelry. Sometimes when I thought about giving up, I'd call just to hear your voice. Just to keep me focused. You'd energize me and I'd go right back to cracking those books. I was doing it for me, and for you, Joi. For us. And now it's our turn." He pulled back to look into her face and was startled by her paralyzed expression. Her face looked as if it were going to explode. "Joi?"

"Did you ever once think about letting me in on it? On what was happening? What you were doing?" She snatched herself away from his grasp. All the feelings she thought she'd controlled broke loose again. Pride for him, then anger at being left out of his plans, anger for his exclusion of her in the name of a "surprise;" anger at herself for not confronting him and Ms. Hat and Heels on the porch that night. And regret for her commitment to Claude and their future children.

"I told you as much as I could on the machine. I wanted to surprise you. To make you proud of me."

"Oh, cheeze!" She rubbed her throbbing forehead.

"Didn't you listen to my messages?"

Joi couldn't admit that after finding him with Ms. Hat and Heels, she had stopped replaying his messages; she just erased them. "Oh, I was never not proud of you," she said sincerely. "You are an extraordinary man."

"Uh-oh." He moved toward her. "This doesn't sound too good," he teased, trying to lighten the mood. "You're mad at me. Even though now, you know why. I haven't seen you since February…what? Eight weeks, and I missed you. I gather your mother didn't give you my message?"

"My mother?"

"It was the long President's weekend and I figured we could spend the three days together. But she said you were out of town."

"You talked to her?" She shook her head in total disbelief. "I never got a message." She recalled those three tortuous days with no word whatsoever from him; that had been the unraveling of their end. Her mother had known how tormented she was about not seeing Pride. How could she? How dare she!

"Umm, I figured as much. I suspect she had a hand in tampering with some of my other more ardent messages. I told you all of this on the machine. Some of them must have gotten through!"

Joi's anger at her mother had escalated to wild proportions. She was barely listening to him as he continued.

"Well, all of this is water under the bridge, as I knew it would be once we hooked up again. None of this will happen again, I promise. No more secrets—no more surprises. We've got some quality time to make up for. Got some cotton candy mix." He yo-yoed his eyebrows, anxious to feel her beneath him again. He reached for her. "Joi?"

She dodged away from him, steeling her emotions and remembering why she had come. "It's all too little too late," she said from the other side of the table. "I have something to tell you, Joe."

"That's the second time in this relationship you've called me Joe. What's up, Joi?" He stood stark still looking as good as a waterfall to a dry-mouthed woman. She wanted to go to him and let him drench her wet in his love.

"I have something to tell you," she repeated, ignoring the prickly sensations that were rising to the surface all over her body. "Only Ella knows and I wanted you to know before Shorty, Edgar and the guys did."

He folded his strong, muscular arms protectively across his chest, shielding his heart. His soft brown eyes searched hers as she nervously played with the back of a chair.

"I'm getting married," she blurted out.

He began to laugh uproariously. He came toward her and she backed away, confused by his reaction. "I accept!" He continued chasing her. "And I won't tell the children that you proposed!"

"Stop it, Joe! It's not me and you," she yelled over his jubilant laughter.

"What?" He froze in his tracks as if he were in a child-hood game of Red Light. The smile slid from his handsome face. "What?" he repeated, facing her and squinting his eyes. "Then who? It's only been a couple of months."

"Only? I did fine without for three years. Then you open me up to love again, and then leave me high and dry and alone for two months." She finally added hurt to her inventory of emotions.

"In the lifetime of love that is to be ours, Joi, two months isn't long at all. Joi, where was your faith and belief in us?" he asked tenderly.

"I didn't know any of this. I thought you were…" She stuttered and tried to swallow burgeoning tears before they reached her eyes. "I thought you were pulling away, letting me down easy."

"Oh, Joi." He started to her, and she stopped him with her hand. "Why didn't you just ask?"

"When? During ten-minute, one-sided, into-a-machine conversations once a day?" It was the first time she had voiced how they had bothered her.

"I'm sorry, Joi. I explained as much as I could without blowing the surprise. I didn't mean to hurt you. I would never do anything to intentionally hurt you—"

"Then I decided to confront you," she talked over him. "And I borrowed Ella's car and saw you waiting on the porch for some woman—"

"Me?" He laughed. "Not me. Why would I want anyone else when I have you?"

"It was Ms. Minerva Chetwynd, but I didn't know that at the time."

"Oh, Joi." He reached out to hold her, to reassure her and soothe her insecurities away, but again she sidestepped him. "With all the things I was juggling—work, school, the jewelry—you were my constant. You were the one thing I counted on. I thought you'd always be by my side."

"It's all too late, Joe." She cleared her throat and threw her head high in resolution. "It's all worked out. Really."

"So you're marrying some other guy to get back at me? Not a way to start a marriage," he said tersely.

"No," she said calmly. "I'm marrying him because he was there in the void you created. And I responded to that and he asked me to marry him and I accepted."

"What the hell are you talking about?" The cool in him grew geyser hot. "You just don't take up with a man because you're lonely, and then marry him out of gratitude!"

Joi sighed heavily, gathering her reserves about her. "I didn't expect you to take this well—"

"Hell no, I'm not gonna take this 'well!' Have you lost your mind?"

"Actually, I've come to my senses. I've come to a realization about my life and where it's going."

"This is some sick joke, Joi. I can't believe our perfect reunion day is ending up like this." He ran his hands through his hair. "Besides, you haven't even been involved with anyone."

"How would you know?"

"Except that engineering inspector, Claude Jeeter—" He stopped. "It can't be him. He's not your type, so I never worried." Surprise registered on his face.

"You should have worried."

"You couldn't possibly have with him what you have with me."

"Had."

"Naw, 'cause it's not over between us, Joi. If ever there was a perfect match on this earth it is you and me. You're going to throw it all away for a Porsche and a boat? He can't love you like I do, Joi. No one can. Does he give you foot and body massages after a hard day? Does he cook for you? Does he make your body quake when he comes near? Does he steal your breath away and replace it with his own?" He stood within inches of her. "Every time he looks at you, does he fall in love all over again?"

She retreated, fighting the intoxicating power of him. "There's nothing more to say." She reached for her jacket. "I just thought I owed you—"

"You don't owe me a damn thing."

"I didn't want it to end this way—"

"Oh? How'd you think it would end? We'd all be friends and double date? You'd have me and my wife over for a

BBQ around the pool?"

"I guess that's it, then." Joi put on her jacket, struggling with the odd emotion of Pride having a wife that was not her.

"I guess it is," he said, blowing out the candles and following her to the door. "You sleep with this guy?" The question formed in his mind and trailed out upon his lips before he realized it. His soft brown eyes turned hard.

"He is my fiancé." She straightened her back and tried to close down her emotions the way Mrs. Claude Jeeter should. She watched his hard stare turn from anger to hurt. "You'll be fine, Joe. Things are really starting to happen for you—"

"I don't need you to tell me that." He reached for the doorknob the same time as she did. Their hands touched. She jerked back quickly at the feel of his razor-hot flesh, searing her own. She didn't trust herself to his touch. "One last thing, Joi." He waited until she looked into his eyes; the hurt turned to compassion. "Do you love him?"

"Of course I do." Her eyes challenged, then flinched.

"You lie like a rug, Joi Martin."

Joi wrung her hands and walked away from the scent of him. She stood by the window with its forest of plants. She had almost made it out of there. All her life her mission had been to "marry well," and now she was. Couldn't he just understand a job well done and leave her alone? She rubbed her temples, massaging a piercing ache which grew there. "I really don't think I owe you any explanation," she said calmly.

"One more thing and I'll let you go. Why, Joi? Why

him and not me?"

"What?" Her eyes fluttered nervously as if they were reacting to the forcefulness of his breath upon them. Her head reeled.

"Why, Joi? Why him?"

"Because you never asked!"

"I'm asking now, Joi. Marry me." He moved toward her and she backed around the sofa in front of the fireplace.

"No. I'm marrying Claude."

"Why him, Joi?" He kept approaching and she kept retreating. "You know I love you and you love me. I love you for who you are right now this very minute—not for who you're going to become. So, why him, Joi? I've built my world around your love. You are my prayers answered— my heaven on earth. All I've done, I've done for us. So, I want to know—why him and not me?"

"Because it's easy and safe!" she exploded under his pressure. "If it doesn't work out between Claude and me, I'd be okay. But if you ever left me, Pride, I'd…I'd…I'd just die! I'd just die…"

She collapsed in tears and he was there to catch her. For the first time she admitted to herself that a little bit of happy with Pride was worth a lifetime of "marrying-well" with Claude. "Every man I ever loved died. My brother, my father and Joaquin. If you died," she sobbed, "I'd want to die, too."

"So you think you're a jinx." He laughed at the absurdness of it, and she began laughing too. He lifted her chin, forcing her wet eyes to his. "Joi, you're my good-luck charm. I am who I have become because of you. Everything

I have, everything I'm doing is because of you." He tried to kiss away her tears, tasting the sweet saltiness. "I'd never leave you, Joi." He rocked her, stroking her face and letting his finger caress her dimple as she began crying in choking tears. "You're the best thing that ever happened to me Joi Martin Pride. You might leave me," he teased, "but I'd never leave you, Joi. You're my *raison d'être*" They chuckled at the French phrase he'd heard her answer to *Jeopardy*. "I love you more than words can say." She clung to him like the life preserver he was, and he beamed pure happiness.

They kissed a hungry kiss, summoning up neglects forgotten and needs unfulfilled but about to be satisfied. As he held her, her toes started to tingle the way a frostbitten body begins to thaw at the touch of warmth. Joi opened her eyes to him and laughed into his chiseled cheeks. She nibble-kissed the sensuous lips that hid beneath his moustache.

She rested her head on his shoulder, and then she saw it—the diamond reminding her of the guaranteed life. It caught the fading sunlight streaming through the window and splashed prisms of color all over the room as if spotlighting all she would lose and all she would gain. She wanted Pride; but she needed Claude to give her the entree into the upper-class world. By choosing Pride, she'd lose a lifestyle most people can only dream about. She had to be practical; she had to think in terms of the long run. Besides, she had already committed to Claude.

"But," she said, rallying her courage and breaking her embrace, "I'm marrying Claude."

"What?"

"I have no choice."

"Unless you're a slave, you always have a choice." He felt his desire for her deflate as his impatience intensified. Or was it the fact that he knew he could not compete materially with this man? His anger returned. "I see. It's about things. Well, Joi, if you're marrying for things then you're right."

"It's not just things—"

"So you say." He gritted his teeth; the tension and release of his jaw vibrated over his face.

"I deserve it all." She couldn't believe she had spoken her mother's words. "And he can give it to me."

"I could have given you the most important part of that—treasures more precious than diamonds and gold. He doesn't know you, Joi. Not like I do." He stared at her; her eyes couldn't sustain the weight of his gaze. "I bet he believes you when you tell him nothing's wrong." He looked at her strangely now. He knew what she wanted, and he knew he couldn't give it to her with a GED or doing his jewelry or anything else. Not in this life, and it hurt. When she didn't reply, he said, "I guess I should wish you the best as I would any stranger. Because that's who you are to me. I knew you were too good to be true. You are not the woman I fell in love with. You are not my Joi. You are a gold-digger and the two of you deserve each other."

He walked unceremoniously to the door. Hurt caused fresh tears to spring to the brim of her eyes. Pride held the door wide open, and Joi began to walk slowly through it. She looked up at him for the last time, but he looked over her, beyond her. He kept the moisture, which exploded from the shards of his broken heart, from gushing from his eyes.

"I'm the only one who'd climb a mountain for you," Pride fired over her head. With his eyes fixed and unseeing, he continued like a recruit giving information to a drill sergeant. "After all your wedding vows are said and done, I'll just be another demon you're running from. Because I'm the only one for you." He still did not dare look at her. "I hope you get the life you deserve. But know this." He hurled his cold brown eyes to her. "If you walk through this door today. There's no coming back. When he dumps you—there's no coming back. I don't want any man's left-overs."

Joi was speechless; there was nothing left to say. She was emotionally drained by this entire ordeal. When she cleared the threshold, Pride slammed the door loudly behind her. She heard something crash against the door and hoped it wasn't the macaroni and cheese. He made the best macaroni and cheese, she thought.

Joi held her head high as she took her final steps down Pride's walkway. By the time she got into the car, her blouse was drenched with tears she refused to admit fell. Well, it's done, she thought. The future Mrs. Claude Jeeter pulled away from the curb and out of Pride's life.

Joi aimed her car to Jacquleen's. "Mother!" Joi shouted and tore through the small house. "Mother?"

"Joie, what is your problem? Screaming like a banshee—"

"You!" She attacked her mother, shoving a pointed finger in her face. "You are my problem."

"What on earth—"

"You've been erasing my answering machine messages from Pride."

"Oh, that." Jacquleen sucked her teeth at the inconsequentialness of it. Then Jacquleen gasped in sudden panic. "You've…you've seen Pride?"

"Mother, whether I have or haven't is not the point. You erased my personal messages, like I am a child who needs protecting from the big bad wolf."

"I was protecting you, Joie," Jacquleen admitted unapologetically.

"You had no right! None."

"He wasn't good enough for you, Joie. He was dragging you down to his level."

"How dare you? Who the hell are you to—"

"I'm your mother."

"So you have the right to sabotage the best man who ever happened to me?"

"He is not. Claude is," she answered self-righteously. Terror registered in her face. "You are still marrying Claude, aren't you?"

"After you've worked so hard to ensure it?" Joi said sarcastically. "Would I sabotage you, Mother?" she spat. "Like mother, like daughter. It would serve you right, if I ran off with Pride. The wedding to Claude is your validation that you did a good job raising a pretentious, manipulative spawn." Joi relished the quiet fear in her mother's eyes. "You don't care about me at all, do you?"

"That's not true, Joie."

"All you care about is your meal ticket to a hassle-free

old age. Lord knows Daddy's pension and life insurance isn't enough to let you grow old in the manner you never lived, but envision yourself deserving of."

"Joie, that's not fair. There was no security with Pride. You'd be a bag lady—"

"You'd be one first, Mother," Joi sniped. "Where do you get off telling me how to spend my life? Because yours was in such a shambles you figure you get a second try with me? Well, you had your chance. So just back off. It's my life, my turn, my decision."

"What are you going to do, Joi?" Her mother dogged her step for step to the door. "You're not going to do anything foolish, are you?" She almost ran into Joi's back when she halted at the door. "You are never going to get a chance like this again, Joi. Everything has worked out for the best. I have to know that the wedding with Claude was still on. Think of the whole wonderful extravaganza and how we would all benefit from the Jeeter—hospitality."

Joi eyed her mother for a lethally long pause, perhaps seeing her clearly for the first time. "Let me ask you this." She stepped up to her mother. "Did you really love Dad?"

Jacquleen recoiled from the verbal assault. "Of course I did. With every fiber of my being. How can you ask me such a question?" Hurt and pain filled her eyes. "But his loving me cut him off from his family and killed him in the end. I figure I owe it to our children to try to make it right again. Since I was the one who denied you all the life of privilege you deserved." She crumpled into guilty tears, under the weight of an admission she had never made to herself or to Royce.

"I am a St. Marie, Mother. Whether I'm rich or poor." Joi wasn't sure whether this act was genuine Jacquleen or vintage manipulation. But she asked softly, "Then why wouldn't you want for me what you and Dad had—not what you didn't? Love."

Joi yanked open the front door as her mother wiped her tears away and rallied herself enough to ask, "Are you still marrying Claude?"

As she traipsed down the walkway, Joi chuckled sardonically at the pure absurdity of her life. She shook her head helplessly. Without turning back to face her mother she said, "Might as well. The man I truly love won't have me. Told me I wasn't the woman he fell in love with; told me I can't ever come back to him. So I got nothing to lose. Only to gain. Right, Ma?" Joi bit back tears. Once again, Jacquleen had won. "Might as well," she repeated. "Claude and I deserve each other—the connoisseur and the neophyte." She walked to her red BMW. She sat in the lap of its luxury. Funny, she thought, the car didn't give her the comfort she needed.

❧

Claude's mother, Connie, and his two sisters, Lauren and Jennifer, flew to Detroit to meet the woman who had snagged the Prince of Jeeter. The meeting was innocuous enough, but Joi got the weird feeling that she was the understudy for the real star who'd later come and claim him.

The time came for Joi to fly to Claude's hometown. She

was quiet as the plane soared and sliced through the pillowy clouds heading for Chicago. Claude held her hand and asked if this was her first flight. She responded no and fought the thoughts of her first flight with Pride. As long as she didn't see him and no one—like Dante or the girls at work—mentioned him, she'd be all right, she told herself. She'd be home free once she relocated to Chi-town. Eventually, her feelings for Pride would disappear like footprints in the sand.

Over the next few weeks, Joi flew to Chicago with Claude three times, first-class. Flying anywhere with Pride became a distant memory. Each time they arrived, Connie and her daughters would have an itinerary planned for the couple, which could include everything from viewing the cathedral, talking with the minister or registering at Tiffany's, Marshall Field's and Crate and Barrel. They selected flowers from the florists and pored over gargantuan books of engraved, vellum invitation samples—complete with tissue paper and stamped return envelopes. After booking the Ritz for the reception and gorging themselves on the sample menu, settling on the ostrich ravioli, they went house hunting and finally decided on a two-story, three-bedroom condo on Lake Shore Drive. To ensure peace, harmony and positive energy in their home, Claude honored the advice of a feng shui consultant by placing an Oriental fountain under the foyer stairwell leading to the second floor. Claude deemed one bedroom the guest room, and the other Joi's study while she was in school. After the first baby was in the works, they'd move to a substantial old home in his old Winnetka neighborhood. Claude was being supportive by being with Joi, but he left most of the decisions up to the women. The only thing he wanted was four French horns to trumpet the wedding march, announcing the beautiful Joi St. Marie soon-to-be-Jeeter as she stood poised at the top of the aisle, commanding everyone to rise and pay homage.

For weeks, Joi had been barraged with wedding gown "suggestions" from Connie via overnight Express Mail. A definitive decision had to be made. In the Jeeter way, her future mother-in-law and her future sisters-in-law accompanied her from bridal salon to salon in an exhaustive trek. Finally, Joi picked a fairytale extravaganza of a gown just to get it over with. It cost more than her yearly salary plus tips at Louie's. For her final fitting, Joi barely recognized herself in the three-way mirror's reflection. She was a vision in mountains of tulle, lace and thousands of hand-sewn beads, which shimmered like liquid. The headdress, a bejeweled regal crown with a gossamer explosion of netting, was placed on her head, and she pirouetted at her image and listened to the designer discuss the care and carriage of the five-foot train by three of her future nieces. Abstractly, Joi wished Ella was there to give her honest opinion on the gown, and that Chantel's son, Jabari, could be the ring bearer. Then she realized that she would have liked Jerona, Camryn and Zanielle to be involved with, if not in, the wedding party. And, of course, her pal, Dante. But none of that was about to happen. It was the Jeeter way. Joi wanted to escape her working-class status, not be exiled from it.

Later that afternoon, a bone-tired Joi staggered into the Jeeter home only to find an obscene population of female strangers yelling "surprise" at the lucky woman and future mother of the heir apparent to the Jeeter throne. Of all the women at the garden bridal shower, Joi only knew her mother who had been flown in as part of the festivities. Her sister, Noel, had sent a gift and a promise to be there on July fifteenth.

Joi thought of her baby sister who had everything and cared about none of it. They had so little in common to be born so close together, but they had had separate rooms all of their lives and little to share but parentage. Joi suspected it was the episode with Noel's brand-new bike that had soured her against her spoiled sister. As the years stretched out so did their similar interests. Now, they only exchanged Christmas cards and birthday calls, although Joi always resented her money ticking away via the phone lines, as Noel lamented the same thing each year: Wade wanting a boy, and how they had three weddings to eventually plan. If it weren't for DNA, Joi doubted she and Noel would ever be acquaintances and certainly never friends. She surmised she felt the normal sibling rivalry for a younger sister who had never understood the sacrifice her parents made for her as she graduated from college and married her college beau the same weekend. After that, the couple remained in Atlanta and now, over ten years later, their entire family was coming to her wedding in Chicago.

Joi looked around at all the luncheon-ladies in attendance at her shower. As she accepted the frilly gifts of sexy lingerie, she noticed how some of the women were overly nice—obsequious really. Others were neutral, and some shot daggers—probably those who thought, by parentage and privilege, they should be seated in the over-decorated chair of honor, about to marry the dashing Claude Bryant Jeeter. These were her future friends, and Joi felt that anyone of them could fill her nuptial shoes. To the life of Claude Jeeter: Add one wife, shake, stir, reproduce, then *voila*—perfection.

She crossed her feet at the ankles and remembered Connie Jeerer's gasp when Joi told the designer that she wore a ten and a half. What—rich people don't have big feet? she had thought. Joi chuckled, realizing she must look the idiot, smiling at herself. One thought sobered her private insanity—Pride never thought her feet were too big. She doubted that his mother, Bernadette, would have either. An uninvited vision of him sprang to her mind— Pride removing her feet from the foot massager, blotting them damp-dry with a fluffy towel before pouring oil into the palm of his hand and beginning to rub her toes—individually.

"Joi?" Jacquleen interrupted, handing her the twenty-sixth elaborately wrapped package while just as many patiently awaited their turn at being disrobed by the future Mrs. Jeeter.

Above the sophisticated cacophony of the afternoon, Joi heard Whitney Houston singing, "I Believe in You and Me." Right song, wrong version, just like this whole wedding thing—right thing, wrong man. Claude was a nice guy and if it weren't for Pride, she could fall for him. But there was a man named Joe Pride and he had been there first. He promised he would always be there for her, and she believed him. There was no pressure with Pride, no

Svengali-esqueness—no need to control. If she suddenly lost her looks in a car wreck, or lost a limb or breast, or couldn't have children or got Alzheimer's, Pride would be there for her. She wasn't too sure about Claude; he wanted a woman who was healthy, whole and fertile, the way he had found her—or the deal was off. He'd leave her if she was broken, barren or disfigured. Claude would be off to find the next princess of perfection to round out his perfect life. It was the Jeeter way.

Still, life was full of chances and this was hers. She'd have to reclaim her heart from Pride and train it to love Claude. She flashed a believable smile as Courtney McLeod Syphax introduced herself to the future Queen of Jeeter.

❧

During her break, Joi disappeared behind the "Employees Only" sign and sat at the back table, poring over back issues of *National Geographic* and planning her honeymoon. Claude had informed her that with his reloca- tion, he had given the new firm a late August available date, meaning they could honeymoon for a month—a wedding gift from Mom and Dad Jeeter. Although Claude had trav- eled extensively, he let his bride select their destinations. Joi plotted the usual Lisbon, Madrid, Majorca and Paris. From there they would journey to Italy. In Rome she'd stroll amid the ruins of the Forum in the footsteps of emperors and visit the Coliseum where gladiators fought to their deaths for the amusement of the patrician class. The honey- mooners would then jaunt across the Italian Riviera: Capri,

Ischia, Procida, Portofino, and then onto the Cinqueterre, those five famous seaside hamlets along the Ligurian coast, before sailing the Greek Islands, spending a weekend in Santorini. Claude didn't want to return to Africa, but Joi talked him into Mauritania, Cameroon and Morocco before adding a trip down the Nile River in Egypt like Cleopatra, for serendipity. In Aswan they would board a traditional Egyptian felucca and sail down to Luxor and the Valley of the Kings where Pharaohs, including King Tut, lay. They would sail on to the old imperial city of Karnak and the Temple of Amun. Back in Aswan again, they would roam south to the Sudanese border, Abu Simbel and the Temple of Ramses II which guards Lake Nasser. All the itineraries were plucked from her dreams and the pages of *National Geographic*. Never in her lifetime did she think she would ever see anyone of them, and now, they were laid out for her like a string of pearls. For Christmas, Claude had said they would be in Bora Bora.

As Joi made notations for the travel agent, she looked up; Marian, her replacement, came through the curtain and smiled. "You are one lucky lady, girlfriend," she said, and disappeared.

Yep, it was the dream of a lifetime, Joi thought. Then why wasn't she floating on clouds of supreme happiness?

She listened to Louie barking at Chantel. She smelled the familiar collision of all sorts of foods, her brand of perfume for a lot of years. She heard the clatter of noisy plates and silverware being dumped into the washer by the busboy. Suddenly, it all sounded like music to her ears—a delightful, familiar song.

Claude had said it was the combination of "some weird separation anxiety" and exhaustion from planning a wedding on such short notice. He predicted that once she got away from the negative environment of Louie's and totally immersed herself into their new life, she'd perk right up. He'd been trying to get her to quit, but Joi had never not worked. In fact, in the surreal whirlwind which had become her life, Louie's was the only reality she had left. Once she let go of that, who was she but a potential bride? And what did Claude think she was supposed to do all day? Look at soap operas, go to lunch and keep hair appointments? Claude hated her short hair and, at his request, she was allowing it to grow for her wedding. There was nothing left for her to do. Everything had been set and done by someone else. Including booking two bands so there would be continuous music at the reception; the invitations already addressed, stamped and sealed with a J pressed into the red wax on the back of each vellum envelope. That is, until Connie Jeeter decided that gold metal tubes with each guest's name engraved in bas-relief on the luxuriant surface was more in keeping with the Cinderella theme of Joi's fairytale wedding gown. Inside each precious metal tube was a rolled scroll of parchment paper strung with gold ribbon which, when unfurled, revealed the formal announcement in gold-inked calligraphy. Now, these gold-tubed invitations waited for that magical moment when they would be mailed out exactly six weeks prior to July 15th. Joi just wished it was all over, honeymoon included, and it was September and her condo was furnished and she was back in school studying.

"It's going to be alright," she reminded herself as she glanced at her watch and stacked the magazines in a neat pile near her locker.

She opened the curtain and was punched in the face by the sight of him—Joe Pride, sitting with the guys in their usual booth. He seemed equally shocked to see her. Her heart leapt to her throat and her knees buckled as she looked away. Her response to him was immediate and involuntary; her bodily juices began to flow at the sight of him. Shorty and the guys had been coming in regularly, but Pride hadn't. She thought that he had decided never to return to Louie's, yet, here he was unnerving her. She eyed Ella who, before Joi could ask, said, "That's your station."

Chantel was too far away to get her attention. Finally, Joi's inner voice said, "This is ridiculous—You shouldn't be flustered by this man." She walked up to the table and the man. She braced herself against the closeness of him.

"Hello, Joe, what will you boys have?" she said in one breath without looking at anyone. She jotted down the usuals for Shorty, Goldie and Edgar. Then the table went quiet. "I Could Love You Like That" by All 4 One played softly on the jukebox. She wondered if Pride recognized the song that had played the first night in her apartment when they slow-dragged.

"I didn't expect to see you here," Pride said. "I thought you'd be gone." His jaw tensed up and released as he stared at her diamond, which was big, bold and eye-level to him.

"Soon," she said, doodling on the pad without looking at him. "What'll you have?"

"Liver and onions, mashed potatoes with gravy, green

beans," he said.

"And milk," Pride and Joi said together.

Her eyes darted to his and somehow got tangled up in their soft brown hue. All they had meant to each other surfaced—and faded. He tossed her a vague, distant glance as if he were looking at a stranger. She tore her gaze away as though his were the blinding light from the Ark of the Covenant.

Joi served their food in silence. Pride sat with his chin in the hollow of his folded hands where his thumbs met and his fingers crisscrossed like an Indian tepee. His index fingers touched his luscious lips and divided his manicured moustache. In an effort to ignore the perfume of his natural scent, she avoided the table.

She went to the other side of the diner, trying to slow her blood after he had set it in motion again. Trying to cool her lips that ached for the taste of his. Trying to numb her skin that craved his touch. But even from there Joi could not block out the sound of a voice she'd know anywhere. When she could no longer stand the way his presence filled her senses, and assaulted her mind, body and soul—she fled to the back and smoked a cigarette. When she returned, Pride was gone.

After the others had finished and were leaving, only Edgar said good-bye. Joi went over to scoop up her tips. Under Pride's cleaned plate, he'd left her the usual five dollar tip—a Lincoln.

CHAPTER 11

The sweltering Chicago heat was at its apex on this July afternoon, but inside the cavernous cathedral it was iceberg cool, as if the Jeeters had flown in igloos from Alaska to assure the comfort of their guests.

Claude's sisters, Jennifer and Lauren, carefully lowered the fairy-tale gown over Joi's head. The day has finally come, she thought, as she twirled in front of the cheval mirror of the cathedral's bride room. Legions of people were abuzz about her, smoothing her gown, flicking her hair, ooohing and aaahing, and every five seconds someone else was knocking on the door. With every entrance, there were more superlatives showered on Joi in an attempt to define just how gorgeous she looked. More accounts of the vast cathedral being filled to the dimmest corners, more tallies of what celebrities, local and national notables, had sat their couture posteriors upon the polished pews. Were they there to see her and Claude marry or to hear Luther Vandross? Joi wondered.

It was time; Joi was escorted from the room to the threshold of the church. She eyed her attendants who were glowing in their beautiful gold gowns with the sweeping backs adorned with mini trains. They proceeded down the aisle in syncopated steps. The wedding coordinator gave Joi a lush bouquet of snowy white, off-white and gold dendrobium, phalaenopsis and cymbidium orchids, which cascaded from her hand to the floor; the same fragrant flowers, wrapped in ribbon, punctuated each pew.

Once the bridesmaids were all in place, two tuxedoed men spent five minutes unfolding a gold carpet that led from the altar where Claude stood to Joi. Then, on cue, just as Claude had arranged, French horns sounded and the crowd rose and turned to pay homage to his soon-to-be wife. Joi's heart swelled with fear and anticipation. Howard, Claude's father, crooked his arm and Joi took it. As if she were a star onstage, Joi step-togethered, step-togethered regally down the aisle. Lights from the cameras of a dozen reporters flashed in her face, and people held their breaths as she glided by. Today, she was a true St. Marie.

A string quartet took over once Joi reached Claude at the altar, and Luther Vandross stepped up to the mike and began his lilting "Here and Now." This crowd was too sophisticated to clap at the song's end. The classical musicians discreetly resumed as Claude took Joi's hand.

"Joi?"

She listened to the minister as he began the ceremony.

"Joi?"

She thought she heard her name, but the buzzing from the crowd was interfering with the minister's words. "Joi!" It was Pride's voice. She hadn't thought about him in weeks. She glanced toward the sound of her name from behind. Her vision was snagged by the sight of Joe Pride, standing at the edge of the altar. When she turned to him, so did Claude. The minister stopped speaking mid-sentence, his face creased into a frown.

"Joi, I love you," Pride said. "You and I belong together. This is a mistake. You know it and I know it. Even he knows it." Pride pointed to Claude, who was shocked speechless.

Raising her veil from her face, Joi was overwhelmed by the delicious sight of him, refreshingly underdressed for the occasion. Amid all of the stifling pretense, he was an oasis of reality. Claude was murmuring something in her ear but she didn't hear him. Suddenly, Pride's calm protest escalated into force. He had tried to open the altar's gate to get Joi, when two well-heeled men came up to his side. "I've come for you, Joi," he said to her. The men tried to grab him, and Pride closed his hands into fists. "Don't touch me, brother, and everything'll be alright," Pride warned, eyeing them with a lethal peripheral glance. They backed off.

An infuriated Claude raged, "What the hell do you think you are doing?" Jacquleen St. Marie gasped and fainted; her two thousand dollar gown, thrown up over her face, kissed the marble floor behind her.

"Doing what I should have done months ago," Pride said. "This doesn't concern you." He dismissed Claude and looked directly at Joi. "Joi," he said and smiled. His soft brown eyes held hers; her heart rejoiced as tears of wonderment and joy slid down her face. She stood rooted to the marble altar.

"Neither of us is blameless," Pride continued. "If I had done things differently, neither of us would be here now. We'd be at the Sleepy Hollow Inn in the Poconos." He chuckled nervously, and she blushed. "Let's not spend the rest of our lives being sorry for chances taken and chances missed."

The crowd hushed so they could hear. Joi was sure that none of them had ever been to a wedding where anyone ever "spoke now or forever held their peace," even before that part of the ceremony was reached. The guests watched with bemused and romantic smiles. A collective gasp sounded as the future Mrs. Claude Jeeter's bejeweled, caramel hands gathered her expensive sparkling lace and took a step toward this uninvited paladin.

Pride released his fingers from his palms and opened his hand to her. "If you want a lifetime of *Jeopardy*, old movies, picnics in front to the fireplace...then I'm your man." She took another tentative step.

"Joi!" Claude spat indignantly. "This is absurd!"

"If you want lazy Sundays in bed, full body massages, foot rubs and nights of honest loving that time can't erase...I'm your man."

The women of the sophisticated crowd were now testifying, while the men signified their encouragement; clearly, there was little allegiance to the Jeeter family as this drama unfolded.

"I want you as you are now, Joi," Pride said. "You're perfect for me just the way you are. You once told me it's never too late. Am I too late, Joi? You game?" His hand was still outstretched for her. She bit her bottom lip, smiled— then she leapt into his waiting arms.

The crowd cheered as Joi said, "Oh, Pride I love you!" She sprayed his handsome face with quick kisses. With wild abandon he carried her up the long aisle on the gold rug. The Jeeter-faithful were visibly appalled, but most of the guests cheered them on.

"Take your woman, man! Just take her!" a man said.

"You go, girl!" a woman urged.

"Life's too short. This ain't no dress rehearsal!"

"Be happy!" was the last comment Joi heard as Pride placed her into a waiting cab.

"Where to?" the cabdriver asked. And before they could answer, he turned around and answered himself. "Straight to hell!"

It was Claude…

"Ahhh!" Joi jolted awake, her heart thumping, her nightgown drenched with sweat. She panted in the still darkness, trying to catch her breath from the phantom dream and trying to figure out where she was. She clicked on the lamp and recognized Claude's room. A sheath of light flashed into the den across the hall where Claude slept. Still shaky, Joi got up, pulled her robe on and tried to reject the images of the dream.

From the den's sofabed, Claude stirred and asked, "You alright?"

"Yeah, I'm fine. Go back to sleep." She stood in the hallway and tried to swallow gasps of air. Between breaths, she could hear Claude's light snore.

Joi padded her way to the kitchen for a drink of water. She took down a tumbler from the glass-paneled cabinet and let the mineral water bubble from its freestanding cooler. As she slowly sipped the clear liquid, she also drank in her surroundings. The high-tech, stainless steel kitchen resembled the one in their new Chicago condo. Only it had an indoor rotisserie, an eight-burner stove and an industrial refrigerator. It all looked so cold and efficient. Joi liked wood and warm colors and curtains and plants; a side-by-side with a door dispenser for water was fancy enough for her.

She looked around at the boxes packed for their Chicago trip and those left to do; the expensive all-black copper pots and pans, utensils and other kitchen gadgets. Pride didn't need any of these gimmicky doo-dads to cook the best meals ever.

She leaned against the cold steel counter and took another long sip, trying not to think about Pride. He would have followed her to the kitchen, making sure she was all right. He would have rubbed her shoulders and they would have discussed her dream and what was bothering her. He was just like that. She sighed and shook her head. Until tonight, sleep had been the only freedom she had. If Pride seeped into her busy days, she could count on the Sandman giving her a sleep so deep nothing penetrated it. But now there he was, his spirit demanding attention. Was it a dream or wish fulfillment, Joi wondered.

Finishing off the water, she went to the refrigerator for juice and found the possibilities staggering: passion fruit juice, kiwi, guava, apple-cran. She just wanted some plain old grapefruit juice. Claude, who purported to love her and know her, ought to at least have her favorite juice handy, she thought. Pride didn't like grapefruit juice, preferring orange, but he had always kept some for her. Did Claude even know her? Or was he supposed to get to know her while she was supposed to fall deeply in love with him? Joi eyed all the fancy marmalades and imported spreads. She liked grape jelly. She thought Godiva chocolates were good, but over-rated; almost any chocolates, as long as they had nuts, were just fine. She preferred balloons to flowers—did Claude know any of this? Pride did. Would it ever cross Claude's mind to give her a foot massage? She had been spared knowing his capabilities in the lovemaking department. She didn't doubt that Claude could make her feel like a woman, but not a natural woman. The intimacy she had had with Pride would be missing as much as the man himself. With Pride it had been that *deja vu*, ESP, telepathic kind of true intimacy; that I-know-what-you-want-and-need-and-where, without ever uttering a word. An intimacy that was as rare as a sighted unicorn streaking across an azure blue sky, and just as whimsical. She wondered if she and Claude would ever have that kind of connection with one another.

Whoever said God didn't have a sense of humor? This was all a cosmic joke. He had given her exactly what she had asked for, so she could discover it was not what she really wanted at all. That God had materialized an almost perfect man from the unlikely environs of the Ford factory and given him to her—only to take him away and replace him with the real Prince Charming she had always thought she wanted. Was it all a spiritual test—her wants against God's will?

Or maybe she had missed the human lesson altogether. Maybe she was only supposed to be Pride's catalyst to have him learn to read, and he was supposed to teach her that a person could experience true love without the material trappings—before giving her the material. Did she and Pride get all they were due from one another? Was that all the Almighty had intended? Bizarrely, the closer the time came, the more palatable this charade was becoming. Like preparing for opening night in a big, Broadway play: the show must go on. Would go on—with her in the lead role.

Like a stage-struck actress, she would love to go running away into the night, but that wouldn't be right, wouldn't be professional. Soon, Pride would be like Joaquin—someone she had once loved but was now gone beyond her reach. Like Joaquin, Pride had been both her freedom and her shelter. He had been so easy to love. Pride made her feel so alive; he had made her feel sixteen again.

But she was grown up and mature, and this called for mature decisions. She knew exactly what she was doing. Claude made her feel safe, sane and secure. She was picking privilege and peace of mind over soul-stirring love and toe-curling passion. It was the right thing to do for her and her children.

Soon, she'd be at that purgatory of a place where she couldn't remember and couldn't quite forget. Where Pride would be just a sunny day she once had along the way. A cotton candy carnival that ended too soon, she thought, and then wiped at something that landed on her face. When she went to flick away the intruder, she looked at her fingers to see if she captured the culprit. She was surprised to find wetness there. She rubbed both her damp cheeks and realized, Pride was still surprising her. She wished he would stop.

❧

"Here you go, sweetie," Joi said and handed Jabari a dish of ice cream surrounded by four Oreo cookies.

"What do you say?" Chantel prompted.

"Thank you." Jabari grinned.

"Nice digs," Ella said while looking around at Claude's posh condo.

"They'll do," Joi teased. "I think that Youth Summit really went well"

"Thanks again for volunteering," Chantel said. "The church has it twice a year. The girls really liked you, Joi. Too bad you won't be here next year."

"I'm sure Chicago has plenty of organizations where I can volunteer my time. As Mrs. Claude Jeeter, I'll only be going to school—so I'll have loads of time to volunteer."

"Hump!" Ella spat and cracked her gum. "Where is his majesty anyway?"

"Playing racquetball."

"Oh, Jabari—" Chantel exclaimed as her son dropped his ice cream on the white carpet then crushed an Oreo under his foot. "That's okay," Joi said soothingly, stooping to help him clean it up. She swallowed her remark that the maid would get the stain out later.

Claude opened the door and entered the foyer with a smile. Once he saw Joi and the other three, a scowl claimed his face and he picked up the mail from a small table.

"Claude. Look who's here," Joi said brightly.

"I see." He stopped rifling through his letters long enough to say, "Ladies."

Jabari ran over to him and grabbed him around his legs.

"Stop that," he snapped. "You're filthy!" He wrenched Jabari's arms away from him. The little boy cried and the three woman stood looking at Claude in shock. "Well, he's got gunk all over his hands and mouth," Claude said defensively. "I'm going to take a shower." He left the foyer as

Chantel calmed her whimpering son.

"Well," Ella said. "We better be going." She grabbed her purse.

"Are you alright, Jabari?" Joi stooped down to ask the little man.

"He hurt my arm," Jabari said, wiping his eyes.

"He didn't mean to. Sometimes men don't realize how strong they are. I'm sorry. Are we forgiven?" He nodded. "Gimme a hug." He did. "And a smile." He complied. "I'll see you on Monday," Joi told her friends.

"Thanks again, Joi," Chantel said as they walked to the door.

Throwing her head toward the direction of the bedrooms and Claude, Ella said, "He's a real piece of work."

"He probably lost the game," Joi offered lamely. "He hates to lose."

"Oh, yeah, well, that explains treating a kid that way," Ella said mockingly, punctuating the statement with a crack of her gum. "Take care, kid," she said to Joi.

Joi closed the door. She was not only livid at the way Claude acted toward her friends, but she hated the look of pity in their eyes for her as they left. She went to the bathroom, knocked on the door and opened it far enough to say, "I'd like to see you when you're finished."

"Of course, you will, my love. Is your company gone?"

Joi left without answering.

Claude took his sweet time in the bathroom. She heard the Jacuzzi running. It gave her time to calm down and decide what she wanted to say without emotion.

"Ah, I feel so much better," Claude said, entering the

living room where Joi watched television. "It's Saturday. You want to eat out or order in?"

"In." Joi didn't want to go out anywhere with him.

"Fine."

"You lost today, didn't you?"

"Yes. Thank you for reminding me, since you know how much I hate to lose. Especially to a lightweight like Jonathan."

"He's your friend, isn't he? Like Chantel and Ella are mine?"

"I suppose. What were you doing with them today?"

"I told you I was volunteering at the Youth Summit—"

"Ah, yes," he cut her off. "Chinese alright?"

"Yes." She got up and joined him at the bar. "Jabari's a sweet little guy." Claude made no comment as he perused the take-out menu. "Smart as a whip. I'd like to send him to parochial school." Joi watched Claude's finger stop by the Moo Goo Gai Pan.

"What? Is that what they came up here for—to beg for money?" Joi looked at him blankly. "I know it's not his fault he was born illegitimately to a single parent. His mother chose to have a child with no man, no means and no responsibility. Giving money to him for school is like flushing it down the toilet."

"Where do you get off deciding who's worthy of a decent life and who's not?"

"It's my money and I decide who gets it. I prefer causes that can benefit mankind. Once we move to Chicago, we won't have to be subjected to their visits. Close chapter." He went back to his menu.

"You sanctimonious, obnoxious son-of-a-bitch!"

"C'mon, Joi, don't overact. People who curse have limited verbal skills and intelligence. Besides, people of my status don't 'show-out.' Certainly, Mrs. Claude Jeeter needs better control over her inappropriate emotions." Joi was so upset she couldn't speak. "As my wife, every Tom, Dick and Harry will be coming to you for donations of your time and money. You have to pick universal organizations like the Cancer Society, heart disease, not the United Negro College Fund or sickle cell—they are too tied to the black community, and we will never recoup our investments. Most of those people don't even vote. It's just a matter of time before that Ella and Chantel ask you for money."

"What makes you think everybody is after your money?"

"You are."

His words slapped her square across her face. The verbal blow knocked the wind out of her. She could feel herself turn red. "Well. There it is," she finally said. She knew this discussion would come sooner or later; she thought it would be two children and a house later.

"Grow up, Joi. It's no disgrace to put money first. Money makes the world go 'round, not love. Money lasts; love doesn't. Money—I have it, I will keep it and I will make more. Money is power. Money can buy anything." He stared at her. "To be so bright you can be unbelievably naive. And I don't want to discuss this anymore. I've had a rough day."

"Try a rough life," Joi said.

"Oh, here we go."

"Don't you dare minimize my life or the people in it. I have tried to overlook your politics, your snide remarks—"

"As the future Mrs. Jeeter you'll have to get on the wagon. Mrs. Claude Jeeter will have to learn—"

"I suppose Mrs. Claude Jeeter will." She slid the two-carat ring from her finger. "Give this to her when you find her." Joi slammed the diamond on the bar.

"Such melodrama on a Saturday afternoon." He had looked at the ring shimmer in the light. "Joi, pick up your ring."

"You pick it up and stick it up your tight, bourgie, Republican—"

"Joi," he said, as she yanked her jacket from the foyer closet. "You are making a mistake of grand proportions!"

"Actually." She stood directly in front of him. "I am correcting one."

"Don't think you can just waltz back in here after a display like this—"

"Ah," she said sarcastically. "You know you are one man too late for that speech." She put her hand on the doorknob. "I have been thrown out by a better class of man than you."

Joi punched the elevator button furiously. When it came she got on. Claude did not follow. When the elevator opened, her red Beamer waited for her at the curb. She stared at it for the moment, then walked over to the doorman. "Would you see that Mr. Jeeter gets these?" She handed her car keys to him, pushed open the door and hailed her own cab.

❧

"I've been expecting you," Jacquleen said as she opened the door to her house.

"So Claude called?" Joi asked, meandering through the hallway to the living room.

"He said you two had an argument."

"No, Mother. We broke up. The wedding is off. I had a week before the invitations went out." She hunched her shoulders and looked at the family pictures on the mantel.

"He said when you'd calmed down and came to your senses, he'd be waiting."

"Oh, really? Well, he said a lot of things." She faced her mother.

"Joi, you've been crying!"

"Some. It's the good kind. You know, when you realize the truth of things. The emperor had no clothes, Ma. There's a side of him we didn't see—or didn't want to see."

"Did he hit you, Joi? If he did I'll go over and kill him myself! There's no reason for a man to hit a woman—"

"Calm down, Ma. He didn't hit me—not with his fists. He beat me up pretty well with his words. Sticks and stones can break your bones but words can kill you." She chuckled wryly. "His words killed that relationship for sure."

"Oh, Joi," Jacquleen said without pretense. Joi noticed she hadn't called her Joie since she had arrived.

"If he's like that before we marry, I can only expect more of the same afterward."

"I hate to admit it but you're right." Jacquleen embraced her daughter. "I thought he was the answer to our prayers," she lamented, guiding Joi toward the sofa.

"All is not lost. Look." Joi presented her mother with an application to the University of Detroit. Joi St. Marie was printed across the top. "Oh, Joi St. Marie—not Martin?" Tears sprang to Jacquleen's eyes.

"Yes. After all, I am a St. Marie." She smiled tenderly at her mother. "They have college programs six days a week geared to the returning adult student. The advisor said there was even a possibility that I would get credit for my life and work experience. I could finish in a year."

"Oh, Joi. I am so proud of you." She wiped her eyes with a tissue from her pocket.

"I am applying for financial aid. I intend to go full-time and take twenty hours a semester. Maybe work part-time at Louie's. I'll have to see after I get accepted. Ma, stop crying." They sat on the couch. "For at least a year I will not be competing with Noel to see who can give you the most extras. So you're gonna have to do your own hair and nails."

Jacquleen laughed through her tears. "Okay. Well, Joi. You may have lost a man but you found Joi St. Marie."

"You got that right. She was there all along, buried, hiding. I guess I should thank Claude for bringing her out again."

"That's one way to look at it."

"I didn't like who I was when I was with him. I wasn't anybody when I was with him—just his extension. He made me feel half charity, half experiment and not at all loved."

"Oh, he was a great charmer on the outside, but ruthless on the in," Jacquleen surmised.

"Make a great snake oil salesman."

"Or politician."

They laughed and genuinely hugged for the first time in years. In finding herself, Joi was able to let go of the resentment; of her mother being able to financially help Noel obtain her college degree. Of her mother being unable to help her finish her degree, yet expecting her to help out with household finances when needed. It was still about money, but now it was in the proper perspective.

"Oh, Joi," Jacquleen said as she stroked her daughter's cheek. "Where did all the time go? How did we get so far apart? When your dad died…well, I had a rough time. We all did. I hated that you had to drop out of school. I had always drummed into you girls the importance of getting your own degree, and when I realized that wasn't going to happen for you, I guess I became obsessed with you getting a man who could take care of you, then you would be financially set no matter what happened to him. Claude was a gift from heaven that turned out to be the devil from hell."

"For me anyway. I'm sure he will find a willing mate."

"To think I championed his cause. Trying so hard, I lost sight of what's really important. My daughter's happiness."

"Spilt milk, Ma."

Jacquleen grabbed a handful of Joi's newly grown hair. "I guess you'll be cutting this?"

"First chance I get." Joi grinned.

Jacquleen saw a spark in her daughter's eyes that she hadn't seen in over ten years. She only wanted what was best for her and that seemed to be someone to care for her. But now, she was looking at a determined woman who was capable of caring for herself. She started crying again. Then she stopped cold. "Joi, this doesn't have anything to do with Joe Pride. Does it?"

"No, Ma. Except maybe inspiration and example. He couldn't even read past the fifth grade level and he went on to get his GED in eight weeks. That's pretty remarkable."

"Yes, it is," Jacquleen agreed quietly and searched Joi's eyes. She believed her; needed to believe her. What would a woman with a college degree, and maybe later a master's or doctorate degree, want with a factory worker?

"I'm working on me, Ma. I don't have time for anything or anyone else…certainly not a man." She rubbed her mother's hand. "Maybe I'm due a good man every ten years. So, when I'm forty-four, I can expect another one to come along. Maybe I'll be ready for him then." As long as Pride stayed out of her sight, she would try to keep him out of her mind. Soon, she'd be totally occupied with studying.

"What will you major in?"

"I'm thinking Literature. Go on for my master's and Ph.D. and teach at the college level."

"I knew it! I'm so happy, I can't believe we're having this conversation." She patted Joi's hand. "Maybe you'll marry someone on the faculty, and the two of you could—"

"Ma!"

"Sorry. Habit." She grinned sheepishly. "Why don't we do something special for Memorial Day? Lunch or dinner and a movie?"

"I'd like that. Wow. Summer's coming—"

"Along with the beginning of your new life."

∽∾∝

"Jacquleen, has Joi stopped by yet? She's not at home," Claude said.

"Yes, Claude, she's been here but she's gone."

"Do you know where she is?"

"No, I don't. She's grown." Jacquleen relished saying that and believing it for the first time in a long while. She could hear Claude squirm on the other end of the line.

"You know, I saw the new riverboat sail by my condo yesterday. Looks like a fine day trip. Would you and a friend like to take the cruise? My treat."

"No, thank you. I don't gamble."

"What would you like? Name it!"

"Actually, Claude, I have everything I want or need." She thought of Joi's reclaimed confidence.

"She told you about our little tiff."

"She told me the wedding was off."

"I am confident we can work it out. We may have said some pretty outlandish things but it's nothing we can't get past."

"Past is what it is. I'm sorry it didn't work out, Claude." Lord knows I am, she thought. "But it's Joi's life and her decision."

"You're mighty cavalier about this. I thought you were on my side."

"I was, but now I'm on Joi's. You have your ring, your car and your answer. It's over. Good luck to you and yours." Jacquleen savored the sound of confusion on his end as she hung up. "Well, that's that."

Joi settled in with her two favorite males, Ben and Jerry, and waited for the ice cream to melt around the edges. She flicked on the television and watched nothing in particular. She didn't feel sad about her breakup with Claude, she thought as she picked up her crossword puzzle. She felt relief as if some grand burden had been lifted from her shoulders. She no longer had to pretend not to notice his off-color comments or make excuses to herself and to her friends for his pretentious behavior. She was now free to enjoy Ella and Chantel without his disapproving glances. She may live in a "hovel" as he once called her apartment, but it was her hovel; her own space. If she had married Claude, she probably would have ended up one of those shallow, pathetic society women who closed their eyes to their husband's cruelties while drowning their sorrows in the finest liquor money can buy. Or she would have wrapped her body in fine fabrics and furs to hide the inner neglect of a shattered spirit. And her poor children would have been strangers to their distant, workaholic father who would shower them with everything but his time and love. He may be right for somebody, but the somebody wasn't her. She dabbed at the chocolate ice cream.

Having been given the opportunity of a lifetime and passed on it, Joi now had a renewed commitment and vitality. Dr. Morton, her college psychologist, would have been proud. Joi was going to finally do what she had always paid lip-service to—work on herself. She fought the reflex to think of Pride. With him she had the most important thing, but threw it away. If only her past could be prologue. But he had made it very clear that she was not to come back. Even when uncontrolled memories of him seeped into her company late at night—of all the wonderful things he had said to her—his last statement to her always put a period to any false hope. "You can't come back. Don't come back. It's over."

∽≈∽

After a week's absence from the diner, Shorty, Edgar and Goldie returned and took up residence in their old booth. Joi was glad to see them. This was to have been her last week. Maybe they'd come to say good-bye.

"How are you all today?" she asked brightly. "It's been awhile."

They each opened menus they had never once consulted during her entire tenure there. "So what's happening?" she continued, noting that they were clearly snubbing the woman who had snubbed their friend.

"Nothing much," Goldie said casually.

"I think she's got a right to know anyway," Shorty said.

"Know what?" Joi asked.

"Why we been out all week," Shorty said, eyeing Goldie and Edgar. "We been spending our lunchtime at the hospital."

"You all don't look sick to me," Joi said, trying to lighten the mood.

"It's not us," Edgar said.

"It's Pride," Goldie said.

The bottom fell out of Joi's world. "What about him?" She couldn't control her racing heart.

"He was hurt bad," Goldie said and looked grimly at Shorty.

"What? How?" she shouted from Shorty to Goldie.

"They didn't think he was going to make it."

"He was sliced up pretty bad."

"Robbery—carjacking."

"Got his car back."

"You know Pride, he ain't gonna give up without a fight."

"That stupid car. Is he all right?" Joi's breathing was shallow and uneven as she rocked from foot to foot and jammed her thumbnail between her teeth.

"Went home today. Got a nurse and all."

"He's got to be rehabilitated."

"Good thing you cut him loose when you did. He's a ruined man now."

Joi jerked off her apron. "Why didn't you tell me?" she screamed as the other customers turned and stared at her.

"We just did," Goldie said.

She pushed the curtain open and came back through with her purse and Ella's car keys.

"Can I borrow your car?" Joi asked Ella without stopping.

"Yeah, sure," Ella said, confused.

"Joi, where you going?" Shorty asked.

"I don't think it's a good idea for you to go—"

"To hell with what you think!" she spat.

"He looks pretty gruesome—" Shorty said to her disappearing frame.

Joi tore through the crowded Detroit streets, crying and blowing the horn until she came to a screeching halt in Pride's driveway behind his car. She flung open her car door. Pride hated for anyone to walk across his lawn. But she did just that as she ran up the steps and began banging on the door and ringing the bell. She alternated between the ringing and the banging, keeping up the noise for a few minutes, then threw herself against the front window. She was unable to see anything inside because of his plants. She went back down the walkway to glance up at his bedroom window, then ran around to the back porch. She returned to the front again, repeating the bell-ringing and door-banging.

Downstairs in the basement, Pride put himself through the paces, lifting weights. He wondered who was keeping up such a racket at his door as he completed another set. Whoever it was would go away eventually. He knew he didn't want to see anyone. Well, one person—and it sure wasn't her at his door.

He had lost weight while he was in school because of his irregular hours, non-meals and infrequent exercising. But he had launched himself on a plan to get his body and strength back. It was also a healthy way to exorcize Joi Martin from his soul. He had gone to his old haunts— caught Joshua Redman on Friday, McCoy Tyner on Saturday, and Al Jarreau at Rudy's on Sunday—but it had all seemed so empty without Joi to play footsie with under the table, and make love to when he got home. While his friends, Mike and Stan, were curiously quiet on the subject of Joi Martin, Rudy and Jerona had asked him about the absence of his lady love. Pride had told them simply that she "was history," in his patented style, signaling the end of any discussion.

After that, folks had seemed to view his stepping out like a debutante's coming-out party. Women had started flocking around him, taking his rare appearances to mean he was ready to hook up with another female. When will women understand that jumping from one relationship into another isn't healthy? he thought. He had done it in his earlier years when he was young, inexperienced and into quantity not quality.

As he went into the fourth set of lifting, he knew that he had messed up two weeks ago with Mavis Stubberfield. After he had slipped on his latex cover and before his final release was complete, he had known he'd made a mistake. Even before his manhood stopped throbbing, he regretted his action, glad he was at her apartment so he could leave. Masturbation by proxy, he had thought, as he dressed to get the hell out of there. He tried to rationalize that it was just a one-night stand and she understood that, and wanted it as much as he did. But when she asked him to stay, his reasons, like that old Earth, Wind and Fire song, had no pride. With the inserting of his selfish manhood, he had unintentionally launched hopes, dreams and expectations which exploded deep in the willing pelvis of Mavis Stubberfield. He was sorry the moment he entered her entrapping canyon. That was probably Mavis banging on his door now. If men had a long way to go to learn when a women said "no" she meant "no," then woman had to understand when a man said he was "not interested," he was not interested. Only one woman could hold his interest. Her name was Joi Martin. He fought thinking about her—all the things they should have said that were left unsaid. All the things they should have done that they never did. He wondered if she ever thought of him.

"Awww!" Pride growled aloud, sprang up and began banging on the punching bag suspended from the ceiling. He'd put as many miles on it as his car. Having the super-imposed, smug face of Claude on it didn't hurt any, but Shorty had made him realize that the breakup with Joi had been just as much his fault as hers.

"Reverse it," Shorty had said. "You with someone morning, noon and night, then all the sudden—poof—you gone. Say you were the one left dangling in the wind. Suppose it was you on the other side of that answering machine, listening to messages, breaking dates and no explanation but 'I got some surprise for you—later.' Tell me that wouldn't drive you crazy?" Shorty had shaken his head in doubt. Before he had left Pride's office, he had turned and said, "Vacations are hardest on the ones left behind; you went away, man. I thought you two had a chance at something really special. Not just 'Let's get together and see where this thing goes.' Naw. Something really special. You just remember three things about pride, Joe Pride. Anger will get you S-O-L, but pride'll keep you there. Pride is a lonely mistress, and that same pride cometh before the fail. Guess what? You've fallen and you all alone. Your daddy,

Jim Pride, would think you was a damn fool. Later."

He and the old widow Covney across the street had spent more nights up alone than he cared to remember. He'd glance over at her lit-up house, knowing she never knew she had company in the unlikely persona and darkness of the Pride household. During those lonely, soul-searching nights, Pride had finally admitted that he had handled the relationship badly. At this point, all he could do was learn from his mistakes. As long as he never had to lay eyes on either of the Jeeters ever again, he'd be alright.

Pride stopped punching and clung to the bag for support. His breathing was labored and sweat commingled with reluctant tears. He looked at his workbench and knew that in the corner tray was an engagement ring of hammered gold. He couldn't give it to Joi and he couldn't give it away. As he tried to catch his breath, the Nefertiti bust he had begun staring at him with her almond-shaped eyes. The divot above her luscious lips caught the dim light. Until that moment, he never realized that her face was Joi's. From the radio, Oleta Adams was telling her man, she didn't care how he got there to her, just get there if he can. "Right here, right now."

"Damn!" Pride shouted at the incessant noise of the intruder. "It better not be any Jehovah Witness or soap salesmen." He let go of the punching bag and took the steps by two, then yanked the door open.

He never thought he'd see her again. He wanted to grab her up and just hold her. But his mind reminded him that she belonged to someone else now.

She gasped at the sight of him. He stood there in shorts

and a cut-off T-shirt, which exposed his washboard abs and his powerful muscled arms. There was a V of sweat from his exposed navel to his handsome face.

"What can I do for you?" he asked coldly, unsnapping, then removing his lifting gloves.

"You're alright?" Relief flushed her face.

"I'm alright." He wiped his thick black eyebrows free of sweat.

"I thought you were—" She stopped, then chuckled wryly. "I suppose Shorty and the boys are having a good laugh about now."

"How's that?" He wondered what she was talking about.

"I didn't mean to disturb you…your workout," she stammered. She gathered her composure and took a deep breath. "Take care." Feeling like a damned fool, she turned to leave. Her crepe, nurse-white shoes made an ungodly noise as she crept across his concrete porch.

He wanted to say something to make her stay just a moment longer; he wanted to say something to hurt her like she had him. "Pride is a lonely mistress." Shorty's words echoed across his wounded soul. His heart vetoed his brain's attempt to maim; instead, he spoke plain, true and honest. "Joi, stay."

She stopped cold in her tracks. The words fell on her ears like manna from heaven. The only true, honest words she had heard in a long time. Until he had spoken them, she hadn't realized how much she ached to hear them. She turned to him. His jaw was resolute, but his eyebrows knitted together at the center of his forehead, giving him what his mother had called that "poor puppy-dog look."

"I still believe in you and me," Pride said. "Stay, but only if you can stay a lifetime."

She looked into his soft brown eyes with the luxurious lashes, searching…searching for what? The door to his house and his heart were wide open, offering all that he could. All she had ever wanted was him. The unbroken dreams of their hearts spoke to one another; the sound of destiny whooshed through her body.

She ran and jumped into his sweaty arms. He laughed with unadulterated pleasure as her body responded passionately to his for all they were and all they could be.

"I love you, Pride." She looked deep into his eyes to his soul; he kissed away her tears. "I've never loved anybody the way I love you," she went on. "I don't know what I'd do without you—"

"You're never gonna have to find out, Joi." He brushed hair back from her face. "We still won't tell the kids you proposed," he said and chuckled, sniffing back tears.

"Suppose I can't have children?" She looked at him in a panic.

"Suppose I can't."

"Oh, I don't care." She hugged him again. "As long as I have you."

"My sentiments exactly. Ummm." He held her tight. "I figure the Lord gave me you, and if you love me for the rest of your days, that's blessing enough for me." He kissed the top of her head. "We'll honeymoon at Niagara Falls."

"Let's go south," she suggested.

"Orlando—Disneyworld?"

"Aruba. Curacao."

"That in South America?"

"Almost."

"I'm game. See why I need you?"

"I'm the needy one, Pride." All along she had thought it was him, but she needed him more than he needed her.

"Let's seal it with a kiss," Pride said.

"Oh, I think we can do better than that, can't we?"

"As a matter of fact, I got some watermelon cotton candy mix for the machine," he teased with a playful glimmer.

"Yeah?" She kissed the lips she had missed. "Maybe for the second time." They giggled and closed the door behind them.

❧

Pride and Joi danced in the stream of sunlight that radiated around the Blue Note in the window. Their friends remarked on their happiness as they consumed food and imbibed the club's best liquor, compliments of the hosts, Rudy and Jerona.

"You guys crashed my bridal shower," Joi said, nuzzling in the arms of her future husband.

"You don't want me here?" He broke his embrace playfully.

"A co-ed wedding shower," Joi pondered. "That's pretty unconventional." She kissed him.

"Why?" Pride held her closer. "We're both getting married."

"Yes, we are," Joi exclaimed. "Happy?"

"Ecstatic."

"How do you feel about your mom not being here?"

"She's been cool since our wedding invitations went out. You know, I've been known to cancel out."

"Oh, really?"

"Ummm hummm."

"You better not cancel out on me," Pride said.

"Never!" They snuggled, kissed and ended up forehead to forehead.

"So, it's a no go with the shower too?" Pride asked.

"When those invites went out, Jacquleen shut down. I've called her but all I get is her machine. And we know how reliable those machines are."

"She'll come around."

"Or she won't. We're both grown. I've made my decision." Joi stretched her arms up around Pride's neck and kissed him passionately. "I got what I want. You're all I need."

"Hey, you two," Jerona yelled from a nearby table. "If you open these gifts, you get to go home and finish what you've started."

⤛⤜

He threw his aristocratic nose up against the windless blue sky of the sunny Sunday afternoon. He sashayed grandly to the door and knocked loudly.

Jacquleen drew her robe about her body and peeked through the glass-paneled side of her door. She thought about not letting him in, but she didn't want her neighbors to see him standing on her porch. Besides, his kind could start a ruckus and draw unwanted attention.

"Yes," she greeted him coldly.

"Hello, Jacquleen," Dante said loudly.

"You're drunk," she said in accusation.

"*Au contraire.* I'm quite sober," he slurred.

"Come in," she ordered, allowing him in only far enough so she could close the door behind him. They stood awkwardly in the hallway, which was shrouded by filtered light. She finally asked, "What do you want?"

"To tell you what you're missing."

"Humph!"

"Your daughter had a very lovely bridal shower given at the Blue Note this fine Sunday afternoon. Besides her hostess Jerona, you would have known Ella and Chantel— but no one else. The decorations were bridal crepe paper bells, the champagne—domestic—flowed like water, and the food was heavenly. Eggs, bacon, sausage, biscuits, waffles, pancakes, home fries—the real kind with onions. Oh, it was a lovely, jazz-brunch bridal shower. And the gifts—" Dante could see how unimpressed Jacquleen was. "Oh, that's right. You were rooting for the other guy. The one with the car, the houses, the beluga caviar, Dom Perignon and all that other stuff that didn't make your daughter at all happy."

Jacquleen twisted her mouth in silent disgust.

"I thought you and Joi were making real progress until Joe Pride came back into the scene. You think by withholding your love you can get Joi to do what you want.

Wrong!" He laughed loudly. "Maybe that crap worked with the old Joi, but not this new one. Lady, you don't know the power of love. Maybe you've never felt it yourself."

"Are you quite finished? I am not about to let you lambaste me in my own house—"

"Well, Jacquleen," Dante interrupted. "You weren't missed." Dante couldn't resist. "A piece of advice, Mrs. St. Marie, from someone who knows a little something about parental disapproval of lifestyle, of profession, of mate. The parent always loses."

Jacquleen sighed her impatience.

"Let me cut to the chase for you. You are alone now and you will be alone later because Joi will be with Joe Pride. I really don't get you, lady. Someone who purports to love her daughter above herself and then acts this way when her grown daughter doesn't dance to her tune. What more does a parent really want than for their child to be healthy and happy—and of course, financially independent?" he added tongue-in-cheek. "Have you looked at Joi lately? I mean, *really* looked at her? Have you *ever* seen her happier? I've known her for over five years and I've never seen her more radiant. Joi is joyous and that alone warms my heart. You should just be happy for her, too. Pride is a good, solid man, easy on the eye. He clearly loves your daughter. If you ask her to choose, you'll lose. And well you should."

Jacquleen bristled momentarily as he continued. "She's a grown woman and she's going on with her life with or without your permission or approval, and where does that leave you?"

Dante fluttered his hand about the entrance and joined

Jacquleen in a quick, unexpected look around her house. The hallway, the living room, the mantel with the family pictures. And all that could be heard was the metered tick of a clock.

"You'll be alone and lonely. You can either hop on the love train or be left at the depot. Your choice. But the train is moving out. I'm through," Dante said, throwing up his hands. He turned for the door and reached for its knob.

A funnel of sunshine spotlighted her robed body before he closed the door in a thud behind him. Jacquleen stood deep in thought, rooted to the spot. The nerve of that man to come here and accuse her of never being in love. She thought of her beloved Royce and how they loved each other despite parental objection. Joi was her father's daughter. Was Jacquleen unwittingly setting up the same demented scenario with Pride; only this time she was cast as Au Claire? The thought made Jacquleen shudder. In one of life's ironic twists, in trying to overcome Au Claire's control, Jacquleen had become her. No matter how old you get, you're never too old to learn or to break a bad habit, Jacquleen thought.

"I guess that fairy told you," a man's voice said from the top of the stairs. "Life goes on. We all go on. It's time for you to let go and grow up, Jackie." He came slowly down the steps and embraced her. "Pride is a good guy. What else do you want for Joi than for her to find a good man who will love and respect her? He don't have all that money, but neither do you. So let it go. The mission to 'marry well' is over. She didn't get the moon, but she got the stars. Now," Louie said, inclining Jacquleen's chin toward him, "when we coming out the closet?"

She looked up at him. His loving gaze began thawing her icy heart. She smiled and joined him in a subtle chuckle.

"C'mon back to bed. It's Sunday for chrissakes," he said. They moved toward the steps. "Joi's happy. It's time for me to make her mama happy again."

"You old coot," Jacquleen teased playfully as she patted his chest.

"I'll just have to show you how young I can be. May not be no har thar." He rubbed his bald head. "But you know where there is har,"

"Louie, you're so bad."

"And you like it, don't ya, Jackie?"

He tapped her behind, and she scampered, laughing, up the steps.

CHAPTER 12

It was a stifling August day. Joi sat in the church's bride room, dressed and ready to marry the man of her dreams. She heard Vivaldi's "Summer Concerto" being played and remembered that she and Pride had selected the classical piece because it was the movement they had fallen to sleep on the one time they had gone to the symphony. Hearing it now meant that the memorial candles were being lit on the altar. One each, for James Pride, Bernadette Noble Pride and Royce St. Marie; they would all be here in spirit to witness their son and daughter marry their love of a lifetime.

She knew the ceremony was running right on schedule. And why wouldn't it, with Dante at the helm? She then heard "All I Ask of You" sung as a duet, the way she and Pride first heard it at *The Phantom of the Opera*. The voices blended magnificently, and Joi remembered all she and Pride had been and done to each other. Her heart soared unencumbered at all they would become today.

Claude had told her she was making "a mistake of grand proportions." Joi imagined that her rejection of him represented the first time Claude Bryant Jeeter had ever been told "no" in his entire life. She didn't doubt that Claude wanted her, like a person would want to win a game or decimate an opponent—for the triumph of winning, not for the love of the game. When he had finally realized that his case was lost, and remembered who he was and that his behavior was not in keeping with the "Jeerer way"—to humble himself for anyone—he had finally relented. Joi couldn't find the words to explain to Claude that he loved from the outside in, whereas Pride loved from the inside out. True love was always from the inside out.

As Joi smiled at her radiant reflection in the mirror, she couldn't ever remember being so happy. She giggled to herself the way she'd caught herself doing a thousand times a day ever since she and Pride had reunited. She was supremely happy. This felt nothing like a mistake to her. This felt like the best day of her life. Like heaven's gates opening. Like wrongs righted, dreams come true and love everlasting.

She had finally got it—God's message. Joe Pride was integral to her, while Claude Jeeter was merely an inter-mezzo—the pause in the middle of the symphony of her life. A period of respite before she got on with the main classical movement. God had showed her what she'd thought she wanted, what she had been trained all her living days to want. Then when she hushed her childhood desires, the quiet of her soul had shouted that all she ever wanted was to be with Pride.

Again, as it had in all her born days, human timing had played tricks on her, but Divine timing was supreme. He had showed her Pride, then Claude, so she could know for herself what she really wanted. The Almighty had every confidence that she would choose Pride because that's who He had intended for her all along. But as was His way, she had to learn the lessons for herself. The quest to "marry well" had been a bad habit; what she had been programmed to want, she didn't want at all. As only He could do, God had also been on Pride's side. He knew that Pride deserved someone who loved him for himself—wholeheartedly, not halfway. God wanted Pride to have a life-mate who was not settling until she could "do better." A mate who could unequivocally withstand the raging of his dissident mother-in-law without questioning her own heart. Not someone who had doubts buried within the depths of her, who would wonder after a year or two if she should have held out longer or married someone else, and therefore keep a practiced eye out for greener grass and husband number two.

So, though it made no human sense, it made God sense; Pride, Claude, Pride—the way it was meant to be. Now, there was nothing between her and Pride but love—pure, solid and strong. Through him, Joi was able to take the narrow-viewed kaleidoscope of her upbringing, where she tried to balance the colorful baubles in the right combination and throw it away. Pride had shown her how to gaze at the immensity of life beyond that slim cylinder. He had taught her that life was made up of tiny, palpable moments laid side by side, interwoven into an expansive mosaic as wide as St. Mark's Piazza in Venice. Joi loved this man.

Dante swept in, interrupting her thoughts. "You are a vision, Lovey. A vision!" He clapped his hands in sheer delight at his friend, and being in charge of this wedding gala. He flitted around the room until Ella and Chantel entered.

"Any sign of my mother?" Joi asked casually, more from curiosity than concern.

"Count your blessings," Dante said without hesitation.

"Maybe her act wasn't just histrionics. Maybe she really won't show. Well, one monkey don't stop no show."

"Joi, Joi, Joi, you are beautiful," Ella gushed as a tear brimmed her eye. Chantel silently agreed while Jabari made faces in the mirror.

"You really think?" Joi smiled and gave them a quick turn of her dress. The off-the-shoulder, sweetheart neckline of the ecru lace gown showcased her coloring magnificently. The long Juliet sleeves covered the gold and pink-stoned friendship bracelet Pride had given her one October night. The tiny, hand-sewn seed pearls of the bodice shimmered in the renegade rays of sunlight escaping through the small, stained-glass window.

"You're not crying, are you?" Joi asked Ella as she completed her turn.

"I feel like the mother of the bride," Ella confessed.

"I wish you were," Dante said. He snapped his fingers at Jabari, who was grabbing Joi's train. "No, son. You are the ring bearer. Where is your pillow?" He mock-scolded as the bridesmaids and flower girls entered.

"Ah, you all are gorgeous!" Joi said, admiring their flowing mauve gowns.

"You the one!" Jerona, Camryn and Zanielle sang in unison.

Ella and Chantel excused themselves. "Next time we see you, Joi," Ella said in parting, "you'll be married to Joe Pride."

"Yes, I will," Joi said, grinning. Her eyes danced at the prospect. "I am so blessed."

"He's pretty blessed, too," Camryn said.

"That's right. Here," Jerona said, as she poised the veil over Joi's head. "You are really tall in those heels." Jerona placed the tulle headpiece on her ringlets of brunette curls. "Got her a tall man, too," Zanielle teased, as she helped Joi pull the veil over her face.

"It's time!" Dante cheered, having entered and left several times. This time he returned with a box of flowers.

"I am ready." Joi stood. "I am so *ready* to marry this man."

Dante gave the two flower girls their baskets filled with white rose petals. He then turned to Joi and handed her a bouquet of ivory spray roses, gardenias, mauve freesia and ecru snapdragons. He smiled at her, dabbed at his eyes with a lace handkerchief and said, "You go, girl. I am so happy for you. Now, don't you cry. You'll mess up the makeup job."

"Yours or mine?" Joi sassed.

Just then Dante noticed, peripherally, that the bridal party was not moving down the aisle. "Amateurs," he sniped and flew off to instruct them for the last time.

Joi beamed at her image in the mirror and couldn't believe this living fantasy. Their song began anew. This time a soloist began "All I Ask of You." This vocalist wasn't Barbra Streisand; she was better because she evoked all the old memories of Pride that Joi's tender heart could stand. She tucked her hanky into the sleeve of her dress, knowing this was going to be a delightfully emotional ceremony. With Rudy and Jerona's gift of the club for the reception, and the music as well, the couple had tapped spectacularly talented singers from the Detroit area. The minister had even asked during rehearsal whether this was an audition for the Top Ten or a wedding ceremony.

Joi chuckled. Then she heard it—the musical introduction. Before Dante flew back in to get her, she was at the top of the aisle. The white carpet was now being laid out before her by the smiling and handsomely tuxedoed Rudy and Mike.

"Well, Miss Thang. A might eager, aren't we? I didn't even have to come get you," Dante said, prancing to her side. "I think the girl wants to marry this guy."

"I swear…" The male lead of the group's clear voice rang out in the All 4 One hit, and Joi smiled beneath her veil. The crowd stood and turned to her.

"Now, remember," Dante reminded. "Step-pause. Step-pause. This is your day. Your show. Take as long as you want! Work it, Lovey."

Just then, Joi felt the presence of another man. She looked alone, but she knew her father, Royce St. Marie, had spanned time and space to be here for her and Pride on their special day. He stepped to her side, bent and gave his beautiful daughter a butterfly kiss before crooking his arm and asking her, "Are you ready, my *Joie de vivre*?"

"Yes, Daddy," she whispered beneath her veil.

Joi's toffee-brown skin made the ecru satin glow as she glided past family, friends and folks she didn't know, moving regally to the one man she knew all too well. The man she'd be spending her lifetime with. A man she'd been looking for all her life and thought she'd never find. A man she had almost lost to misplaced dreams and foolish pride. She smiled when she saw Pride's handsome image before her and slowed a little, savoring the sight of him standing there waiting for her. It was like those little sexy games they had played, delaying the inevitable and making the destined tryst all the sweeter. As Joi approached the base of the altar, she handed off her bouquet to Jerona. Pride came down to meet her and offered both his hands to her as he sang along with the vocalist.

"Oh, Shorty, he's singing to her," Ruby said and blotted her eyes. Pride had insisted that they sit in the seats that would have been reserved for his parents.

Pride folded Joi's hands into his as they faced the minister. "Dearly beloved," he began, "we are gathered here in the sight of God to join this man and this woman…" Even those guests who could not hear the minister, could hear the sentiments perfectly expressed in the words of the songs selected by the bride and groom, and tears began to flow freely in the church. Dante sat near the back, fighting tears, then finally giving up the battle and blowing his nose noisily. When the male vocalist finished "I Swear" and seamlessly folded into "I Believe in You and Me," the couple went to opposite sides of the altar and extinguished their separate candles, then rejoined each other and ascended the altar to light the Unity candle. The name Pride and Joi embossed in gold lettering with their marriage date beneath the double-ring motif was a keepsake.

"Just beautiful," Dante exclaimed aloud.

The couple set fire to their one candle and joined the minister at the altar's center. Pride began to slow dance with Joi and sing along. He spun her slowly in one direction, and when her train wrapped around her ankles, he rewound her.

"Nothing has changed," the minister remarked. "His mother couldn't keep him from fidgeting in church either." The crowd chuckled while Jerona and Camryn rearranged the train behind her.

"Joi and Joseph have prepared their own vows," the minister spoke to the congregation. "They will share them with us. Joi."

Joi turned slightly to him. "Pride," Joi began, when, suddenly, Pride whipped back the veil from her face. Joi was shocked and excited by his action and laughed.

"I want to see what you say to me," he said quietly. "No more miscommunications."

Joi beamed. "That's why I love you," she said simply. "You don't care about propriety or customs. You care about you and me. You make me feel like we are the only two people in the universe. You make me feel important, respected, listened to—you make me feel special." Tears spilled from her eyes. "You walked into my life when I needed you most. I was trying to please everybody else and I lost myself. With your patience, love and understanding, I found me again…and I thank you. I have to live another lifetime to give to you what you have given me." Joi's tears streamed down her face. "I love you because you are strong, intelligent, determined, unafraid and have a good heart and a slow hand." She blushed and he smiled. "I love you for who you are, and for who I am when I am with you. I look forward to spending the rest of my living days with you, with our children and our grandchildren. I love you." Her bottom lip trembled as she bit back tears, and Pride wiped them from her cheeks.

"Joseph," the minister prompted.

"There are no words in any language that can come close to expressing my feeling for you. I guess my *raison d'être* comes closest." He smiled and his soft brown eyes shimmered with tears he had tried to hold at bay. "When I look at you, I see everything I want and need in this life— every hope and dream. I knew from the first moment I saw you that you were my prayers answered. You saw in me something that I didn't see in myself, and I can never repay you for the vision you have given me. Knowing you has made my life complete. You are the center of my joy." His smile sent the tears in his eyes southward. "I have never given myself to anyone the way I have and will continue to do with you. I promise to never close you out, always let you in. My arms are your shelter and will never let you down. I'll build your dreams with my two hands. Above it all, Joi, I want you to remember that you are never alone. Remember that there is no place on this earth I'd rather be than with you." He cleared his throat. "All I want in return for loving, honoring and protecting you is—forever. Eternity with you and me. I always want you near me, beside me, even when you're old, gray and toothless." The crowd chuckled. "I want us to laugh into old age together. It's our memories that will keep us company. I love you, Sparkle. Now and forever."

"Just perfect," Dante said aloud, dabbing at the corner of his eyes. When he thought he couldn't take the emotional roller coaster anymore, he looked around—and saw him. "Oh!"

No one saw or heard Claude climb into a back pew. He watched the nuptials, knowing at some point Joi would come to her senses, and when she did, he would be there to drive her back to his world. But Claude looked at her. She was beautiful, happy, alive. He realized that she had never once looked at him the way she was looking at Joe Pride.

Claude stood, and Dante's heart stopped. Should he go back there and ask Claude to leave? Should he remind him that this wedding was by invitation only, and no Jeeter made either list? Should he approach him with "I didn't think Jeeters crashed parties?" Suppose he made a scene? Dante didn't want anything to ruin this for Joi. He decided to ask Claude to leave.

By the time Dante turned to assume the task at hand, Claude was gone. Only Dante heard the sound of burning rubber speeding away from the church. It sounded like a mad Porsche, Dante thought with a wicked smile. He turned back to the altar just in time to see the minister pronounce Pride and Joi man and wife.

"You may kiss your bride," he said.

First, Pride kissed Joi passionately, then pecked her on the lips as if not wanting to let her go. Then he placed his damp cheek to hers and fluttered his wet eyelashes.

"Ah, butterfly kisses," Jacquleen St. Marie recognized from the first pew. Tears trickled down her face and fell upon her silk blouse. Louie handed her a tissue.

Dante clapped for the newlyweds before anyone else did. "Well, alright now!" Dante looked at the black rings of mascara on his handkerchief. "Oh, I know I look a sight," he muttered to himself. "Well, hell, it's not my wedding."

After Pride and Joi jumped the broom into the land of matrimony, the minister introduced "Mr. and Mrs. Joseph Pride!" to the congregation.

Well-wishers rushed the newlyweds with kisses and hugs.

"Your vows were beautiful," Jacquleen told her daughter. "Both of you." She smiled warmly at her new son-in-law.

"Glad you could make it, Mother," Joi said playfully as Pride reprimanded her lightly on the fanny. "What? I meant it," she said to her new husband.

"I plan to make your daughter very happy, Mrs. St. Marie."

"I think you've already accomplished that," Jacquleen admitted quietly.

"C'mon, people, work with me," Mike said as he instructed the bride and groom on how to pose for their pictures. "Let's take these shots so we can go and party." Camryn shot her husband a mock-shocked look. "Just the family now," Mike said.

"C'mon, Shorty and Ruby," Pride directed as the delighted pair stood in for Pride's parents. "Mrs. St. Marie," Pride said. "That means you too."

Jacquleen was humbled by Pride's easy invitation and acceptance of her when she had been so unaccepting of him. "Please Joe, call me Jacquleen," she said and tiptoed to her daughter's side. Pride and Joi exchanged knowing glances.

At Rudy's, the music was loud and romantic the way it couldn't be at the church. Guests dined on exotic hors d'oeuvres, drank from the open bar or placed a glass under the fountain which splashed champagne. Mike took more pictures while Stan ran the videotape, which captured the couple singing to each other and dancing alone in a single spotlight as the Four Tops crooned "I Believe in You and Me." Mr. and Mrs. Pride decided they would leave, and, on film, Stan caught the perfect ending to the reception as the couple climbed into the decorated LTD and pulled away from the curb.

"Be happy, Joie," Mrs. St. Marie said, waving tearily at the car until it was out of sight. She said good-bye to Louie and strutted to her own car.

"Well, ain't that a blip?" Ella asked Chantel as they watched Joe Pride's new mother-in-law drive off in the opposite direction.

"Well, they make me believe in love again," Chantel said wistfully. "I'm happy for them."

"They have a connection we don't. That marriage was heaven-sent. Joi taught Pride how to dream, and he gave her permission to be...herself. That's gut-bucket, death-do-you-part love." Ella stared off into the sunset as Chantel grabbed the ever-hyper Jabari by the hand.

"Neither one of them thinks they're good enough for the other. Yeah." Ella smiled. "They'll be just fine."

∽℘∾

In the early sun of an October morning, the Sunday paper bounced on the porch of the Phoebus Road bungalow, just missing the freshly planted chrysanthemums, the recently mowed lawn and the new stones leading from the driveway to the front walk. Inside, by the door, stood a new antique desk the Prides had picked up on one of their weekend drives to the country; it held two pairs of keys, one to the LTD and the other set on top of the five-inch-thick Comparative Literature textbook, belonged to the Mustang convertible, a gift from Pride. In the living room over the fireplace hung their wedding portrait, crowned by the broom over which they had jumped. On the mantel beneath this shrine to their undying love was the Unity candle. Framed next to it was an acceptance letter for Joi S. Pride to the University of Detroit's Literature Department. Replacing all of Pride's trophies were mementos from their travels, and the little treasures they had wrapped in love notes and stuck in each other's pockets to discover during their workday apart.

Upstairs, one bedroom had been converted into a study for Joi where a desk, bookshelves and trophies peacefully coexisted. The second bedroom nearest to the master bedroom remained untouched, though there was a crib tucked in the closet beside four rolls of wallpaper decorated with pretty little black children holding bouquets of colorful balloons and cotton candy.

In the master bedroom, the fresh air from the open window billowed the sheers as Pride and Joi snuggled and giggled under the comforter. Pride's hands slid down Joi's abdomen, tracing the faint tan line left from their Aruba/Curacao honeymoon. On her nightstand, glasses from Saturday night's ice cream sodas and the remote control sat quietly from last night's use. They had watched

Cabin in the Sky and Joi had sung along with Ethel Waters, "Happiness is just a man called Joe." On the dresser, a breeze gently ruffled a magazine open to an article. "Local man takes the art world by storm" it read. It was accompanied by a picture of the Pride family—Joe and Joi—standing by his Nefertiti and his more recent John Coltrane sculpture. Over the easy chair by the closet lay two freshly ironed uniforms—one was pink and white, and the other had "PRIDE" emblazoned over the Ford company emblem. Under the bed were two pairs of shoes—one pair of slightly scuffed black brogan work shoes, and one pair of pristine white waitress shoes. The clock radio on his nightstand clicked on, and Marvin Gaye sang, "You are my pride and joy."

"Listen, Joi!" Pride exclaimed.

They couple stopped their love-playing long enough to peek out of the covers and laugh uproariously. They just laughed…and laughed…and laughed…

❧

❧

❧

2007 Publication Schedule

January

Rooms of the Heart
Donna Hill
ISBN-13: 978-1-58571-219-9
ISBN-10: 1-58571-219-1
$6.99

A Dangerous Love
J. M. Jeffries
ISBN-13: 978-1-58571-217-5
ISBN-10: 1-58571-217-5
$6.99

February

Bound By Love
Beverly Clark
ISBN-13: 978-1-58571-232-8
ISBN-10: 1-58571-232-9
$6.99

A Love to Cherish
Beverly Clark
ISBN-13: 978-1-58571-233-5
ISBN-10: 1-58571-233-7
$6.99

March

Best of Friends
Natalie Dunbar
ISBN-13: 978-1-58571-220-5
ISBN-10: 1-58571-220-5
$6.99

Midnight Magic
Gwynne Forster
ISBN-13: 978-1-58571-225-0
ISBN-10: 1-58571-225-6
$6.99

April

Cherish the Flame
Beverly Clark
ISBN-13: 978-1-58571-221-2
ISBN-10: 1-58571-221-3
$6.99

Quiet Storm
Donna Hill
ISBN-13: 978-1-58571-226-7
ISBN-10: 1-58571-226-4
$6.99

May

Sweet Tomorrows
Kimberley White
ISBN-13: 978-1-58571-234-2
ISBN-10: 1-58571-234-5
$6.99

No Commitment Required
Seressia Glass
ISBN-13: 978-1-58571-222-9
ISBN-10: 1-58571-222-1
$6.99

June

A Dangerous Deception
J. M. Jeffries
ISBN-13: 978-1-58571-228-1
ISBN-10: 1-58571-228-0
$6.99

Illusions
Pamela Leigh Starr
ISBN-13: 978-1-58571-229-8
ISBN-10: 1-58571-229-9
$6.99

2007 Publication Schedule (continued)

July

Indiscretions
Donna Hill
ISBN-13: 978-1-58571-230-4
ISBN-10: 1-58571-230-2
$6.99

Whispers in the Night
Dorothy Elizabeth Love
ISBN-13: 978-1-58571-231-1
ISBN-10: 1-58571-231-0
$6.99

August

Bodyguard
Andrea Jackson
ISBN-13: 978-1-58571-235-9
ISBN-10: 1-58571-235-3
$6.99

Crossing Paths, Tempting Memories
Dorothy Elizabeth Love
ISBN-13: 978-1-58571-236-6
ISBN-10: 1-58571-236-1
$6.99

September

Fate
Pamela Leigh Starr
ISBN-13: 978-1-58571-258-8
ISBN-10: 1-58571-258-2
$6.99

Mae's Promise
Melody Walcott
ISBN-13: 978-1-58571-259-5
ISBN-10: 1-58571-259-0
$6.99

October

Magnolia Sunset
Giselle Carmichael
ISBN-13: 978-1-58571-260-1
ISBN-10: 1-58571-260-4
$6.99

Broken
Dar Tomlinson
ISBN-13: 978-1-58571-261-8
ISBN-10: 1-58571-261-2
$6.99

November

Truly Inseparable
Wanda Y. Thomas
ISBN-13: 978-1-58571-262-5
ISBN-10: 1-58571-262-0
$6.99

The Color Line
Lizzette G. Carter
ISBN-13: 978-1-58571-263-2
ISBN-10: 1-58571-263-9
$6.99

December

Love Always
Mildred Riley
ISBN-13: 978-1-58571-264-9
ISBN-10: 1-58571-264-7
$6.99

Pride and Joi
Gay Gunn
ISBN-13: 978-1-58571-265-6
ISBN-10: 1-58571-265-5
$6.99

Other Genesis Press, Inc. Titles

A Dangerous Deception	J.M. Jeffries	$8.95
A Dangerous Love	J.M. Jeffries	$8.95
A Dangerous Obsession	J.M. Jeffries	$8.95
A Drummer's Beat to Mend	Kei Swanson	$9.95
A Happy Life	Charlotte Harris	$9.95
A Heart's Awakening	Veronica Parker	$9.95
A Lark on the Wing	Phyliss Hamilton	$9.95
A Love of Her Own	Cheris F. Hodges	$9.95
A Love to Cherish	Beverly Clark	$8.95
A Risk of Rain	Dar Tomlinson	$8.95
A Twist of Fate	Beverly Clark	$8.95
A Will to Love	Angie Daniels	$9.95
Acquisitions	Kimberley White	$8.95
Across	Carol Payne	$12.95
After the Vows	Leslie Esdaile	$10.95
(Summer Anthology)	T.T. Henderson	
	Jacqueline Thomas	
Again My Love	Kayla Perrin	$10.95
Against the Wind	Gwynne Forster	$8.95
All I Ask	Barbara Keaton	$8.95
Ambrosia	T.T. Henderson	$8.95
An Unfinished Love Affair	Barbara Keaton	$8.95
And Then Came You	Dorothy Elizabeth Love	$8.95
Angel's Paradise	Janice Angelique	$9.95
At Last	Lisa G. Riley	$8.95
Best of Friends	Natalie Dunbar	$8.95
Beyond the Rapture	Beverly Clark	$9.95
Blaze	Barbara Keaton	$9.95
Blood Lust	J. M. Jeffries	$9.95

Other Genesis Press, Inc. Titles (continued)

Other Genesis Press, Inc. Titles (continued)

Eden's Garden	Elizabeth Rose	$8.95
Everlastin' Love	Gay G. Gunn	$8.95
Everlasting Moments	Dorothy Elizabeth Love	$8.95
Everything and More	Sinclair Lebeau	$8.95
Everything but Love	Natalie Dunbar	$8.95
Eve's Prescription	Edwina Martin Arnold	$8.95
Falling	Natalie Dunbar	$9.95
Fate	Pamela Leigh Starr	$8.95
Finding Isabella	A.J. Garrotto	$8.95
Forbidden Quest	Dar Tomlinson	$10.95
Forever Love	Wanda Y. Thomas	$8.95
From the Ashes	Kathleen Suzanne	$8.95
	Jeanne Sumerix	
Gentle Yearning	Rochelle Alers	$10.95
Glory of Love	Sinclair LeBeau	$10.95
Go Gentle into that Good Night	Malcom Boyd	$12.95
Goldengroove	Mary Beth Craft	$16.95
Groove, Bang, and Jive	Steve Cannon	$8.99
Hand in Glove	Andrea Jackson	$9.95
Hard to Love	Kimberley White	$9.95
Hart & Soul	Angie Daniels	$8.95
Heartbeat	Stephanie Bedwell-Grime	$8.95
Hearts Remember	M. Loui Quezada	$8.95
Hidden Memories	Robin Allen	$10.95
Higher Ground	Leah Latimer	$19.95
Hitler, the War, and the Pope	Ronald Rychiak	$26.95
How to Write a Romance	Kathryn Falk	$18.95
I Married a Reclining Chair	Lisa M. Fuhs	$8.95
Indigo After Dark Vol. I	Nia Dixon/Angelique	$10.95

Other Genesis Press, Inc. Titles (continued)

Indigo After Dark Vol. II	Dolores Bundy/ Cole Riley	$10.95
Indigo After Dark Vol. III	Montana Blue/ Coco Morena	$10.95
Indigo After Dark Vol. IV	Cassandra Colt/ Diana Richeaux	$14.95
Indigo After Dark Vol. V	Delilah Dawson	$14.95
Icie	Pamela Leigh Starr	$8.95
I'll Be Your Shelter	Giselle Carmichael	$8.95
I'll Paint a Sun	A.J. Garrotto	$9.95
Illusions	Pamela Leigh Starr	$8.95
Indiscretions	Donna Hill	$8.95
Intentional Mistakes	Michele Sudler	$9.95
Interlude	Donna Hill	$8.95
Intimate Intentions	Angie Daniels	$8.95
Jolie's Surrender	Edwina Martin-Arnold	$8.95
Kiss or Keep	Debra Phillips	$8.95
Lace	Giselle Carmichael	$9.95
Last Train to Memphis	Elsa Cook	$12.95
Lasting Valor	Ken Olsen	$24.95
Let Us Prey	Hunter Lundy	$25.95
Life Is Never As It Seems	J.J. Michael	$12.95
Lighter Shade of Brown	Vicki Andrews	$8.95
Love Always	Mildred E. Riley	$10.95
Love Doesn't Come Easy	Charlyne Dickerson	$8.95
Love Unveiled	Gloria Greene	$10.95
Love's Deception	Charlene Berry	$10.95
Love's Destiny	M. Loui Quezada	$8.95
Mae's Promise	Melody Walcott	$8.95

Other Genesis Press, Inc. Titles (continued)

Magnolia Sunset	Giselle Carmichael	$8.95
Matters of Life and Death	Lesego Malepe, Ph.D.	$15.95
Meant to Be	Jeanne Sumerix	$8.95
Midnight Clear	Leslie Esdaile	$10.95
(Anthology)	Gwynne Forster	
	Carmen Green	
	Monica Jackson	
Midnight Magic	Gwynne Forster	$8.95
Midnight Peril	Vicki Andrews	$10.95
Misconceptions	Pamela Leigh Starr	$9.95
Montgomery's Children	Richard Perry	$14.95
My Buffalo Soldier	Barbara B. K. Reeves	$8.95
Naked Soul	Gwynne Forster	$8.95
Next to Last Chance	Louisa Dixon	$24.95
No Apologies	Seressia Glass	$8.95
No Commitment Required	Seressia Glass	$8.95
No Regrets	Mildred E. Riley	$8.95
Nowhere to Run	Gay G. Gunn	$10.95
O Bed! O Breakfast!	Rob Kuehnle	$14.95
Object of His Desire	A. C. Arthur	$8.95
Office Policy	A. C. Arthur	$9.95
Once in a Blue Moon	Dorianne Cole	$9.95
One Day at a Time	Bella McFarland	$8.95
Outside Chance	Louisa Dixon	$24.95
Passion	T.T. Henderson	$10.95
Passion's Blood	Cherif Fortin	$22.95
Passion's Journey	Wanda Y. Thomas	$8.95
Past Promises	Jahmel West	$8.95
Path of Fire	T.T. Henderson	$8.95

Other Genesis Press, Inc. Titles (continued)

Path of Thorns	Annetta P. Lee	$9.95
Peace Be Still	Colette Haywood	$12.95
Picture Perfect	Reon Carter	$8.95
Playing for Keeps	Stephanie Salinas	$8.95
Pride & Joi	Gay G. Gunn	$15.95
Pride & Joi	Gay G. Gunn	$8.95
Promises to Keep	Alicia Wiggins	$8.95
Quiet Storm	Donna Hill	$10.95
Reckless Surrender	Rochelle Alers	$6.95
Red Polka Dot in a World of Plaid	Varian Johnson	$12.95
Reluctant Captive	Joyce Jackson	$8.95
Rendezvous with Fate	Jeanne Sumerix	$8.95
Revelations	Cheris F. Hodges	$8.95
Rivers of the Soul	Leslie Esdaile	$8.95
Rocky Mountain Romance	Kathleen Suzanne	$8.95
Rooms of the Heart	Donna Hill	$8.95
Rough on Rats and Tough on Cats	Chris Parker	$12.95
Secret Library Vol. 1	Nina Sheridan	$18.95
Secret Library Vol. 2	Cassandra Colt	$8.95
Shades of Brown	Denise Becker	$8.95
Shades of Desire	Monica White	$8.95
Shadows in the Moonlight	Jeanne Sumerix	$8.95
Sin	Crystal Rhodes	$8.95
So Amazing	Sinclair LeBeau	$8.95
Somebody's Someone	Sinclair LeBeau	$8.95
Someone to Love	Alicia Wiggins	$8.95
Song in the Park	Martin Brant	$15.95

Other Genesis Press, Inc. Titles (continued)

Soul Eyes	Wayne L. Wilson	$12.95
Soul to Soul	Donna Hill	$8.95
Southern Comfort	J.M. Jeffries	$8.95
Still the Storm	Sharon Robinson	$8.95
Still Waters Run Deep	Leslie Esdaile	$8.95
Stories to Excite You	Anna Forrest/Divine	$14.95
Subtle Secrets	Wanda Y. Thomas	$8.95
Suddenly You	Crystal Hubbard	$9.95
Sweet Repercussions	Kimberley White	$9.95
Sweet Tomorrows	Kimberly White	$8.95
Taken by You	Dorothy Elizabeth Love	$9.95
Tattooed Tears	T. T. Henderson	$8.95
The Color Line	Lizzette Grayson Carter	$9.95
The Color of Trouble	Dyanne Davis	$8.95
The Disappearance of Allison Jones	Kayla Perrin	$5.95
The Honey Dipper's Legacy	Pannell-Allen	$14.95
The Joker's Love Tune	Sidney Rickman	$15.95
The Little Pretender	Barbara Cartland	$10.95
The Love We Had	Natalie Dunbar	$8.95
The Man Who Could Fly	Bob & Milana Beamon	$18.95
The Missing Link	Charlyne Dickerson	$8.95
The Price of Love	Sinclair LeBeau	$8.95
The Smoking Life	Ilene Barth	$29.95
The Words of the Pitcher	Kei Swanson	$8.95
Three Wishes	Seressia Glass	$8.95
Ties That Bind	Kathleen Suzanne	$8.95
Tiger Woods	Libby Hughes	$5.95

Order Form

Mail to: Genesis Press, Inc.
P.O. Box 101
Columbus, MS 39703

Name _____
Address _____
City/State _____ Zip _____
Telephone _____

Ship to (if different from above)
Name _____
Address _____
City/State _____ Zip _____
Telephone _____

Credit Card Information
Credit Card # _____ ☐ Visa ☐ Mastercard
Expiration Date (mm/yy) _____ ☐ AmEx ☐ Discover

Qty.	Author	Title	Price	Total

Use this order form, or call 1-888-INDIGO-1	Total for books _____ Shipping and handling: $5 first two books, $1 each additional book _____ Total S & H _____ Total amount enclosed _____ *Mississippi residents add 7% sales tax*

Visit www.genesispress.com for latest releases and excerpts.